U0004165

長腿叔叔
Daddy-Long-Legs
中英雙語典藏版

珍·韋伯斯特——著、繪

艾柯——譯

晨星出版

導讀

陽光少女情

東海大學中文系教授 許建崑

　　閱讀《長腿叔叔》這本書，大部分的人都可以分享到故事主人翁的陽光少女情。喬若莎，後來改名為茱蒂的女孩，小時候在孤兒院長大，被留下來直照顧較小的孩子。她心甘情願嗎？直到有天，一位匿名的理事願意送她去讀大學。能夠離開孤兒院和勢利的院長，茱蒂當然樂意，可是要被送到另一個陌生的環境，她心裡慌恐不安。她看見資助人的身影投射在牆壁上，像一隻長腳蜘蛛，所以她惡作劇地稱資助人為「長腿叔叔」。「長腿」暗寓著「蜘蛛」的意思。對於這位有錢的資助人，掌控著她的生活與未來，她心裡很不舒服，卻必須假裝恭順，而且在大學四年之中，每個月都得寫信報告學習境況。這本書就在孤女茱蒂的書信報告中展開了！

感恩與自尊的爭鬥

　　得到別人的幫助，應該感恩在心，可是被迫在大眾面前說出感謝的話，只會傷害受助者的自尊。茱蒂被規定寫信給資助人，卻得不到回信，最多只是從秘書先生處寄來金錢和口諭，內心很不平衡。多麼難堪的事啊！

　　同學們之間談起家世。茱蒂又難過了，她的姓氏是孤兒院院長翻閱電話簿，從第一頁上抄來的；她的原名又是從一塊墓碑上看到的。她怎麼可能原諒院長的「隨便取材」？脫離孤兒院，進入大學，她趕快為自己改了名字。暑假中，同學們歡喜回家度假，而茱蒂卻又百般尷尬，她無處可去，更不願意回到孤兒院。她甚至詛咒院長「永遠去世」了！

　　這樣的孩子忘恩負義嗎？將心比心，對於心靈曾經受傷的孩子，我們很難去苛責。

積極的態度驅退自卑

　　茱蒂的心眼可真多呢！她想了解她的資助人模樣，故意在信裡畫了個金甲蟲，說是其他理事們的長相。你瞧！如果她的資助人也長得像金甲蟲，要怎麼辦呢？她還在信中談起與英俊的男士散步、聊天、喝茶等等，希望引起資助人的忌妒，趕快跳出來，好驗證真實的身分！要是資助人生氣了，斷絕對她的資助，又要怎麼辦呢？

　　她從不掩飾自己的情緒，不管是快樂或難過，總要把生活中的點點滴滴寫進信裡。她的本意未必是讓資助人「分享」，或者是「捉弄」有錢人。儘管茱蒂也試圖在信裡使用小手段，表現個人的意願，來爭取較多的自由、關懷或物質；但是在書信往返之中，她無法隱藏個人純真而善良的本性。她退回多餘的零用錢，贏得學校的獎學金，投稿賺得些微的稿費，來減少對資助人的依賴，以便早日可以償還債務。她的努力，要讓人打從心底疼起來。

　　她是奉命寫信的，可是不寫信，又如何吐露心聲呢？身為孤兒，她可以向誰訴說呢？除了用文字以外，畫畫也是一種方式。茱蒂喜歡用簡單的線條構圖，來表現他的生活與快樂。茱蒂畫了自畫像，把自己孤兒的心情與模樣具體化了，五十碼短跑賽的佳績、每天的例行學習與工作、增胖九磅的模樣，都從筆下透露了。日常所見農莊的美景、下雨的景緻、越過小溪逃走的九隻小豬，還有小鹿、牛隻、馬匹、始祖鳥、貓咪、蜘蛛、蜈蚣等有趣的動物形象，甚至畫了一幅與松鼠、蜈蚣、雲雀分享下午茶的情景，靈動的筆觸讓讀者親如目睹。

自信與夢想的實現

　　茱蒂積極奮鬥的態度，讓她能夠勇敢地揮別過去，走向開朗的未來。她的自信心又如何培養呢？她把童年的不幸當作一段不尋常的人生經歷，使她能站在一個「旁觀者」的角度來省視生命，這是家境優越的孩子所不曾有過的經驗。剛上大學時，她功課不頂好，數學和拉丁文兩科不及格，還參加補考呢。在自由、獨立的生活環境中，她迷戀起小說和詩歌，這些作品給了她許多人生啓示，也讓她堅定成爲作家的夢想。

夢想是可以實現的，她努力學習，功課好了，也讀出學問的滋味。《簡愛》、《咆哮山莊》、莎士比亞戲劇、邏輯辯論、法文、化學、生物學，每一本書、每一科目都樂趣無窮。積極的態度，讓茱蒂獲得「脫胎換骨」的機會。茱蒂的興趣還有許多，當籃球隊員、戲劇演員，甚至是競選班代表，以便「熱心從政」。從書中讀來，她改變了在孤兒院中幾乎是「顧影自憐」的習慣，使她陰鬱的反抗轉變爲「無時的快樂」。她甚至在寢室裡的三面鏡子之前，覺得自己「很漂亮」！這不是人生信念的具體表現嗎？

成爲偉大的作家，是茱蒂的第一意願，也是作者自身的投影。書中提到史蒂文生撰寫《金銀島》，只拿到三十鎊的權利金，當作家能得到的報酬，少得可憐；或許到學校裡教書來養活自己，才比較實際。這是作者的自我嘲諷吧！不然作者爲什麼還要繼續寫作？

邂逅在文學的河流中

到底茱蒂後來如何幸福？和她在一起的幸運兒是誰？而長腿叔叔又是誰？還請讀者自己在書中尋找答案吧！

作者珍‧韋伯斯特一八七六年七月二十四日誕生於美國紐約州西邊的佛萊德尼亞。父親是個出版商，母親是馬克吐溫的姪女，家裡已經有濃濃的文學氣息。瑪莎女子大學畢業之後，她開始以寫作爲生。

一九一二年，她三十六歲，寫了這本《長腿叔叔》，書中時空背景自然都擺在她所熟悉的康乃迪克州與麻薩諸塞州。三年後，她又寫了續集，讓前集中的好友莎利擔任孤兒院的新院長，改善管理制度，也實現作者關懷孤兒以及改良教育的初衷。作者後來與律師馬吉尼結婚，隔年生下女兒，自己卻一病不起，像彗星般地劃過了美國文壇。《長腿叔叔》和《續集》，也成了作者永久的代表作。

好的作品不會寂寞，它會以不同形式，在不同的地方出現。英國人改編爲音樂喜劇片《茱蒂的愛》，搬上了舞台。美國人也改拍爲黑白電影。

台灣電視公司在民國八十年十月購買了卡通影片版權，爲茱蒂改了個中國式的名字叫「周蒂蒂」，還請張衛健唱主題曲，歌名是〈夢中天使〉，喜歡的朋友可以上網去抓。這齣卡通影片在九十年十二月第四台卡通工作站上又重播了一次。今年三月，還製成 DVD，供愛好者收藏。電腦網路上也有人設站，銷售《長腿叔叔》周邊的書籍和禮物。由於「長腿叔叔」的義行，香港的學生團體發起運動，要幫助失學學童回到學校。

　　亮麗的陽光純情少女，建構了《長腿叔叔》，在時光的流逝中，還是有許多人用不同的文字翻譯、改寫和出版。親愛的朋友，拿起書來，直接進入茱蒂的世界，有什麼好猶豫呢？

譯者的話

一生做一次孤兒

艾柯

大多數人一出生就被無所不在，理所當然的愛包裹著。

所有的一切都是如此地毫無疑問，順理成章。人們視生命中一切的美好爲理所當然。

但是，終於有一天，當青春的熱潮蕩起，叛逆的種子萌發，我們的視角卻開始傾斜了。我們開始想逃離無所不在的關懷，懷疑起原本視爲理所當然的愛，有時候我們甚至會因此失去所擁有的一切。

我害怕的是，當愛無所不在時，或者在我們視爲理所當然的愛中，卻不覺地喪失了愛的感覺。人類的天性中原就有愛的因數，可是這種愛的潛能卻於幼小時，在父母的過分呵護下，無形中被扼殺了。

與其這樣，不如嘗試著做一次孤兒——一生嘗試著做一次。

海倫·凱勒在《假如給我三天光明》中這樣寫到：「如果每個人在他的人生初識階段患過幾天盲聾症，這將是一種幸福。黑暗會使他更珍惜視覺，啞默會教導他喜慕聲音。」

同樣地，我想，如果每個人在他人生之初的一段時間裏做一次孤兒，或許也是一種幸福。孤獨使我們能更珍惜相聚，隔絕會告訴我們如何去愛。無獨有偶，據說在一些佛教國家，男人一生中要進寺廟做一次和尚，其意是體驗苦修和頓悟，這種感覺也許能讓人一生都慈悲爲懷。

對於無所不在的親情來說，嘗試做一次孤兒，首先要學會捨棄。我曾經做過這樣一個心理測驗：把自己最心愛的七樣東西按順序列在紙上，既可以是親人和朋友，也可以是一件事或物，然後，按順序一一放棄——這真是殘酷的選擇。雖然是一種心理類比，但那種痛楚卻像真的要割捨一般隱然在心，那一瞬間，我突然發現，自己實際上竟然有如此之多割捨不下的東西。

當一切不可避免都被捨棄，回歸爲零的時候，我們需要重新開始，需要重新建立聯繫，（《小王子》一書中，在那隻等愛的狐狸心目中，愛就是馴養，而馴養的意思就是「建立某種聯繫」。）需要學會愛與被愛——我們需要重新學習和感悟生命中那些曾經視之爲理所當然的東西。

在此我所謂的捨棄並不是一種生存狀態，而是一種心理狀態，是一種在缺失愛的狀態下體會愛，在被親人放逐的情形下感悟親情。

同樣的，一生中做一次孤兒，並不是要在生活中眞正發生什麼。現實意義的孤兒，面對著一切不可挽回的局面時，那種傷痛將永遠銘記在心中。而我們需要做的不過是一種心靈體驗，做一些假設，假設我們一生下來就無依無靠，假如我們有一天突然失去了許多，以此試著把自己推向心靈的孤寂狀態。

身爲一位孤兒的感覺並不好，然而人們對於我們所擁有的總是毫不在乎，卻一心留戀已經喪失的，這正是人性的悲哀和缺陷所在。於是，一生做一次孤兒的體驗也就變得非常必要了。

那些生活在幸福和愛中的人們常常抱怨，他們得不到任何的愛，於是他們反抗，他們出走，因爲他們從來就不曾嘗過失去愛的滋味。

一無所有後才會無所不有，失去後才會珍惜所有，學會施與才懂得感恩，這是我在《長腿叔叔》中所體悟到的。

每個女孩子看了《長腿叔叔》後，都希望自己變成一個孤兒，羨慕那種無拘無束和自由放任的生活，幻想著也能夠遇到自己的白馬王子——長腿叔叔。而我想告訴大家的是，生活需要奇蹟，而最大的奇蹟就是你自己。

給你愛的人和愛你的人親筆寫封信，無論他們遠在天涯還是近在咫尺——如果能做到這一點，也就達到了我們出版這本書信體小說的目的了。

目録

導讀

002

譯者的話

006

憂鬱的星期三

011

**喬若莎・艾伯特小姐
給長腿叔叔史密斯先生的信**

019

CONTENTS

Blue Wednesday
167

The Letters of
Miss Jerusha Abbott
to
Mr. Daddy-Long-Legs Smith
174

予你

憂鬱的星期三

　　每個月的第一個星期三眞是糟糕透頂——這是一個讓人在憂慮中迎接它到來，到來時堅忍地度過，然後匆忙忘掉的日子。這一天，每層地板都必須光潔照人，每張椅子都要一塵不染，每條床單都不可以有半點褶皺。除此之外，還要把九十七個活蹦亂跳的小孤兒梳理一遍，給他們穿上漿過的格子襯衫，並且一一囑咐他們要注意禮貌。只要理事們一問話，就要回答：「是的，先生」、「不是的，先生」。

　　這眞是個令人沮喪的日子，可憐的喬若莎・艾伯特作為孤兒院裏最年長的孩子，不得不首當其衝。不過，這個特別的星期三跟往常一樣，終於要結束了。喬若莎逃出廚房，她剛剛在那裏為訪客們做了三明治，接下來要回到樓上完成她每天的例行工作。她特別照顧第六室，那裏有十一個四歲到七歲不等的小孩子，和十一張排成一列的小床。喬若莎把他們都叫來，幫他們整理好皺巴巴的衣服，把鼻涕抹乾淨，排成一行，然後領著他們往餐室走去。在那裏，他們有半個小時可以盡情地享受喝牛奶、吃麵包，再加上好吃的梅子布丁。

　　她疲憊地跌坐在窗臺，把漲得發疼的太陽穴靠在冰冷的玻璃上。從早晨五點鐘起，她就手腳不停地忙碌著，聽從每個人的命令東奔西跑，而且不時被神經兮兮的女監事臭罵，催得她暈頭轉向。李皮太太在私底下，可不像她面對理事和來訪的女士們時，表現得那樣冷靜、自負。喬若莎的目光掠過孤兒院高高的鐵欄杆外一片結凍的開闊草地，望向遠處起伏的山巒，山上散落著的村舍在光禿禿的樹叢中，露出房舍的尖頂。

這一天終於過去了。就她所知，應該算是圓滿落幕，沒有出什麼差錯。理事們與參訪團繞過一巡，看了報告書，喝過茶，現在正要趕著回到自家溫暖的爐火邊。起碼要再過一個月，才會想起他們照管的這些磨人的小東西。喬若莎傾身向前，好奇地看著那一連串的馬車與汽車，挨挨擠擠地穿過孤兒院的大門，內心不禁一陣渴望。幻想中，她跟著一輛又一輛的車，來到座落在山坡上的一棟大房子。她想像自己穿著一件貂皮大衣，戴著天鵝絨裝飾的絲質帽子，靠在車座上，漫不經心地向司機說：「回家！」不過一到家門口，整個畫面卻又變得模糊。

喬若莎的想像力豐富，李皮太太提醒她若不克制，會讓她惹上麻煩。但是，不論她的想像力有多麼豐富，都無法帶領她走進那扇她一直渴望進入的大門。她只有站在門廊上的資格。小喬若莎可憐兮兮，但積極且冒險心旺盛，只是在她十七年的歲月裏，從未踏進任何一個正常的家庭。她無法想像，那些沒有孤兒干擾的人們，他們的日常生活會是如何。

喬……若……莎……艾……伯……特

有人要……妳

去辦公室，

而我想啊，

妳最好動作快一點！

湯米‧狄倫剛加入唱詩班。他邊唱邊走上樓梯，從走廊走向第六室，聲音越來越近，越來越響亮。喬若莎將思緒從窗外拉回來，好面對生活裏的麻煩事。

「是誰叫我？」她打斷湯米的詠唱，急切地問道。

李皮太太在辦公室，

我覺得她好像很火大，

阿……門！

湯米依然虔誠地吟頌著，他的腔調並非幸災樂禍。就算是心腸最硬的小孤兒，面對一個做錯事的姐姐，要被叫去見那個討厭的女監事時，也是會感到同情的。況且湯米挺喜歡喬若莎的。雖然她偶爾會使勁扯他的胳膊，而且幫他洗臉的時候，幾乎要把他的鼻子給揉掉了！

喬若莎默默地朝辦公室走去，額頭上出現兩道皺紋。會是哪裡出了差錯？三明治切得不夠薄？有殼掉在杏仁蛋糕裏？啊！還是哪個來訪的女士看到蘇西‧華生襪子上的破洞了？

還是……哎，糟糕！是不是那個六號房的頑皮小寶貝，把調味醬弄倒在理事身上了？

低矮長廊上的燈早已熄滅。當她下樓時，最後一個理事站在那兒，正好要離開。在辦公室敞開的門裏，喬若莎看了一眼這個人，覺得他好高好高，他正朝著在院子外等候的汽車招手。當汽車靠近時，刺眼的車燈將他的影子清楚地投射在大廳的牆上，影子把手腳都滑稽地拉長了，從地板一直延伸到走廊的牆壁。它看起來真像人們俗稱的「長腿叔叔」——一隻晃來晃去的大蜘蛛。

喬若莎緊鎖的眉頭舒展開來，輕鬆地笑了。她是個天性樂觀的人，一點小事都能把她逗樂，在使人感到壓抑的理事身上發現笑料，對她來說，確實是一件預想不到的好事。這段小插曲使她高興得在走進辦公室見李皮太太時，臉上仍舊掛著一絲笑意。令人驚訝的是，女監事也衝著她笑，雖然不是真的在笑，至少還算和藹可親。她幾乎像對待來訪的客人一樣，滿臉喜悅。

「喬若莎，坐下，我有些話要跟妳說。」

喬若莎跌坐在最近的一張椅子上，屏息以待。霎時，一輛汽車從窗外駛過，車燈的閃光照到窗戶上。李皮太太望著遠去的車子問道：

「妳有看到剛剛離開的那位先生了嗎？」

「我看到了他的背影。」

「他是我們最富有的理事之一，捐了很多錢給孤兒院。不過我不能透露他的姓名，因為他特別要求我保密。」

喬若莎的雙眼微微張大。她不太習慣被女監事叫到辦公室討論理事們的怪癖。

「這位先生已經照顧過孤兒院裏的幾個男孩子。妳記得查理‧班頓和亨利‧傅理茲吧？他們都是被這位先生……這位理事，送去上大學的孩子。兩人都很用功，以良好的成績來回報他慷慨的資助。這位先生從不要求其他的報償。不過到目前為止，他仁慈的對象僅限於男孩子，我從未能讓他對女孩們留一點心，不論她們有多麼出色。這麼說吧，他一點也不喜歡女孩子。」

「是的，女士。」喬若莎喃喃答道，心想此刻似乎該回應些什麼。

「今天的例會裏，有人提起妳的前途。」

李皮太太略微停頓了一會兒，然後又慢條斯理地說下去，這讓她的聽者頓時神經緊繃，坐立難安。

「妳知道──通常孩子們過了十六歲以後就不能留下來了。不過妳算是個特例，妳十四歲讀完孤兒院的課程，表現良好──我不得不說，妳的操行並非一向優良──但由於妳其他的表現不錯，所以我們讓妳繼續讀村裏的高中。現在妳也快畢業了，我們再也不能負擔妳的生活費了。不過妳想想，即便如此，妳也比其他人多享受了兩年的教育。」

李皮太太全然無視喬若莎這兩年為了自己的食宿，工作得有多賣力，永遠都是孤兒院工作第一，功課擺第二。尤其是遇到像今天這種日子，她還得留下來打掃。

「而我剛才說了，有人提出妳的前途問題；會議上也討論了妳的表現──徹徹底底地討論了一番。」

李皮太太用一種責備的眼光盯著她的犯人，而這個囚犯也表現出一副有罪的樣子。倒不是因為她真的記得做過了什麼壞事，而是覺得李皮太太似乎認為她應該要這樣。

　　「當然啦，以妳來說，給妳安排一個工作就行了。不過妳在學校裏有某些科目表現突出，英文寫作甚至可以說是非常出色。而妳們學校的理事——普查德小姐，正好也在參訪團裏。她跟妳的作文老師談過，為妳說了一番好話，還讀了妳的一篇作文——題目是〈憂鬱的星期三〉。」

　　這回喬若莎可真的知罪了。

　　「我認為妳嘲笑這個為妳做了很多事的孤兒院，是忘恩負義的行為。要不是妳寫得很逗趣，我想不會有人原諒妳。幸好那位……就是剛剛離開的那位，有很強的幽默感，讀過那篇不中肯的文章後，他決定資助妳去念大學。」

　　「念大學？」喬若莎的眼睛睜得好大。

　　李皮太太點點頭。

　　「會後他留下來和我討論條件，很不尋常的條件。我覺得這位先生有點古怪。他認為妳很有天分，他希望把妳培養成為一位作家。」

　　「作家？」喬若莎腦袋一片空白，只能重覆李皮太太的話。

　　「那只是他的理想，不管怎樣，以後自然會知道。他會給妳充足的零用錢。那對一個沒有理財經驗的女孩子來說，實在是太多了，不過這些瑣事他安排得很周全，我也不便多說什麼。這個夏天妳暫時先留在這裏，之後好心的普查德小姐會替妳打理所有行囊。妳的食宿與學費都會直接付給學校，在校四年間，妳每個月還會有三十五元的零用錢。這讓妳可以跟其他學生平起平坐。這些錢每個月都會由這位先生的私人祕書寄給妳，而妳每個月都要回封信表示一下，作為回報。並不是要妳為零用錢向他道謝，他對這方面一點都不稀罕，而是妳要寫信告訴他，妳求學的過程和日常生活的細節。就像是寫信給妳的父母一樣，如果他們還在世的話。」

「這些信將由祕書轉交給約翰·史密斯先生。這位先生的本名當然不是約翰·史密斯先生，不過他希望保持神祕。因此對妳而言，他將永遠只是約翰·史密斯先生。他要求妳寫信的原因在於，他認為沒有什麼比寫信更能培養寫作技巧。由於妳沒有家人可以聯絡，他才希望妳寫這樣的信給他；另一方面，他也想隨時知道妳的求學情況。但他絕不會回信，也不會很特別地去注意妳的來信。他很討厭寫信，也不想讓妳造成他的負擔，除非有任何緊急事件需要回覆──比如妳被學校開除了。不過我想這應該是不會發生的──妳可以跟他的祕書格利茲先生聯絡。每個月的書信是妳絕對要遵守的義務，這也是史密斯先生唯一的要求，所以妳一定要一絲不苟地寫信，就當作妳在付賬單一樣。我希望妳以尊敬的語氣，並且好好發揮妳寫作的長才來寫這些信。妳一定要記得，妳是在寫信給約翰·格利爾孤兒院的理事。」

喬若莎的眼睛轉向房門口。她興奮得有些暈頭轉向了，只想快點從滔滔不絕的李皮太太身邊逃開，好好思考一下。她起身試探性地退了一步，而李皮太太卻舉手示意她留下來。這麼好的說教機會，她怎能輕易放過呢？

「我相信妳一定很珍惜這個從天而降的好運吧？世上沒有幾個像妳這種出身的女孩子，能獲得這種好運。妳一定要記得……」

「我會的，女士。謝謝您，我想如果沒有其他事的話，我得去幫弗萊迪‧柏金斯修補褲子了。」話才說完，她就把房門帶上。走了。

李皮太太目瞪口呆地望著門，她的長篇大論正說到興頭上呢！

喬若莎‧艾伯特小姐
給長腿叔叔史密斯先生的信

9月24日於佛格森樓215室

我最親愛的，送孤兒上大學的好心理事：

我終於到了！昨天搭了四個鐘頭的火車，感覺好新奇啊！不是嗎？我從來沒有坐過火車呢！

校園好大，是個很容易把人搞糊塗的地方——我只要一離開房間就會迷路，等我對周圍環境熟悉一些再對您描述我的校園，並報告我的功課。現在是星期六晚上，要到下星期一早上才開課，不過我還是想先寫封信，讓您熟悉一下。

寫信給陌生人是件挺奇怪的事。對我來說，寫信本來就夠奇怪的……目前為止，我這輩子就只寫過三、四封信，要是寫得不好，請您多多見諒。

昨天早上出發前，李皮太太與我嚴肅地對談。她告誡我今後一輩子該如何為人處世，尤其是對有恩於我的好心先生，更要注意自己的言行，一定不能忘記，對您要非常地「尊敬」。

不過，對一個自稱約翰‧史密斯的人，怎麼尊敬得起來呢？您爲什麼不挑個有個性點的名字啊？我感覺自己就好比在給拴馬椿或衣架寫信一樣。

　　整個夏天我想了很多關於您的事。這麼多年來，突然有人關心我，讓我覺得自己好像找到家一樣，有了歸屬感。這感覺令人陶醉。但不論如何，我必須承認，當我想到您的時候，我的腦子總是空蕩蕩的。因爲我只知道三件事：

　　一、您長得很高。

　　二、您很有錢。

　　三、您討厭女孩子。

　　我想我可以稱呼您爲：「親愛的厭女先生」，不過這有傷我的自尊。或許我可以稱呼您：「親愛的有錢人」，不過這樣又侮辱到您的人格，好像您唯一值得一提的只有錢。此外，「富有」是一種很膚淺的特徵。因爲您也許不會一輩子都這麼有錢，有很多聰明人在華爾街慘遭滑鐵盧的。不過您的身高永遠不變，所以我決定稱呼您：「親愛的長腿叔叔」。希望您別介意，這只是個私底下的暱稱，不必告訴李皮太太。

　　再兩分鐘，十點的鐘聲就要響了。我們的一天被鐘聲分成好幾段，我們吃飯、睡覺和上課都照著鐘聲來進行。這讓我十分有朝氣，因爲我總感覺自己像匹拉消防車的馬。

　　就這樣，該熄燈了，晚安！

　　瞧！我多守規矩——多虧了約翰·格利爾孤兒院的訓練。

尊敬您的喬若莎·艾伯特

10月1日

親愛的長腿叔叔：

我喜歡大學，也喜歡把我送來這裏的您──我真的非常非常快樂，經常都興奮得睡不著覺。您無法想像這裏跟約翰‧格利爾孤兒院有多麼地不同。我從不知道世上還有這樣的好地方，我深深地爲那些不是女孩，不能來上大學的人感到難過。我相信您以前讀的大學一定沒有這般美好。

我的房間位在一棟大樓裏，在新醫務室蓋好前，它曾暫時被當做傳染病房使用。這層樓還有另外三個女孩子──一個戴眼鏡的高年級女生，老是要人家安靜一點，還有兩個新生，莎莉‧馬克白與茱莉亞‧平萊頓。莎莉有一頭紅髮和一個翹鼻子，爲人友善；茱莉亞出身紐約名門，還沒注意到我。她們倆住同一間房，那個高年級女生跟我一樣，住單人房。因爲房間很少，一般來說，新生是不能住單人房的。但我沒向學校要求就得到一間。我猜是註冊處的人覺得，讓有教養的女孩跟孤兒住在一起不太妥當。您瞧，身爲孤兒還是有好處的呢！

我的房間在西北角，有兩扇窗，窗外景色宜人。跟二十個人在同一個宿舍裏住了十八年，如今獨處一室，我覺得很輕鬆。我第一次有機會可以真正認識喬若莎‧艾伯特，我想我會喜歡她的。

您會嗎？

長腿叔叔

星期二

　　她們正在招募籃球隊的新血，我要去爭取這個機會。沒錯，我是長得很瘦小，不過我反應敏捷、身體強壯。當其他人跳到半空中時，我可以從她們的腳底下搶到球。練球真是有趣啊！午後，操場前滿樹的紅葉、黃葉，空氣中瀰漫著燃燒落葉的氣味，大家在此又叫又笑。這是我見過最快樂的一群女孩了，而我是其中最快樂的那一個。

　　本來打算寫封長信跟您談談我的功課（李皮太太說您想知道），不過第七堂課剛結束，再過十分鐘，我就要換好運動服到空地上集合了。您一定也希望我入選吧？

您永遠的喬若莎·艾伯特

附記：

　　（晚上九時）莎莉·馬克白剛才探頭進來說：「我想家想得快受不了了，妳呢？」

　　我笑了笑說：「才不呢！」我想我挺得過去。至少我是絕不會染上思鄉病的，沒聽說過有人想念孤兒院的吧，不是嗎？

10月10日

親愛的長腿叔叔：

　　您聽過米開朗基羅嗎？他是中世紀義大利的著名畫家，上英國文學課的人好像都知道他。我說他是個天使，惹得全班哄堂大笑。可那名字聽起來很像天使，您說不是嗎？上大學最糟糕的是，大家都認爲你應該懂得一些你根本沒學過的東西，這有時眞的讓人十分尷尬。不過，現在只要女孩們提到我不懂的事，我就閉口不言，然後回去查百科全書。

　　上學第一天，我就鬧了一個大笑話。有人提到梅特林克，我問她是不是我們學校的大一新生。這個笑話傳遍整所大學，眞是羞死人了。還好，我在課堂上的表現並不俗，甚至比某些人還要聰明。

　　您想知道我房間的佈置嗎？它就像是一曲棕黃相間的交響樂。淡黃色的牆壁，配上我買來的黃色丹寧布窗簾和靠墊，一張三塊錢的二手紅木書桌、一把籐椅、一條正中有墨水漬的棕色地毯，我把椅子放在有墨漬的地方。

　　窗戶很高，坐在椅子上看不到窗外。我把梳妝臺上方鏡子的部分拆掉只留下桌子並鋪上桌布，然後將它移到窗前，坐在上面看窗外正好合適。我還把抽屜一層層打開變成階梯，上來下去，舒服極了。

　　這些是莎莉‧馬克白幫我在高年級學生辦的拍賣會上挑的

長腿叔叔

東西。她從小到大都住家裏，對於家具擺設頗有經驗。對於以前那個從沒拿超過五毛錢的我來說，完全沒辦法想像──原來用一張真的五元鈔票去買東西，還能找些零頭回來，是一件多麼有趣的事！不過我向您保證，親愛的叔叔，我對於您給的零用錢絕對心存感激。

莎莉算是全世界最有趣的人了，而茱莉亞‧平萊頓則相反。註冊處的人安排這兩人一起住，可真古怪。莎莉對於每件事都覺得很有趣，甚至連考試不及格也一樣。而茱莉亞則不然，事事都讓她不開心，她對人從未表現出親切的態度。也許她相信，只要是平萊頓家的人，就一定可以上天堂毋須任何善行──茱莉亞跟我是天生的冤家。

現在您一定急於知道我的功課吧？

一、拉丁文：第二次迦太基戰爭。昨晚，漢尼拔和他的部隊紮營在特拉西美諾湖旁。他們埋下了伏兵對付羅馬人，凌晨四點打了一仗，羅馬人撤退。

二、法文：讀了二十四頁《三劍客》，學了第三組不規則動詞的變化。

三、幾何學：學完圓柱體，現在正在學圓錐體。

四、英文：學習表達能力。我的風格日益清晰、簡練。

五、生理學：進行到消化系統，下節課要學膽和胰。

正在接受教育的喬若莎‧艾伯特

附記：長腿叔叔，我希望您滴酒不沾，酒會傷肝。

星期三

親愛的長腿叔叔：

我改名字了。

在學校的名冊上我仍叫喬若莎，不過在其他場合我就改名叫茱蒂了。要為自己取小名實在很悲哀，不是嗎？不過茱蒂也不是我憑空捏造的名字，弗萊迪‧柏金斯在牙牙學語時，都是這樣叫我的。

我希望李皮太太以後在給小寶寶取名字時，能多動一點腦筋。她總是從電話簿上尋找要給我們取的姓氏——您要是翻開第一頁就會看到艾伯特了。而她取名字也都是信手拈來。我的名字喬若莎，是她從一塊墓碑上看到的，我一直都很討厭這個名字，不過我挺喜歡茱蒂的。這是一個傻呼呼的名字。擁有這名字的女孩，應該有雙藍眼睛、甜甜的、嬌生慣養，被全家人疼愛，什麼都不用煩惱，與我截然不同。真是那樣該有多好啊！不管我犯了什麼錯，都沒人會說是我的家人把我慣壞的。不過這樣假裝一下也挺好玩的，以後就請叫我茱蒂吧！

您知道嗎？我現在有三副真羊皮手套了。以前我有雙有指的手套，是掛在聖誕樹上的禮物，但從來沒有手指分開的那種真羊皮手套。現在我會時不時地拿出來戴在手上，好不容易才忍住，沒有把它戴到教室去。晚飯鈴響了，再見！

星期五

　　叔叔，您知道嗎？英文老師誇獎我上一篇作文，別出心裁。她真的這麼說了！想想我這十八年來受的訓練，似乎不太可能有這結果，不是嗎？約翰‧格利爾孤兒院的宗旨，就是要把九十七個小孤兒，變成九十七個相貌和言行舉止都一樣的人。而我不尋常的藝術天分，是小時候在門板上畫李皮太太培養出來的才能。

　　我對小時候的家說長道短，希望您不要不高興。不過您大權在握，如果我冒犯了您，您隨時可以停止您的資助。這樣說是不是不夠禮貌？不過您不能期望我有什麼教養，孤兒院畢竟不是淑女訓練學校。

　　叔叔，您知道的，在大學裏真正困難的不是功課，而是娛樂。很多時候，我都聽不懂女孩們在談些什麼，她們的玩笑似乎都與她們的過去聯繫在一起。這個過去人人有份，卻與我無緣，我在她們的世界裏就像一個外國人，聽不懂她們的語言。這是一種十分悲哀的感受，我這一生有太多這種感受。高中時，女孩們都一群一夥地冷眼看著我。我很奇怪，與眾不同，人人都知道這一點。我似乎感覺到「約翰‧格利爾孤兒院」就寫在我臉上，然後會有一些好人走過來安慰我。我恨他們每一個人──尤其是那些好人。

　　這裏沒有人知道我是在孤兒院長大的小孩。我告訴莎莉‧

馬克白我父母雙亡，是一位好心的老先生送我上大學——這些都是事實。我不希望您覺得我很愚蠢，我只是真心渴望自己可以跟其他女孩子一樣，不過孤兒院那可怕的陰影卻籠罩著我的童年，把我和大家隔絕開來。若能忘懷此事，把它逐出腦海，我想我應該可以變得跟其他女孩一樣可愛。我不認為自己和她們真有什麼區別，您說是吧？

不過，無論如何，莎莉‧馬克白都喜歡我！

您永遠的茱蒂‧艾伯特（原名喬若莎）

長腿叔叔

星期六上午

　　我剛才又把信重讀了一遍，調子似乎很沉重。但是您可能猜不到，我星期一早上要交一篇專題作文、又要複習幾何學而且還得了感冒，不停地打噴嚏。

星期日

　　昨天忘了寄信，今天再發點牢騷吧。早上來了個主教，您猜他都說了些什麼？

　　「聖經給我們的最佳許諾是：『常有窮人和你們同在』，他們可使我們永遠慈悲為懷。」

　　您瞧，窮人成了有用的家畜。要不是我已經變成有教養的小姐，我可能會在禮拜結束後，跑去告訴他我的想法。

10月25日

親愛的長腿叔叔：

　　我加入籃球隊了。您真該看看我左肩上的瘀傷，又青又紫的，還有橘黃色的劃痕。茱莉亞‧平萊頓也報名了，不過沒入選，真棒！

　　您瞧，我心胸多狹窄。

　　大學越來越有趣了。我喜歡這些女孩、喜歡老師、喜歡上課、喜歡校園也喜歡那些好吃的食物——每週吃兩次霜淇淋，從不吃在孤兒院常吃的玉米粥。

　　您只要我一個月寫一封信，不是嗎？我卻每隔幾天就寄一封給您！我對這些新奇的經歷是如此地興奮，一定要找個人傾訴，而您是我唯一認識的人。請原諒我的興奮吧！我很快就會安定下來的。如果您嫌煩，可以把它們丟到廢紙簍裏，我保證十一月中旬以前不再寫信就是了。

茱蒂在打籃球

噪噪不休的茱蒂‧艾伯特

11月15日

親愛的長腿叔叔：

　　請看我今天的學習內容：

　　正稜錐體平截頭凸面的面積，等於底邊總長和梯形一邊的高度乘積的一半。

　　聽起來似乎不對，但實際上非常正確。我還驗算過呢！

　　您還沒聽我提起我的衣服，是吧？叔叔，我有六件漂亮的新衣服——是專門為我添購的，不是那種確已不合身的衣服。也許您無法理解，這在一個孤兒的生命中代表什麼意義，但這些都是您給我的，我非常非常地感激您。可以受教育固然不錯，不過沒有什麼事比擁有六件新衣服，更讓人感到快樂了。這些都是參訪團的普查德小姐替我挑選的衣服，感謝上帝，幸好不是李皮太太。一件是綴著石竹花的絲綢晚禮服（我穿上很美）、一件藍色禮拜服、兩件餐服。其中一件餐服是紅色布料，上面鑲著東方花邊（我穿上後像個吉普賽人），另一件則使用玫瑰紅印花布料製成。最後兩件則是一套日常穿的灰色套服，還有一件是平時上課穿的。這些服裝對茉莉亞・平萊頓來說，可能算不了什麼；可是對茱蒂・艾伯特來說——天呀，實在是太了不起了！

　　我猜您現在一定這樣想——她是一個如此輕浮淺薄，多麼愚蠢的女孩子啊！讓這樣一個女孩子受教育，真是浪費錢！

　　不過叔叔，要是您一輩子除了花格布，沒穿過別的衣服，您就會明白我的感受了。我上高中以後，穿的衣服比花格布還不如呢！

　　捐贈二手衣的濟貧箱。

　　您無法想像，我是多麼害怕穿那些可怕的救濟服去學校。我擔心鄰座的女孩就是衣服的主人，而她會偷偷將這事告訴別的女孩，在背地裏嘲笑我，並對我指指點點。想到身上穿的也許就是自己討厭的人扔掉的衣服，我就心如刀絞。即使我今後一輩子都能穿上長統絲襪，也無法抹去這些環繞在我心頭上的傷痕。

最新戰報！

戰場消息：

　　十一月十三日星期四的四點時分，漢尼拔擊敗了羅馬人的先鋒部隊，帶領迦太基部隊翻山越嶺，進入卡西利濃平原。有一隊帶著輕便武器的努米底亞人與馬克西馬斯的步兵交戰，一共兩場戰役，還有幾次小衝突。羅馬人被擊退了，他們損失慘重。

　　很榮幸做您的戰地特派記者。

您虛榮的朋友

茱蒂‧艾伯特

附記：

　　我知道我不該奢求得到回信，也被告誡過不要拿這個問題來打擾您。不過長腿叔叔，就此一次，下不為例——您是老態龍鍾呢，還是半老？頭髮全部脫落了呢，還是微禿？您對我來說，就像幾何定理般抽象，是我這個腦袋難以想像的人。

　　一個身材高眺的男人，他厭惡女孩子，卻又對一個鹵莽無禮的女孩慷慨相助。他究竟會是什麼模樣呢？

　　盼覆。

12月19日

親愛的長腿叔叔：

　　您對我的問題置之不理，但您知道嗎？對我來說，那些問題非常重要。

　　您禿頭嗎？

　　我畫了您的長相——一切都很順利，但是到了頭頂就把我難倒了。我無法確定您的頭髮是白的、黑的、灰的，或者已經禿頭了呢？。

　　這是您的畫像：

但有幾個問題——我到底該不該加點頭髮上去呢？

您想知道您的眼睛是什麼顏色嗎？是灰色的喔，眉毛突出得像廊簷一樣（小說中稱為懸崖），嘴巴則像兩角下垂的直線。對啦，您瞧，我曉得很！您肯定是一個精神飽滿、脾氣暴躁的老傢伙。

（做禮拜的鐘聲響了！）

晚上9點45分

我給自己訂了一條雷也打不動的嚴格規定：絕不⋯⋯絕不在晚上唸書，只看小說，不管隔天有多少考試——我不得不這樣。您知道的，我已經白白浪費了十八年。叔叔，您無法想像我有多麼無知，我才剛開始明白自己是如此地淺薄。有個正常家庭、朋友和圖書館爲伴的女孩子，自然而然會知道很多事情，但那些卻是我前所未聞的事。

例如：我從沒聽過經典童謠《鵝媽媽》、讀過《藍鬍子》、《劫後英雄傳》、《灰姑娘》、《魯賓遜漂流記》、《簡愛》、《愛麗絲夢遊仙境》，或者吉卜林的片言隻語。我不知道亨利八世曾經再婚、雪萊是詩人、人類的祖先是猴子，也沒有聽說過伊甸園這個美麗的神話。我不知道 R.L.S 是羅伯特·路易斯·史蒂文生的縮寫，更不知喬治·艾略特是女性。我從未看過名叫《蒙娜麗莎的微笑》的畫作（這是眞的！請別懷疑），也從未聽說過什麼福爾摩斯。

現在這些我都知道了喔，還知道了其他一大堆的事情。但你也知道，我還是必須奮發努力好跟上進度。喔！不過這是件有趣的事！我盼望黃昏早些降臨，好在門口掛上「讀書中」的牌子。我要穿上我舒服的紅睡袍和毛茸茸拖鞋，把枕頭堆在椅背上，打開手邊的檯燈，然後埋頭讀啊，讀啊，一直讀下去。一本書嫌不夠，我常常找來四本書同時進行。現在，我正在讀丁尼生的詩、《浮華世界》和吉卜林的《山中的平凡故事》。另外，您聽了請不要笑話我，還有一本是《小婦人》。因爲，我發現自己是大學裏，唯一沒有受過《小婦人》薰陶的女孩。不過我沒告訴任何人（我可不想被當作怪胎），我只是悄悄地溜出去，用上個月剩下的 1.12 塊零用錢買了它。如果再有人提起醃酸橙，我就知道她在講些什麼了。

（十點鐘聲響了，這封信被打斷了多次。）

星期六

先生：

　　我很榮幸向您報告我在幾何學方面的新探索。上週五，我們放棄了平行六面體的功課，轉而學習截頭棱柱體。學習的道路真是艱難坎坷。

星期天

　　下個星期是聖誕假期，因此走廊上堆滿行李箱，堆到幾乎無法通行的地步，大家都興高采烈到把學業全都拋在腦後。我也要好好享受自己的假期了，一個德州的新生也準備留下來，我們計劃要出外遠足。如果有冰的話，我們還要學溜冰呢！再加上，這裡有一整座圖書館的書任我閱讀──我有整整三個星期可以在裏面讀書！

　　晚安，叔叔，我希望您和我一樣快樂！

您永遠的茱蒂

附記：

　　別忘了答覆我的問題。您若無法提筆，可以請祕書打個電報。只要說：

史密斯先生是禿頭

或

史密斯先生不是禿頭

或

史密斯滿頭白髮

　　您可以從我的零用錢裏扣去二角五分。明年一月再見，祝您聖誕快樂！

寫於聖誕假期的尾聲（確切的日期不明）

親愛的長腿叔叔：

　　您那裏下雪了嗎？從我的小閣樓望去，大地一片白雪茫茫，雪花如爆米花般紛紛揚揚地飄落下來。此刻正是傍晚，太陽西下（一種冷黃色調），落到寒冷的紫色山頭後方。我坐在高高的窗臺上，藉著最後一點餘暉，寫信給您。

　　意外地收到您寄來的五枚金幣！我還沒有養成收聖誕禮物的習慣，您就已經給我這麼多東西了——我所擁有的一切，您知道的——我覺得自己已經擁有太多了，但是我還是很高興。

您想知道我用這些錢買了什麼嗎？

一、一隻裝在皮盒中的銀手錶，它使我能夠準時溫習功
　　課。

二、馬修‧阿諾德的詩集。

三、一個熱水瓶。

四、一條船用小毯子（我的小閣樓很冷）。

五、五百張黃色稿紙（我很快就要開始當作家了）。

六、一本同義詞詞典（可以增加作家的辭彙量）。

七、（我不太想告訴您最後一件，不過還是告訴您吧）

　　一雙絲襪。瞧，長腿叔叔，我對您沒有任何保留。

　　如果您一定要知道我為什麼買絲襪的話，我會告訴你。事
實上，促使我去買絲襪的動機，極其淺薄。起因是茱莉亞‧平
萊頓每晚來我的房間做幾何題時，她都穿著絲襪盤腿坐在我的
床上。不過等著瞧，等她一放完假回來，我就要走進她的房
間，穿著絲襪坐在她的床上。叔叔，您瞧，我真是個壞胚子，
不過至少我很誠實。您早就從約翰‧格利爾孤兒院的紀錄裏，
知道我的不完美了，不是嗎？

　　總而言之（這是英語教師每句話的開場白），我對您送的
這七件禮物，都心存感激。我假裝它們是裝在一個大箱子裏，
從加州的家裏寄來的禮物。爸爸送錶、媽媽送毯子、祖母送熱
水瓶 —— 她老怕我在這種季節裏著涼 —— 稿紙是弟弟哈里送
的、妹妹伊莎貝爾送我長統襪、蘇珊姨媽送詩集、哈里舅舅
（小哈里與他同名）送詞典。他本想送巧克力，可是我堅持要

同義詞詞典。

您不會反對扮演這裏全部的家庭成員吧？

現在我該跟您談談我的假期了，但也許您只關心我的學業本身。希望您能體會「本身」這一詞的微妙涵義，這是我掌握到的最新辭彙。

那位來自德州的女孩名叫藍儂拉‧芬頓（這名字幾乎和喬若莎一樣可笑，不是嗎？）我喜歡她，不過更喜歡莎莉‧馬克白。我可能不會再像喜歡莎莉一樣喜歡任何人──除了您。我應該永遠把您放在首位，因爲您是我全家人的化身。每當天氣晴朗時，藍儂拉跟我還有兩個二年級的女孩子，就會散步到鄉間。我們穿著短裙和針織外衣，戴上線縫的帽子，拿著光滑的棍子四處敲敲打打。有一回我們走到四哩外的鎮上，在一家大學女生常去的餐館用餐。我要了紅燜龍蝦（三角五分）至於甜點呢！則是蕎麵餅和楓糖漿（一角五分），既營養又便宜！

對我而言，這尤其有趣，因爲跟孤兒院太不一樣了──每回我離開校園，總覺得好像逃獄的犯人。啊，我曾不假思索地談起我的感受，幾乎說破了自己的祕密，我得趕緊收住話題。守口如瓶眞非易事，我天性誠實坦率，要不是有您可以傾訴，我非憋死不可。

上星期五，佛格森樓的舍監舉行拉糖蜜聚會，還邀請了其他宿舍沒有回家的同學一起參加。就這樣，二十二名不同年級的學生友好地聚集在一起。廚房很寬敞，石造牆壁上掛著一排排銅鍋銅壺，最小的雙耳壺竟和煮衣服的鍋一般大，因爲佛格

森樓住了四百名女生呢！頭戴白帽、身上圍著圍裙的廚師，找出二十二套一模一樣的白圍裙和白帽子，不知道他是從哪裡弄來的，把我們全都裝扮成廚師。

　　眞的很有趣，雖然我吃過更好吃的糖蜜。當一切終於結束時，我們每個人、整個廚房，連同門板全都黏答答的。然後我們依然戴著白帽，圍著圍裙，每人一把大湯匙或大叉子抑或是平底鍋，列隊穿過空蕩蕩的大廳到達教師休息室。那裏有半打教授和講師正在打發寧靜的夜晚。我們爲他們唱校歌然後送上糖蜜，他們雖然一臉猶豫，但還是很有禮貌地接受了。最後我們離開休息室，留他們在那裡安靜地吮吸一大堆黏答答的糖蜜。

　　所以您瞧瞧，叔叔，這就是我的求學過程！您眞的不認爲我應該當個藝術家而不是作家嗎？

　　再過兩天假期就要結束，我又可以高興地見到同學們了。我已經感到有些寂寞，九個人住著原本是四百人住的房子，確實令人坐立不安。

　　可憐的叔叔，您一定累了！我本來打算要寫封簡短的感謝函——不過我一提筆，就寫了十一頁。

晚安，謝謝您惦記著我——我本來應該是要無比快樂的，可惜心頭有一小朵烏雲籠罩著我——因為二月要考試了。

愛您的茱蒂

附記：

致上對您的愛意會不會不太恰當？如果是這樣，請您原諒。我總得愛個什麼人吧，而可以選擇的對象只有您和李皮太太。所以您瞧，親愛的叔叔，您可得為我忍耐一下，因為我實在無法愛她呀！

考試前夕

親愛的長腿叔叔：

您真該看看全校同學都在啃書的情景！我們根本快要把才剛過完的假期都忘得一乾二淨了。因為四天以來，我背誦了五十七個不規則動詞，希望老天保佑我考試前不要全都忘記了才好。

許多同學把讀過的課本賣掉，但我決定全部留下來。畢業後，可以把學過的東西展示在書架上，不懂的細節還可以隨時查詢。這比全部記在腦海裏要方便得多，當然也會更爲準確。

茱莉亞‧平萊頓今晚來我的宿舍做禮貌性拜訪，一坐就是一個小時。她談到自己的家族，而我卻無法打斷這個話題。她問起我外婆家的姓氏——您聽過有人會如此冒昧地問一個孤兒這種問題嗎？我沒有勇氣說不知道，只好胡編亂造，信口說了腦海中浮現的第一個姓氏，蒙哥馬利。她又追問，是麻薩諸塞州的蒙哥馬利家族，還是維吉尼亞州的蒙哥馬利家族？

她的母親姓路德福特，這個姓氏可以追溯到方舟時代，還曾經和亨利八世聯姻。她的父系則始於亞當之前，最早的源頭是一群毛色豐潤、尾巴奇長的良種猿猴。

今晚本想給您寫一封親切、愉快而有趣的信，但是我太睏了，而且心中充滿憂慮。唉！新生可眞苦！

快要考試的茱蒂

星期日

最親愛的長腿叔叔：

我有個很不好很不好的消息要告訴您，不過我不會從這裏開始寫，我要先讓您的心情高興起來。

喬若莎‧艾伯特已經開始要當作家了！她寫了一首名叫

〈在我的閣樓〉的詩，刊登在第二期《月刊》上，並且刊在首頁喔！這對一名新生來說，真是莫大的榮耀。昨天晚上我從教堂出來，英語老師叫住我，說我的詩寫得很動人，只是第六行的韻腳太多了。如果您想看，我會寄一份給您。

　　讓我想想還有什麼趣事——喔，對了！我正在學溜冰，已經算是可以自由自在地滑來滑去。還有，我也學會了如何從體

育館的屋頂用繩索爬下來。另外，我的跳高成績有三尺六，希望不久就可以跳過四尺。

今天早晨阿拉巴馬主教的講道十分精采。他的題目是：「不要論斷人，免得被論斷」，意思是說，要原諒別人的缺點而不要求全責備，希望您聽過這一節。

這是個陽光燦爛，讓人眼花繚亂的冬日下午。結冰的雪花掛在松樹枝頭，大地白雪皚皚。只有我除外，我的內心被悲傷壓抑著。

現在要告訴您那壞消息了——勇敢些，茱蒂！妳一定要說出口。

現在您的心情真的很好嗎？我的數學和拉丁文作文兩門課不及格，我正在補習，準備下個月補考。如果讓您生氣了，我很抱歉。不過我卻不是很在意，因為我從許多課外讀物中學到了很多東西。我讀了十七本小說和許多詩歌，包括《浮華世界》、《理查‧費福羅》、《愛麗絲夢遊仙境》等必讀之書。還有愛默生的《隨筆集》、羅克哈特的《司各脫生平》、吉蓬的《羅馬帝國》第一卷和半本塞利尼的《生平》——他真有意思！他常在清晨外出閒逛，殺一個人後再回去吃早餐。

所以您瞧，叔叔，這比死讀拉丁文的收穫還要豐富多了吧！如果我保證以後絕不再考不及格，您能原諒我嗎？

您悲傷的茱蒂

長腿叔叔

最親愛的長腿叔叔：

　　這是本月中旬額外寫的一封信，因爲今晚我感到十分寂寞。窗外狂風暴雨，校園裏漆黑一片。加上我喝了黑咖啡，難以入眠。

　　今晚我辦了一個晚餐派對，受邀的人有莎莉、茱莉亞和藍儂拉·芬頓。我備有沙丁魚、烤鬆餅、沙拉、牛奶軟糖和咖啡。茱莉亞說她玩得很愉快，不過只有莎莉留下來幫忙洗盤子。

　　我本可以利用今晚的時間學拉丁文，但是，說實在的，我對拉丁文總是漫不經心。我們學完了李維和《論老年》，正在上《論友誼》（讀作該死的依西西亞）。

　　您介不介意充當一下我的祖母？莎莉有祖母，茱莉亞跟藍儂拉不但有祖母，而且還有外祖母，她們今晚一直都在比較彼此的祖母。我完全無法想像。我眞想有這樣一位親戚，一位和藹可親的老人。所以如果您不反對的話，我想在您八十三歲生日時送一件禮物給您：一頂史上最可愛，綴著紫色緞帶和蕾絲花邊的帽子，這是我昨天在城裏的商店看到的。

　　噹！！！！！！！！！！！！

　　教堂的鐘敲了十二下，我想我終於有點睏了。

晚安，祖母我好愛您
茱蒂

3月5日

親愛的長腿叔叔：

　　我正在學寫拉丁語作文。我一直在學，並且會繼續學下去。我正準備要繼續學習，因為下星期二第七節課即將補考，我得努力爭取及格，否則就要留級。所以下次寫信時我如果不是安然無恙，愉快地擺脫了不及格的陰影，就是已經支離破碎了。

　　考完試後，我會寫封像樣的信給您，今晚我要認真學習拉丁文的奪格絕對句。

茱蒂

3月26日

長腿叔叔史密斯先生：

　　先生，您從不回答任何問題，亦不曾對我的所作所為表示出些許興趣。您可能是那些理事中最可惡的一個。您讓我受教育，完全是出於一種道義和責任，毫無半點關懷和愛意。我對您一無所知，甚至不知道您的名字，寫信給「一個東西」實在毫無意義。我懷疑您根本讀都不讀我的信，就將它們扔進廢紙簍。今後，除了學業之外，我再也不在信上寫其他事情了。上星期補考數學跟拉丁文，我兩科都通過了，一點問題也沒有。

您最真實的喬若莎・艾伯特

4月2日

親愛的長腿叔叔：

我是個壞孩子。

請原諒我上星期寄給您那封蠻橫無禮的信——寫信那晚，我覺得非常孤獨，渾身不舒服，喉嚨還隱隱作痛。當時我不知道自己得了扁桃腺炎和流行性感冒，現在，我住進大學病房已經六天了。今天他們第一次讓我坐起來，還給我紙筆，護士長兇極了。我總是心神不安，倘若得不到您的原諒，我永遠都好不起來了。

這就是我現在的模樣，繃帶繞過我的頭綁了個大結，像兔子的耳朵。

這樣您會對我產生一點同情嗎？我的舌下腺腫起來了，我已經學了一年的生理課還不知道舌下腺在哪裡，教育是多麼無用呀！

　　我不能寫了，坐久後感覺有點虛弱，請原諒我的粗魯和忘恩負義，因為我從小就缺乏教養！

愛您的茱蒂·艾伯特

4月4日住院中

最親愛的長腿叔叔：

　　昨天傍晚，坐在病床上望著窗外的雨景，我深感體制之下的人生真是無聊透了。就在那時，護士送了一個白色大盒子給我，裏面裝滿鮮豔的玫瑰花。更令人愉快的是，上面還附有一張措辭優雅的便箋，一筆性格的左斜體，一點點爬升上去。叔叔，謝謝您！我要對您說一千個謝謝！這是我生平第一件真正的禮物，我高興極了，像個孩子似的躺下來大哭了一場。

現在我能確信您讀過我的信了，我以後會寫得更有趣些，這樣才值得用紅緞帶紮起來，放在保險櫃裏。不過請找出那封糟糕透頂的信燒掉它，我不想您再次讀起它。

謝謝您使一個生病、悲傷又神經兮兮的新生高興起來。也許您有很多親愛的家人與朋友，無法明白孤獨是什麼樣的滋味，可是我懂。

晚安！我保證以後絕不再胡鬧了，因為我現在知道您是一個活生生的真人。而且我也保證，以後不再拿問題來煩您了。

您還討厭女孩子嗎？

您永遠的茱蒂

星期一第八節課

親愛的長腿叔叔：

但願您不是坐在癩蛤蟆上的那位理事。聽說當時砰地一聲十分響亮，那有可能是一位比您胖得多的理事。

您記得約翰·格利爾孤兒院洗衣房的窗外，那些覆蓋著鐵條的防空洞嗎？每逢春季蛤蟆鼓噪時，我們常常捉那些蛤蟆藏在窗外的洞中。有時牠們爬進洗衣房，就會引起一陣愉悅的騷動，我們也會因而受到嚴厲的懲罰。但是捕捉蛤蟆的行為並未

就此停止。

有一天——對了，我不拿細節來煩您——一隻又肥又大，黏黏糊糊的蛤蟆，不知怎地，躍進了理事休息室的大皮椅子裏。結果，下午開會時——您一定在場，而且一定記得當時的情景。

現在冷靜地回想起來，我受到懲罰也是罪有應得，如果我沒有記錯的話，懲罰的份量也算是恰如其分。

不知道為什麼我竟如此懷舊，莫非是春天和蛤蟆觸動了我貪玩的天性？現在這裏沒有不許捕蛙的禁令，但我已經沒有捕蛙的想望了。

星期四作禮拜後

您知道我最喜歡哪本書嗎？我指的是現在。雖然我的愛好三天一變，但目前我最喜歡《咆哮山莊》。愛蜜麗·勃朗特寫這本書時還很年輕，從未到過哈渥教區之外的地方。她一生從未接觸過男性，如何能創造出希斯·克利夫這樣一個人來呢？

我就沒辦法跟她一樣。但我明明也同樣年輕，又沒出過孤兒院的大門——早已具備了成功的種種條件才對。我有時很氣餒，覺得自己不是天才。長腿叔叔，如果我成不了偉大的作家，您會對我感到失望嗎？春天裏，一切都那麼美好、青翠、

長腿叔叔

欣欣向榮，我眞想丟下功課，跑去和大自然玩耍。野外有無數新鮮事物，如果可以經歷書中的故事，那肯定會比寫書有趣多了。

哎呀！！！！！！！

我這一聲叫喊，把莎莉、茱莉亞還有（眞倒楣）走廊那頭的大四生都招來了。因爲我見到一條蜈蚣，就像下面的圖一樣：

但牠實際上比這幅圖還可怕。我剛寫完上句，正在斟酌下句時，噗噠！牠從天而降落在我身旁，我爲了躲開牠打翻了桌上的兩隻杯子。莎莉用我的梳子背面拍打牠，弄死了前半截（這把梳子我再也不能用了），後面的五十雙腳跑到梳妝臺下，不見了。

老舊的宿舍爬滿了長春藤，其中隱藏著無數的蜈蚣，簡直比老虎蹲在床下還可怕。

星期五晚上9時30分

　　真是屋漏偏逢連夜雨。今天早晨我沒聽見起床鈴，睡過頭了。然後急急忙忙地穿衣服時，又不小心扯斷鞋帶，還把領口的鈕子從脖子上扯下來。我沒有趕上早餐，第一節自習課也遲到了，鋼筆漏水，居然又沒帶吸墨紙。上三角幾何課時，教授與我在對數方面的一個小問題上出現分歧，查了查書，竟然她才是對的。午餐吃爛羊肉和大黃莖，這都是我不愛吃的食物，因為它們的味道和孤兒院的伙食一樣。郵差什麼也沒送來，只有賬單（不過說真的，除了賬單我也不曾收到過別的東西，我的家人從來不寫信）。下午的英語課突然改成寫作課，一進教室，映入眼簾的是：

> 我別無他求，
> 也不復遭到拒絕。
> 我為此獻上我的生命，
> 那位無所不能的商人笑了。
> 巴西？他擺弄著鈕釦，
> 對我看也不看，
> 但是，夫人，難道我們今天
> 就沒有其他可以呈獻？

這是一首詩，我不知道作者是誰，也不明白它的含意。到教室時，只見它工整地抄在黑板上，要求我們加以評論。當我讀完第一段時似乎有些懂了。無所不能的商人，是指賜福給行善者的神祇，可是看到祂在第二段中擺弄鈕釦，這推測似乎有些褻瀆神明，我又慌忙改變了主意。班上其他同學與我陷入相同的窘境，整整三刻鐘，我們面對著一張白紙，腦子裏空空如也。受教育真是個極其磨人的過程。

這還沒完，更倒楣的事還在後面。

由於雨天不能打高爾夫球，只好到健身房去。我旁邊那個女孩的體操棒「砰」地一下，打到我的手肘。回到宿舍，我的天藍色新春裝送來了，可是裙子太小，緊到完全沒辦法坐下來。星期五是打掃宿舍的日子，清潔女工把我桌上的紙弄得亂七八糟。飯後甜食吃「墓碑」（一種香草牛奶凍）。做禮拜的時間又延長了二十分鐘，宣講的是為婦之道。還有，當我好不容易鬆了口氣，坐下來看《貴婦人的畫像》時，阿克莉這個笨手笨腳、死氣沉沉、面孔長得像生麵糰的女孩跑來問我，星期一的課是從第六十九段還是從第七十段開始。這個女孩上拉丁語課時坐在我旁邊，因為她的姓和我一樣都是 A 字母開頭（我真希望李皮太太給我起了個 Z 字母開頭的姓，比如紮布里斯基）。她坐在我旁邊整整一個鐘頭，剛剛才走。

您有聽過這麼一連串叫人喪氣的事嗎？生活中，並非僅在大難臨頭時才要顯現英雄本色，人人都能勇於面對危險或不幸。但要能對日常的煩擾付諸一笑，還真需要點強大的心理素質才行。

今後，我要培養這種心理素質。我要把生活視為一場競技，盡可能熟巧地、公平地投入。勝也罷、敗也罷，我都會聳聳肩，一笑置之。

不管怎樣，我要做一個堂堂正正的人。親愛的長腿叔叔，您再也不會聽到我對茱莉亞穿長統絲襪，或是蜈蚣從天而降這樣的事發出怨言了。

請速覆信。

永遠是您的茱蒂

5月27日

長腿叔叔：

親愛的先生，今天收到李皮太太的來信，她希望我品學兼優，表現良好。如果我這個夏天無處可去，她願意讓我回孤兒院去工作來賺取自己的食宿，直到大學開學為止。

我恨約翰·格利爾孤兒院。

我寧死也不回去！

您最誠實的喬若莎·艾伯特

親愛的長腿叔叔：

您真好！

能到農莊去我實在是太高興了，因為我這輩子還沒去過農莊；而且我也恨死回到約翰·格利爾孤兒院，去洗一整個夏天的盤子。我早已失去謙卑的心，我害怕哪天情緒失控，一怒之下把孤兒院裡的杯盤全部摔碎。

請原諒我匆匆止筆，不能繼續談我的近況。我正在上法文課，我擔心老師很快就會叫我了。他果然叫我了！

Au revior（再見）

Je vous aime beaucoup（我好愛您）

茱蒂

5月30日

親愛的長腿叔叔：

您到過我們的學校嗎？（這只是一句客套話，請別在意。）五月時節，這裏的景致美妙極了。灌木叢中花團爛漫，樹枝上泛起一片青綠色——連最蒼老的松樹也煥然一新，草皮上點綴著黃色蒲公英，還有幾百個穿著藍白和粉紅衣裳的女孩，每個人都歡天喜地，無憂無慮的樣子。不僅是假期即將來臨的緣故，還有伴隨而來令人期待的一切，考試的憂慮也就此拋到九霄雲外去了。

這真是令人心曠神怡，而我是裏面最快樂的一個！因為我再也不是在約翰‧格利爾孤兒院裏了，不再是誰的保姆、打字員或會計（您知道如果沒有您，我早該是了）。

> 我對過去所做的一切壞事，我很抱歉
> 我曾經對李皮太太很無禮，我很抱歉
> 我曾經打弗萊迪‧平頓，我很抱歉
> 我曾經把鹽倒進糖罐裏，我很抱歉
> 我曾經在理事的背後扮鬼臉，我很抱歉

我以後要聽話、溫柔、善良地對待大家，因為我太快樂了。這個夏天我要開始不斷寫作，朝一個偉大的作家之路邁進。這算不算是個崇高的目標？我在培養一種美好的氣質！儘管寒冷和冰霜會使它低落，但燦爛的陽光將會使它迅速高漲起來。

這是每個人的必經之路，我不相信所謂逆境、憂傷或失意會造就道德力量的理論，我深信幸福的人才會熱情洋溢。我也不相信厭世者（好字眼，剛剛學會的），長腿叔叔，您不是一個厭世者吧！

我一開始就告訴您學校的風景，是希望您能來稍微參觀一下，我可以陪您到處走走，告訴您：

「親愛的叔叔，那是圖書館，這是煤氣廠。您左手邊的哥德式建築物是體育館，它旁邊的都鐸式建築，是新建的醫務大樓。」

哦！我很會帶人參觀喔！過去在約翰‧格利爾孤兒院我常常帶人參觀，今天還領人走了一整天，真的，不騙您！而且是一位男士！

這是個很棒的經歷，因為我從未跟男人說過話（除了偶爾出現的理事，但他們不算）。對不起，叔叔，當我那樣談理事的時候，並不是故意要冒犯您，我並沒有把您看成他們其中的一員，您只是偶然加入理事會。所謂理事，應當是肥胖、傲慢、一副慈善模樣，喜歡摸人腦袋，身上還會掛一個金懷錶。

那樣看起來就像一隻金甲蟲，但這是除了您以外其他理事的畫像。

不過——言歸正傳：

我和一名男士散步、聊天、喝茶。他是一位很了不起的人物——茱莉亞家族的傑維‧平萊頓先生。簡單地說，就是她的叔叔（詳細說來，我應該告訴您，他的身材和您一樣高），他到城裏辦事順便來學校看姪女。他是茱莉亞爸爸最小的弟弟，但茱莉亞和他並不親密。好像在她的童年時代，他看了她一眼，覺得沒有多大的好感，就再也不注意她了。

無論如何，他來了，端坐在接待室裏，帽子、手杖、手套放在一邊。莎莉和茱莉亞的第七節是朗讀課，不能缺席，所以茱莉亞衝進我的房間求我陪他到處走走，等她上完第七堂課，再領著她叔叔去找她。出於禮貌，我勉強答應了，但我對平萊頓家族的人，實在沒有多大的好感。

不過他是一個溫文儒雅、情感豐富的人——一點也不像平萊頓家族的人。我們度過了一段美好的時光，從那時起，我就渴望能有個叔叔，您來作我的叔叔好嗎？我覺得叔叔比祖母還好。

叔叔，平萊頓先生讓我想起您，像二十年前的您。您瞧，我對您多麼熟悉，儘管我們還沒有見過面。他高高瘦瘦、臉色黝黑、輪廓很深，雖然沒有開懷大笑，但只要把嘴角一咧，就能讓人覺得很舒服。儘管認識不久，我卻和他一見如故。

我們走遍了中央廣場到遊樂場的每個角落。他說他走累了，要喝杯茶，提議我們去學院附近的小吃店。小吃店不遠，就在校門外的小路旁。我對他說，該叫茱莉亞和莎莉一起去，但他卻說，他不願自己的姪女喝太多茶，這會使她變得神經質，所以我們就直接去了。我們一起坐在走廊上的一張雅致的小桌子旁，享用茶、蛋糕、霜淇淋和餅乾。因為是月底，大家的零用錢都快花光了，所以店裏沒人。

我們玩得很開心，但一回到學校他就得去趕火車，因此匆匆見了茱莉亞一面就走了。茱莉亞對於我把他帶出去很惱火，看來他是位非常富有又討人喜歡的叔叔。知道他很富有讓我感覺好過一些，因為茶和點心很貴，每樣要六角錢呢！

今天早上（今天是星期一）快遞送來三盒巧克力，分別送給茱莉亞、莎莉和我。您覺得如何呢？一個男人送來了巧克力！

我開始感到自己像個女孩子，而不是個孤兒。

我希望您哪天能來吃茶點，讓我看看自己喜不喜歡您。可是如果我不喜歡，那豈不太糟糕了？不過，我相信自己會喜歡您的。

好了，向您致意！

我永遠不會忘記您
茱蒂

附記：

今天早晨照鏡子，我發現自己長了個酒窩，以前我從來沒有看到過。真奇怪，您知道這是從哪裡來的嗎？

6月9日

親愛的長腿叔叔：

今天眞高興！我剛考完最後一科──生物學。接下來呢，我要到農莊去住三個月！

對於農莊我一點概念也沒有，我這輩子不曾去過，甚至連看都沒看過（從火車上的窗戶往外看到的除外）。不過，我想我會喜歡農場，我也會開始喜歡自由自在。

我現在還不太習慣在約翰・格利爾孤兒院之外的地方生活。每當想到這一點，我就感到一陣心神不定，覺得自己好像應該跑快點、再快一點；邊跑邊回頭張望，看看李皮太太是不是在我背後伸手，要將我抓回去。這個夏天我對誰都不用顧忌了，對嗎？

您徒有其名的權威嚇唬不了我，您離我太遠了，對我沒有傷害。對我來說李皮太太已經永遠去世了。山普夫婦不會監督我的品行吧？我想不會！我已經長大成人了！萬歲！

就寫到這裏吧！現在我要離開您去收拾自己的行李了，還有三個裝有茶壺、盤子、枕頭和書籍的大箱子。

您永遠的茱蒂

附記：這是我的生物學試卷，您認爲您可以及格嗎？

星期六晚上於洛克威洛農莊

最親愛的長腿叔叔：

我才剛到農莊還沒開始整理行李，就已經迫不及待地想告訴您，我是多麼喜歡農莊。這真是好棒好棒的地方！房子是方形的，如下圖：

而且它十分古老，大約有一百年歷史了。我無法畫出的那一面，有一個露臺，它接著一個門廊。圖畫得不好，不能展現出它的真面目——那些像雞毛撢子似的東西是楓樹，在車道旁帶刺的是松樹和鐵杉。這棟房子座落在山頂上，放眼遠眺，綠色的草地會一直延伸到遠處的一座小山上。

康涅狄格州的地形就像頭髮上燙出的波浪，洛克威洛農場就坐落在浪尖上。穀倉原本在道路的那邊，正好擋住了視線，幸好天上來了一道閃電把它夷為平地。

這裏住著山普先生和山普太太，還有一個雇來的女工和兩個男工。工人們都在廚房吃飯，山普家跟茱蒂則是在餐廳裏用餐。晚飯有火腿、蛋、餅乾、蜂蜜、果凍、蛋糕、泡菜、奶酪還有飯後茶，和一大堆的談話。我這輩子從來沒講過這麼多話，不管我說什麼都很好笑。我猜是因為我從不曾到過鄉間，而我的問題來自於，我對所有事物都不太瞭解。

那個打了叉叉的房間不是凶案現場，而是我住的房間。它又大又方正，十分寬敞。裏頭有可愛的老式家具，而窗戶得用棍子撐開，上頭還掛有鑲著金邊的綠色塗漆，一碰就會掉色。此外，這房間內還有一張方形大木桌——我打算整個夏天都趴在上面寫小說。

喔！叔叔，我實在太興奮了！我盼望著天亮，好去四處探險。現在是晚上八點半，我要吹熄蠟燭想辦法讓自己入睡，我們必須五點起床。您曾經擁有過這麼有趣的體驗嗎？我不敢相信我真的是茱蒂！您和仁慈的上帝給予我太多了，我一定要做一個非常、非常、非常、非常好的人，來報答您。我會這麼做的，您等著瞧吧！

晚安！

茱蒂

長腿叔叔

附記：

　　您要是能聽到青蛙的鼓噪和豬仔的尖叫聲，該有多好呀！還有那一輪彎月，從我的右臂看上去就能看到月亮！

7月12日於洛克威洛農莊

親愛的長腿叔叔：

　　您的祕書怎麼會知道洛克威洛農莊呢？（這不是客套話，我確實很好奇。）因為這個農莊過去曾為傑維・平萊頓先生所有，現在，他把農場送給他的保姆——山普太太了。多麼有意思的巧合啊！她到現在還稱呼他「傑維少爺」，說他小時候是多麼可愛。她將一小撮他小時候的捲髮珍藏在盒中，是紅色的——至少是微紅色的！

　　打從山普太太知道我認識他，就對我另眼相待。認識平萊頓家族的一員，在洛克威洛可算是最好的引見詞了，而平萊頓家族的驕傲是傑維少爺——我很高興茱莉亞屬於底層的一支。

　　農莊越來越好玩了，昨天我還坐了運草的馬車。我們有三隻大豬和九隻豬仔，您應該看看牠們的吃相，真不愧是豬！我們還有無數隻的雛雞、小鴨、火雞和珍珠雞。您本可住在農場，怎麼偏要住在城市裏，真是不可思議。

　　我每天的工作就是揀雞蛋。昨天在穀倉裏，我想爬過去掏一個黑母雞偷走的鳥窩，卻不小心從樑上摔了下來。當我帶著膝蓋的傷回去時，山普太太一邊幫我包紮，一邊自言自語地說：「天呀！傑維少爺也從同一根樑上摔下來過，就像是昨天的事情一樣，連膝蓋受傷的位置都一模一樣啊！」

這裏的景致優美無比，山谷、河流、青鬱鬱的山丘和遠處莽莽蒼蒼的高山，全都令人回味無窮。

每個星期我們做兩次奶油，並且把奶油放置在由石頭砌成的冷藏室裏，有一道小河從下面潺潺流過。鄰近的農民有脫脂器，但我們並不喜歡這種新鮮玩意兒，依然用鍋子攪拌，儘管麻煩些，但品質更好也值得這麼做。我們有六頭牛，我全替牠們取好了名字：

一、西爾維亞，因爲她在林中出生。

二、萊茲比亞，以卡圖勒斯作品中的人物命名。

三、莎莉。

四、茱莉亞，一隻有花斑的
　　無趣動物。

五、茱蒂，以我來命名。

六、長腿叔叔。您不會介意
　　吧，叔叔？牠是純澤西
　　血統而且性格可愛。牛
　　看起來像這樣 —— 您
　　瞧，牠眞是名副其實。

我還沒有時間開始我的巨作，因為農莊讓我忙個不停。

您永遠的茱蒂

附記：

一、我學會做甜甜圈了。

二、您如果想養雞的話，我推薦奧爾平頓種，牠們腿上不
　　長毛。

三、我真想送您一塊我昨天做的新鮮奶油，我成了一個不
　　錯的擠奶姑娘。

四、這是未來的大作家——喬若莎・艾伯特趕牛回家圖：

我不會畫牛！

星期日

親愛的長腿叔叔：

您不覺得很有趣嗎？昨天下午當我正要開始寫信給您時，才剛提起筆寫下：「親愛的長腿叔叔」，忽然想起我答應山普太太要採些黑莓當作晚餐甜點，就把信紙留在桌上出去了。當我回來時，您知道我發現什麼坐在信紙中央嗎？是一位真正的「長腿叔叔」——大蜘蛛！

我輕輕拈起牠的一隻腳，放到窗外。我絕對不會傷害牠，因為牠總讓我想到您。

在教堂催人入眠的佈道聲中，有人懶洋洋地搖著芭蕉扇，除了牧師的聲音外，就只有窗外樹叢中蟋蟀的唧唧聲。我一直睡到大家起立唱讚美詩才醒過來，我為剛才沒有用心聽佈道感到內疚。真想明瞭那個人選擇這首讚美詩的心理，請聽：

> 來吧，丟下你的玩物和塵世的消遣，
> 與我在天國攜手歡騰。
> 要不，朋友，你我從此永別，
> 任你淪入地獄受盡磨難。

我發現和山普夫婦討論宗教很不妥當。他們的上帝（那是他們從清教徒的祖先那裏，完整無缺地繼承下來的）狹隘、吝嗇、不講理、不公正、報復心強而又冥頑不靈。謝天謝地，我的上帝不是自什麼人遺傳下來的。我可以自由地創造自己的上帝！祂善良、富有同情心、有想像力、寬宏大量而又通情達理──還富有幽默感。

我非常喜歡山普夫婦，他們的行動超越了他們的信仰，勝過他們的上帝。我這麼一說，把他們嚇壞了，認為我褻瀆了上帝，但我真的認為他們勝過了上帝。於是我們不再辯論這方面的話題了。

現在是星期日的下午。

阿馬薩（男雇工）和嘉麗（女雇工）剛剛駕著馬車走了。阿馬薩精神抖擻，鬍子刮得乾乾淨淨的，繫著紫色領帶，戴著鵝黃色鹿皮手套。嘉麗戴著一頂綴有紅玫瑰的大帽子，身穿一襲藍色裙裝，頭髮捲成緊緊的小卷。阿馬薩花了整整一個上午的時間，洗刷那輛輕便馬車；嘉麗則沒有去教堂，假裝留下來做飯，實際上是在燙她那身細布衣服。

再過兩分鐘，等我寫完這封信，我就要沉醉到一本書裏去了。那是我在樓上發現的書，書名是《在小徑上》，扉頁上有著小男孩稚拙的筆跡寫道：

    傑維·平萊頓

    如果這本書迷了路，

　　　　　請揪著它的耳朵，

　　　　　　送它回家。

　　他十一歲時生了一場病，曾來這裏療養，於是把《在小徑上》這本書留在這裏了。看來他讀得很認真──到處都有他骯髒的小手留下的污漬。閣樓的一角還留有一輛水車、一個風車和一些彈弓。山普太太常常談起他，以至於讓我覺得他依然還是個可愛、頭髮蓬亂的骯髒孩子，並沒有長成一個戴著絲帽，拿著手杖的紳士。他拿著球拍在樓梯爬上爬下，從不記得關紗門，老是吵著要餅乾吃（我知道山普太太對他有求必應，他一張口要，準會應許他）。他似乎非常富有冒險精神，勇敢而正直，可惜他是平萊頓家族的人，但他實際上比這家人還要更好一點。

　　　　　　　　　　您充滿感情的孤兒茱蒂·艾伯特

附記：

　　第一章講印地安人、第二章講路上的強盜，我屏住呼吸，第三章講什麼呢？卷首上寫著「印地安人躍到半空中，落地身亡」。

　　茱蒂和傑維怎麼能不開心呢？

9月15日

親愛的長腿叔叔：

　　昨天在轉角雜貨店的麵粉秤上量體重，我胖了九磅。讓我向您推薦洛克威洛，那是休養身體的最佳去處。

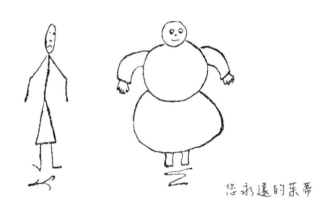

您永遠的茱蒂

9月25日

親愛的長腿叔叔：

　　上星期五返校，您瞧——我已經是大學二年級的學生了。離開洛克威洛雖然心裏很難過，不過很高興又開學了，回到熟悉的地方感覺真好。我已經開始習慣大學生活，能應付自如了。事實上，我開始覺得自己是一個社會人了——就好像我真的是屬於它，而不是被人勉強收留的。

我所說的這些，您或許根本無法理解。一位當上理事的大人物，怎麼能夠理解一個卑微孤兒的想法呢？

現在，叔叔，您聽聽這個。您猜我跟誰同住？莎莉‧馬克白與茱莉亞‧平萊頓。這是真的，我們有三間臥室和一間書房！請看下圖：

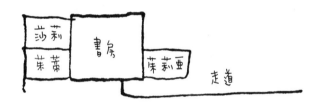

從去年春天，莎莉跟我就決定住在一起；但不知道為什麼，茱莉亞打定主意要跟莎莉住一起。我猜不出來，因為她們倆一點共同點也沒有。也許平萊頓家族的人生性謹慎，因循守舊（好字眼！），總之，我們住在一起了。想想看，約翰‧格利爾孤兒院的孤兒喬若莎‧艾伯特，與平萊頓的家族成員住在一起，這裏果然是一個民主國家！

莎莉要競選班代表，除非一切徵兆都是假象，否則她一定會當選的。這滿是密謀的氛圍真該讓您見識一下——我們多像個政治家。喔！叔叔，我告訴您，當我們婦女爭取到權利後，你們男人就得小心點了！下星期六投票，不管誰當選，晚上都將會舉行火炬遊行。

　　我開始修化學了。一個不尋常的學科，我從沒有聽說過這種學科。現在正學到分子和原子，下個月我就能告訴您更多具體的細節。

　　我也開始學習辯論和邏輯，還有世界史、莎士比亞戲劇、法文。像這樣持續個幾年，我一定會變得學識淵博。我比較想選經濟而不是法文，不過我不敢，因為我擔心自己若不繼續修法文，教授可能不會讓我通過。畢竟六月份的考試我是勉強才通過，但我得說這應該歸咎於我高中的基礎太薄弱了。

　　班上有一個同學法文說得和英文一樣流利。她小時候隨父母出國，在修道院學校讀了三年。您可以想像她是多麼地鶴立雞群，那些不規則動詞對她來說，就像遊戲一樣。我多麼希望小時候父母把我丟到法國修道院，而不是什麼孤兒院。唉，不對，我不是這個意思。因為如果真是那樣的話，我又怎麼能認識您呢？哪怕不會法語，我也要認識您。

　　晚安，叔叔，我現在要去拜訪哈莉‧馬丁，談談化學反應，順便談談我對下一屆班代表的看法。

您積極參政的茱蒂‧艾伯特

10月17日

親愛的長腿叔叔：

假如體育館的游泳池都裝滿了檸檬果凍，人在裏面游泳的話，會浮起還是下沉？

晚餐後，當我們正在吃檸檬果凍時，有人提出這個問題；我們激烈地爭論了半個小時，還是沒有結論。莎莉認爲她可以在裏面游泳，而我則斷定，即使是世界上最頂尖的游泳好手，也會沉下去。能死在檸檬果凍中不也很有趣嗎？

我們還討論了其他兩個問題。

第一，八角形的屋子裏的房間是什麼形狀？有的同學斷定房間是方形的，我想它們一定像片餡餅一樣，您說呢？

第二，如果坐在一個四周全是鏡子的巨大空心球裏，鏡子要在何處才會只照到背，而不照到臉？我越想越糊塗，您看，我們用多麼深奧的哲學概念來打發時間！

我跟您提過選舉的事嗎？三個星期前選完了，不過時光飛逝，三個星期前的事，好像已經是遠古的歷史了。莎莉當選了，我們當晚帶著「莎莉萬歲」的標語遊行，還有一個十四人的樂隊（三個口琴和十一把梳子假裝的口琴）。

現在，我們258室的人都成了重要人物。茱莉亞和我也沾了不少的光——跟一個領袖住在同一個屋簷下，也是要承受社會壓力的。

晚安，親愛的叔叔！

尊敬您的茱蒂

11月12日

親愛的長腿叔叔：

　　昨天與大一生的籃球比賽我們贏了。當然啦！我們歡欣雀躍。不過要是能打贏大三生就好了。若真能如此，我們願意打得全身青一塊紫一塊，包上繃帶在床上躺一個星期。

　　莎莉邀我去她家度過聖誕假期，她住在麻薩諸塞州的烏斯特。她人是不是很好？我很想去，除了洛克威洛外我從沒去過別人家。而山普家都是大人跟老人，所以不算。但是馬克白家有一屋子小孩（其實是兩個或三個），有媽媽、爸爸和祖母，還有一隻安哥拉貓，是一個相當健全的家庭！我一想到假期就好興奮！能夠收拾行李準備遠行，比留下來更加有趣。

　　第七節課就要結束了，我得趕緊去排練。我參加了感恩節的演出，我演的是一位閣樓王子。身著天鵝絨上衣，頭上有金黃色的捲髮，多有意思！

您的茱蒂

星期六

　　您想知道我長得什麼模樣嗎？附上我們三人的照片，是藍儂拉‧芬頓拍的。

　　面帶笑容的是莎莉、目空一切的高個子是茱莉亞、頭髮被風吹到臉上的小個子是茱蒂，實際上她比照片上漂亮，只是陽光刺得她睜不開眼睛。

12月31日於麻薩諸塞州，烏斯特的「石門」

親愛的長腿叔叔：

本想早些寫信給您，謝謝您耶誕節寄給我的支票；不過在馬克白家的生活實在太充實了，我幾乎找不出完整的時間，可好好坐在桌子邊寫一封信。

我買了一件並非必要，只是想要的衣服。今年聖誕節，長腿叔叔寄來了禮物，家人則送來了愛。

在莎莉家，我度過最美好的假期。她住在一棟舊式的大房子裏，屋外牆壁漆成白色，背靠著街道，完全就是我在約翰·格利爾孤兒院時經常看到的那種房子。住在裏面是什麼樣的感覺，令人十分好奇。我從不敢奢望能親眼看到，而現在，我就在這裏啊！一切都是如此愜意、舒適、自在而美好。我在房間裏走來走去，仔細觀賞他們的陳設，並沉醉其中。

這是養兒育女最理想的所在。有陰暗的角落可以玩捉迷藏，有壁爐可以爆玉米花，下雨的時候可以在閣樓上玩耍和嬉戲。樓梯扶手滑溜溜的可以當溜滑梯，而扶手尾端有個舒適的扁平旋鈕。廚房寬闊明亮，有一位性格開朗活潑的胖廚子，他在這個家裏已經十三年了，常常留一小塊麵包讓孩子們烤著玩。光是看到這樣的情景，就會讓人想重返童年。

至於那些家庭成員，我做夢都想不到，他們會是這般友善。莎莉有爸爸、媽媽、祖母、一個滿頭捲髮，可愛活潑的三

歲小妹妹。一個進門老是忘記擦腳，不大不小的弟弟。還有一個高大英俊的哥哥叫吉米，他現在是普林斯頓大學的大三生。

在飯桌上是最美妙的時刻——每個人又說又笑，誰也不讓誰。飯前也不用祈禱，不用為到嘴的每口食物感恩，這真是一種解脫。（我確實對神明不夠尊敬，如果您像我一樣對一切都要千恩萬謝，想必也會如此的。）

我們做了如此多的事情，都不知該從何說起。馬克白先生有一家工廠。聖誕夜前夕，他在裝飾得很漂亮的包裝間裏，為員工的孩子們準備了一株聖誕樹和許多的聖誕禮物。當晚由吉米扮成聖誕老人，莎莉跟我則幫忙分發禮物。

天啊，叔叔，這種感覺真好玩！我覺得自己像約翰‧格利爾孤兒院的理事一樣和善。我親吻了一個可愛又黏答答的小男孩——不過，我好像沒有摸他們的腦袋！

耶誕節第二天，他們在家裏為我辦了一場舞會。

這是我第一次參加舞會——大學的舞會不算，因為我只能和女生跳舞。我穿了一件嶄新的白色晚禮服（您的聖誕禮物——多謝了！），戴著白色的長手套，還有可愛的白色鞋子。我沉浸在完全、徹底和絕對的幸福中。唯一令人遺憾的是，李皮太太沒能看到我跟吉米‧馬克白開舞。拜託您，下次去約翰‧格利爾孤兒院時，告訴她一下。

您永遠的茱蒂‧艾伯特

附記：

如果我沒能成爲偉大的作家，反而變成一個平凡的女孩子。叔叔，您會不會大失所望？

星期六6點30分

親愛的長腿叔叔：

我們今天步行去城裏，不過，老天啊！遇上了傾盆大雨。冬天就要像冬天，應該下雪而不是下雨啊！

茉莉亞那位討人喜歡的叔叔，今天下午又來造訪——帶來一盒五磅重的巧克力。您瞧，和茉莉亞同房還是大有好處的。

他似乎覺得聽女孩們的談話很有趣，因此故意錯過一班火車，跟我們在書房裏喝茶。爲了得到校方的許可，我們可花了好大一番的功夫。讓爸爸或祖父來訪已經夠難的了，叔叔更難一些，至於哥哥或表兄弟則幾乎是不可能。茉莉亞必須在公證人面前發誓他是她的叔叔，再把公證人的證明帶回來（我還知道點法律吧！）。儘管如此，我依然懷疑，一旦院長看到傑維叔叔那麼年輕英俊，我們的茶究竟喝不喝得成還是個問題。

無論如何，我們還是一起喝了茶，配上黑麵包和瑞士奶酪做的三明治。他幫我們做了三明治，但自己就吃了四塊。我告訴他，我去年夏天是在洛克威洛度過的，我們高興地聊起山普夫婦、馬兒、牛還有小雞。以往他熟知的馬兒中，除了葛洛佛，都已經死了。上回他去時牠還是隻小馬——可憐的葛洛佛，現在已經非常老了，只能夠跛著腳移動。

他問我，山普夫婦是不是還把甜甜圈放在黃色的鍋子，用藍色的盤子蓋著，放在餐櫥的底下。的確如此，一點也沒錯！他還問我，夜間牧場的一堆石頭下是不是有個土撥鼠洞——還真的有！夏天，阿馬薩抓到一隻又大又肥的灰色土撥鼠，應該是傑維少爺在小時候抓到的那隻，牠的第二十五代孫子。

我當面稱呼他傑維少爺，他顯得一點也不在意。茱莉亞說，她從沒看過他這麼友善——他通常是很難親近的。不過我想，是茱莉亞不懂得訣竅。我發現，面對男人必須懂很多的秘訣。如果撫摸得當，他就會發出呼嚕聲，不然就會吼你了（這個比喻不是很優雅，但我只是比喻。）。

我們正在讀瑪麗‧巴斯格謝夫的日記，內容真讓人震驚不已。您看：「昨天，失望籠罩了我整個身心，使我發出痛苦的呻吟。最終我無法控制自己，以致於將餐廳的掛鐘丟到大海裏。」

我希望自己不要成為一個天才，天才一定都很令人討厭，而且老是損壞家具。

老天啊！這樣的傾盆大雨怎麼一直下個不停！

我們今晚恐怕要游泳去教堂了。

您永遠的茱蒂

1月20日

親愛的長腿叔叔：

您有沒有一個小女孩在襁褓中被人偷抱走？

也許我就是她！如果我們是在小說裏，故事可能就會是這樣收尾，不是嗎？

對自己的身世一無所知，實在太奇怪了 —— 令人有點興奮也覺得有些浪漫，畢竟有那麼多的可能性。可能我不是美國人也說不定，在美國有很多人不是美國人。或許，我的祖先是古羅馬人。可能，我是北歐海盜的女兒。又或者，我是俄羅斯流亡者的孩子，理應關在西伯利亞的監獄裏。還是我是吉普賽人 —— 這很有可能是真的，我喜歡到處流浪，儘管至今我仍沒有機會好好地流浪。

您知道我過去的一大污點嗎？我曾從約翰·格利爾孤兒院逃跑過，因為我偷餅乾吃，他們要處罰我。這件事記錄在案，任何理事都可以自由地翻閱。不過，叔叔，這怎麼能怪我呢？

當您把一個飢餓的九歲小女孩放在餐廚室，一罐餅乾就在她手邊，然後留下她一個人就離開；之後您突然跑回來，當然會發現她嘴邊有餅乾屑。最後，您把她一手提起來，搧上兩個耳光；接著又在飯桌上，當布丁送上來時命令她走開，還告訴所有孩子，那是因爲她偷東西。您能期望她不逃走嗎？

　　我只跑了四英里路就被他們抓回來了。整整一個星期，當其他的孩子在外面玩耍時，我卻像隻頑皮的小狗被拴在後院的柱子上。天啊！下課鐘響了，下課後我要開個會。我很抱歉，今天本來打算寫一封有趣的信給您的。

　　再見，親愛的叔叔！

茱蒂

附記：有一點我能肯定的是，我不是中國人。

2月4日

親愛的長腿叔叔：

　　吉米送給我一面普林斯頓的校旗，和我房間的牆壁一樣大。我感謝他還記得我，卻不知道如何使用這面旗子。莎莉和茱莉亞不讓我掛起來。今年我們的房間以紅色爲基調，如果我再加上橙色和黑色，可想而知會變成什麼模樣。旗子是用暖和的厚實毯子做成的，丟掉實在可惜。做成浴衣應該不至於太不像樣吧，正好我那件縮水不能穿。

最近我絲毫沒有談到我的學業。雖然從信上沒有提到，但實際上我是把全部時間都用來看書的。畢竟同時修五門課，著實讓人暈頭轉向。

化學老師說：「學問的考驗就在於對細節的熱情。」

歷史教授則說：「不要過分注意細節，高瞻遠矚才能掌握全局。」

您瞧！在化學課和歷史課之間，我們需要多麼小心地見風轉舵啊！我比較喜歡歷史課的做法。威廉一世於一四九二年征服英國，而哥倫布則是在一一〇〇或一〇六六年，或者其他什麼年代發現美洲大陸，歷史課教授是全然不計較這些細枝末葉的。歷史課輕鬆愉快，化學課則不然。

　　第六節課鈴聲響了──我又要去實驗室研究酸、鹽和鹼。鹽酸把我做化學實驗的圍裙，燒了一個像盤子一樣的大洞。從理論上來說，我可以用強氨把洞中和，對嗎？

　　下星期要考試，我可不擔心！

永遠是您的茱蒂

3月5日

親愛的長腿叔叔：

　　三月的春風緩緩吹拂，滿天的烏雲湧動著，松樹上的小鳥正吱吱叫個不停，似乎在召喚著我。我真想闔上書本，起身到山頂去追逐微風。

　　上個星期六同學們玩追逐遊戲，在濕漉漉的野外草地上跑了五英里。由三個女孩裝作狐狸，帶上一筐五彩紙屑逃走，二十七名獵人則在半個小時後出發尋找她們。我扮成獵人。到路程的一半，就有八名獵人掉隊了，剩下我們十九個人窮追不捨。我們沿著紙屑翻山越嶺，穿越玉米田後踏入一片沼澤，只好輕輕地從一塊高地跳到另一塊高地，半數以上的人都踩入水中。我們常常找不到她們的蹤跡，在沼澤地裏就浪費了二十五分鐘。接著又沿著叢林翻越一座山丘，到達一個穀倉的窗戶。穀倉的門上了鎖，窗戶又高又小。她們真狡猾，不是嗎？

我們並沒有爬進窗戶，而是繞到倉庫的後邊，找到一些紙屑；在確認她們的足跡後，我們爬過一個低矮的棚屋，又越過了一道籬笆。狐狸們以為能在這裏難倒我們，但是卻沒有得逞。再穿過綿延了兩英里的草地，因為紙屑越來越少，所以追蹤也越來越困難；原定兩堆紙屑的距離不得超過六英尺，可她們的六英尺未免也太長了。最後，我們足足跋涉了兩個小時，才終於在水晶泉的廚房裏找到那群狐狸們（水晶泉是個農場，女孩們常滑著大雪橇，或坐著運草用的車到那裏吃晚餐，那裏有雞和雞蛋餅乾）。我們發現那三隻狐狸正在安靜地喝牛奶、吃蜂蜜和餅乾，她們還以為，我們會卡在倉庫窗戶那邊而追不到她們呢！

雙方都堅持自己贏了，我認為是我們獲勝，您說呢？她們還沒有回到校園就被我們抓到了。我們十九個人一坐下來，就像蝗蟲一樣吵著要吃蜂蜜；蜂蜜不夠了，水晶泉太太（這是我們對她的暱稱，她本姓約翰遜）就立刻拿出一罐草莓醬和一罐糖漿（上星期剛做的），還有三個黑麵包給我們。

直到六點半我們才回到學校。晚飯時間已經開始半小時，所以我們沒有換衣服就直奔餐廳，絲毫沒有因為吃過點心就沒了胃口。晚上的禮拜大家都請假了，理由很充分，我們的靴子沾滿了泥巴。

我還沒跟您提到考試的事，每科我都輕而易舉地通過了。

我現在知道訣竅，再也不會不及格了。儘管如此，我也不可能以優異的成績畢業，就因為我大一時那可惡的拉丁文和數學。不過我不在乎，當您心情好時不會有什麼不順心的事（這是從書上抄來的，我正在讀英國古典文學）。

說到英國古典文學，您曾讀過《哈姆雷特》嗎？如果不曾，現在就開始吧！它絕對是一部曠世巨作。我很早就聽人說過莎士比亞，卻不知他的文筆是如此之美妙，我還以為他徒有虛名呢！

很久以前，我剛開始識字時，就自己發明了一種遊戲。每晚入睡前，我都把自己想像成手邊正在看的那本書中的人物，一個最重要的人物！

目前我是奧菲莉亞——通情達理的奧菲莉亞！我要讓哈姆雷特隨時都很開心，並且安撫他、指引他；當他感冒時我要為他戴上圍巾，我會將他的哀傷都趕跑。國王跟皇后最後會死於一場海難，所以連葬禮都不用辦，我和哈姆雷特將毫無阻礙地統治丹麥王國。我們會把國家治理得井井有條，他管理政府，我主持慈善事業，我會成立許多第一流的孤兒院。如果您或其他理事想參觀的話，我會很樂意當個導遊，我想您會得到很多有用的啟發。

我向您致意，先生。

您最充滿敬意的丹麥皇后奧菲莉亞

3月24日，也許是25日

親愛的長腿叔叔：

我不相信我能去天堂——在塵世擁有這麼多，死後再能進天堂就太過分了。聽聽發生了什麼事吧！

喬若莎‧艾伯特贏得了《月刊》雜誌每年舉辦的短篇小說獎（獎金二十五美元），參賽者大多數是四年級的學生，而她還只是個大二生。看到自己榜上有名，簡直不敢相信那是真的，也許我真的能成為一名作家。真希望李皮太太給我起的名字不是這麼蠢該有多好，這名字一聽就知道是女作家，不是嗎？

而且，春天裏我們要在露天表演戲劇《皆大歡喜》；我被選中飾演賽麗亞，她是羅賽林的表妹。

最後，下週五茱莉亞和莎莉還有我要去紐約採購春裝，並在那裏住一晚。翌日清晨，將和「傑維少爺」一起去看戲，是他邀我們去的呢。茱莉亞要回家住一宿，莎莉跟我則住在馬沙華盛頓飯店。您聽過比這更令人興奮的事嗎？我這輩子從沒去過飯店，也沒去過劇院。只有聖公會舉辦慶典，邀請孤兒們參加時去過一次。不過那不是真正的演出，不能算數。

您猜我們要看什麼戲目呢？《哈姆雷特》！你想想！我們在莎士比亞課上讀它讀了四週，我早就倒背如流了。

這一切讓我太興奮了，我幾乎無法入睡。

晚安，叔叔。

這世界真的太太太美好了！

您永遠的茱蒂

附記：我看了一下日曆，是二十八日。

又一個附記：

我今天看到一位公車司機，他一隻眼睛是藍色的，另一隻是棕色的，是不是很像偵探小說裏的壞蛋？

4月7日

親愛的長腿叔叔：

天啊！紐約真大！相較之下，烏斯特不值得一提。您告訴我，您真的住在那麼嘈雜、人潮洶湧的城市裏嗎？我只住了兩天，但我恐怕幾個月也無法恢復。我不知道怎樣向您描繪我的見聞，不過我猜您都知道，因為您自己就住在那裏。

那些街道真有趣，不是嗎？還有人群、商店，櫥窗裏有那麼多美麗的東西，讓人想花上一輩子，每天穿戴不一樣的配件。

莎莉、茱莉亞和我星期六早上一起去購物。茱莉亞帶我們走進我生平見過最華麗的地方。白色和金色的牆、藍色的地毯、藍色絲質窗簾和鍍金椅子；一位穿著黑絲拖地裙，十分美麗的金髮小姐笑臉相迎，我以為我們是來拜訪的人，於是上前去和她握手。不過我們似乎只是要買帽子而已，至少茱莉亞要買帽子。她在鏡子前面坐下來，試了一打帽子，一頂比一頂漂亮，她從中選擇了兩頂最漂亮的帽子。

能坐在試穿鏡前買下任何一頂你選上的帽子，而且完全不用考慮錢的問題；我無法想像，人生還有什麼能比這更快樂的事了。

買完東西，我們到雪莉飯店與傑維少爺會合。您一定去過雪莉飯店吧？請把它與孤兒院的飯廳比較一下，您就能想像我的感覺了。孤兒院的飯廳只有鋪著油布的桌子、不可以打破的白陶盤子和木柄刀叉。

吃魚時，我拿錯了叉子，不過好心的服務員又給了我另一把，所以沒有人注意到。

用過午餐，我們前往劇院——它真是好壯麗、好神奇，我無法相信我就置身於——我每晚都夢見的地方。

莎士比亞多麼奇妙呀！

《哈姆雷特》在舞臺上比我們在課堂上分析的還要更好，我原本就喜歡它。但現在，天啊！

我想如果您不介意，我想去演戲，不當作家了。我轉學去戲劇學校好嗎？我會在演出時為您保留一個包廂，還會從舞臺上在舞臺燈下，對您笑一笑。您只需在外衣別上一朵紅玫瑰，拜託。這樣我才能確定我笑對人了。如果我搞錯了，那可真難為情。

星期六晚上返校，我們在火車上用晚餐，餐桌上擺著粉紅色的檯燈，還有一個黑人侍者。我無意中提及自己以前從沒聽過火車上有提供餐點服務的事。

「天哪，妳到底在哪長大的？」茱莉亞問我。

「一個小村莊。」我淡淡地回答茱莉亞。

「難道妳都沒旅行過嗎？」她問我。

「在上大學之前沒有，而且距離只有一六〇英里遠，不用吃飯。」

她對我產生了好奇心，因為我說了這句可笑的話。其實我很小心，但一遇到新鮮事就會脫口而出──我常常大驚小怪。這真是一種奇異的經驗。在約翰‧格利爾孤兒院待了十八年，忽然陷入這個「世界」，著實讓人頭暈目眩。

不過我現在慢慢習以為常，不會像以前一樣犯那麼多錯；而且我跟其他女孩子在一起時，不再手足無措了。以前，只要人家一看我，我就渾身不自在，好像他們能透過我的冒牌新衣看到裏面的花格布衣服似的。但我再也不讓花格布衣服影響我了──不要為明日憂慮，因明日自有明日的憂慮。

我忘了告訴您，我們收到的花。傑維少爺送我們每個人一大把紫羅蘭和鈴蘭。他真好，不是嗎？過去我對男人沒有好感──全是基於對理事的評價──不過現在正在回心轉意中。

寫了十一頁，信太長了，別擔憂，就此擱筆。

您永遠的茱蒂

長腿叔叔

4月10日

親愛的大富翁先生：

　　隨信附上您的五十元支票，非常謝謝您；不過我不認為自己應該收下這筆錢。我的零用錢足夠買自己需要的所有帽子了。我真後悔寫了那麼多關於帽店的蠢話，其實我只是少見多怪罷了。

　　無論如何，我並沒有在乞討！我也不願再接受您額外的恩惠。

您的喬若莎‧艾伯特

4月11日

最親愛的叔叔：

　　您能原諒我昨天寫的那封信嗎？我一寄出去就後悔了。想取回來時，那個可惡的郵差卻不肯還給我。

　　現在是半夜，想起自己以怨報德就無法入睡。心裏除了痛罵自己是個卑鄙小人外，又能說些什麼呢！我將通往書房的門關上，以免吵醒了茱莉亞和莎莉；並從歷史筆記本上撕下一頁，坐在床上寫信給您。

我只想告訴您，您寄支票來是好意，我卻如此無禮，十分抱歉。您是一位這麼好心的老人，才會連一頂帽子這樣的小事都要費心，我本應滿心感激地把支票退回去才是。

可是不管怎樣，我都該還給您。這件事對我來說，跟其他女孩子擁有截然不同的意義。她們能理所當然地接受別人的東西；她們有爸爸、哥哥、姑姑和叔叔，而我卻沒有任何這種親人。我想像您是屬於我的，當然僅僅只是想像，我也知道您絕對不屬於我。我孤單一人獨自面對整個世界，一想起來就有些心驚膽戰，不過我把這些都拋在腦後，繼續假裝。只是，叔叔，您看不出來嗎？我不能再接受您的金錢，多過於我所應受的。因為這些錢，有朝一日我必須全數歸還給您。更況且，即使我如願以償成為了一個偉大的作家，也無法償還如此巨大的債務。

我喜愛那些美麗的帽子和飾物，但是我不該拿我的未來做抵押。

您會原諒我的，不是嗎？原諒我這麼魯莽。我有一想到事情就衝動下筆的壞習慣，而且還沒來得及仔細想想，就寄出去了。雖然有時候我看起來魯莽又不知感恩，但是我真的不是故意的，我打心眼裏感謝您所給予我的生活、自由和獨立。我的童年充滿了陰鬱的反抗，而現在我時時刻刻都很快樂，幾乎不敢相信這一切是真的。我覺得自己像故事書中的女主角。

現在已是凌晨兩點一刻了，我要悄悄地溜出去寄信了。您將會在上一封信寄達後不久，就收到這封。這樣您才不會有太長的時間把我想得太壞。

晚安，叔叔！

永遠都愛您的茱蒂

5月4日

親愛的長腿叔叔：

上星期六開運動會，場面十分壯觀。一開始，各班級同學穿著白色校服列隊入場。大四學生撐著藍色和金色的日本陽傘；大三學生手持黃白相間的旗幟；我們班拿著豔紅的氣球——非常動人，尤其它們老是脫手飄走；大一新生則戴著綠色皺褶紙做成的帽子，垂下長長的飄帶。另外還有從城裏請來的樂隊，他們穿著藍色制服替我們表演；以及十多個喜劇演員像馬戲團的小丑一樣，在比賽期間給觀眾助興。

茱莉亞扮成肥胖的鄉下人，拿著麻布雞毛撢子、留著鬍子，並且撐著一把鬆垮的傘。又高又瘦的帕齊·莫里哀娣扮演茱莉亞的妻子，歪戴著一頂可笑的綠色無邊女帽。她們走到哪裏都會發出一片笑聲，茱莉亞扮得非常、非常成功。真想不到平萊頓家族的人，也可以表現得這麼富有幽默感——願傑維少

爺原諒我的不敬。我從不把他當做平萊頓家族的人，就像我從不認爲您是理事一樣。

莎莉跟我參加了比賽，所以不在進場隊伍中。而您猜怎麼著？我們雙雙獲勝！至少贏了某些項目。我們嘗試跨欄賽跑，結果輸了，但莎莉在撐竿跳方面獲勝（七呎三吋），而我在五十米短跑上獲勝（八秒）。

茱蒂贏了五十碼短跑賽

雖然我最後跑得上氣不接下氣，不過很好玩。全班揮著氣球歡呼，並叫著：

> 茱蒂‧艾伯特
>
> 棒不棒？
>
> 她眞棒！
>
> 誰最棒？
>
> 茱蒂‧艾伯特

長腿叔叔

　　叔叔，這是實至名歸。比賽完後我用小跑步回到休息室，她們用酒精給我擦身，還給我一塊檸檬含在嘴裏。您瞧，我們多專業啊！能為班上爭光是件好事，獎牌獲得最多的班級可以拿到年度冠軍獎盃。大四班今年以七個獎牌贏得這個獎盃。組委會在體育館請所有得獎者吃飯，有油炸軟殼蟹和做成籃球形狀的巧克力霜淇淋。

　　昨晚花了個大半夜看完《簡愛》。長腿叔叔，您是不是很老了？還記得六十年前的事嗎？那時人們是那樣說話的嗎？

　　傲慢的布蘭奇夫人對僕人說：「僕役，住嘴，照我說的去做！」而羅徹斯特先生用「蒼穹」這個詞意指天空。另外，故事裡有一個瘋女人——笑起來十分歇斯底里；她放火燒床簾，撕破結婚禮服的面紗，還會咬人——十足是勸懲惡揚善的通俗劇。儘管如此，還是讓人愛不釋手。但更令我不解的是，我看不出是怎樣的女孩會寫出這樣一本書，更何況作者還是一個在牧師家庭長大的女孩子。勃朗特家有些事使我很感興趣：她們的書、她們的生活、她們的精神，以及她們從哪得來的素材？當我讀到小簡愛在慈善學校中的種種遭遇時，我憤怒極了，不得不出去走走。我完全能理解她的感受。因為我認識李皮太太，所以我知道布洛克赫斯特先生是怎樣的人。

　　叔叔，別生氣，我不是說約翰‧格利爾孤兒院跟沃德慈善學校一模一樣。我們吃得飽、穿得暖、洗浴方便，地窖裏還有旺盛的爐火。不過兩者有個極相似之處，那就是我們的生活都單調無聊。除了星期天的霜淇淋之外，沒有任何讓人感到高興的事情。過去十八年來，我只有經歷過一次冒險，就是隔壁的柴房著火了。我們半夜爬起來並穿好衣服，這樣的話，萬一我們的房子也著了火，就能夠立即逃跑。不過火勢並沒有蔓延，我們只好又爬上床睡覺。

每個人都喜歡一些意外的驚喜，這是人類的天性。不過我從來沒有感受過驚喜，直到李皮太太把我叫去，並告訴我，有位約翰・史密斯先生要送我上大學。可是她如此慢吞吞地向我透露這個消息，讓我只輕微地震撼了一下。

您知道的，叔叔，我認為一個人最重要的素質就是想像力。唯有這樣，人們才能設身處地為他人著想，才能變得友善、富有同情心而且體貼。這種稟賦應該從童年就開始培養，但是約翰・格利爾孤兒院在它一萌芽時，就把它踩死了。義務雖是一件值得鼓勵的素質，可是我不認為小孩子應該懂得它的意思——這討厭又可恨的字眼。他們應該要以愛為出發點，去做一切的事情。

您等著看我如何管理孤兒院吧！這是我上床睡覺前最喜歡玩的遊戲。我鉅細靡遺地規劃每一個細節——用餐、穿著、讀書和遊戲——還有處罰。因為即使是最乖的孤兒，有時也會犯錯。可是不管怎樣，他們都應該是快快樂樂的樣子。我認為，一個人不管他成長的過程中會遇到多少困難，都應該給他一個快樂的童年可以回首。如果我將來有孩子的話，不管我有多麼痛苦，我都要讓他們無憂無慮地成長。

（教堂的鐘聲響了——我會找時間寫完這封信的。）

星期四

今天下午我上完課回來時，發現一隻松鼠坐在茶几上吃杏仁。天氣暖和了，我們把窗戶打開時，常常會有這樣友善的訪客。

親愛的蝸蝝太太，
要一塊方糖還是兩塊？

星期六上午

今天是週末沒課。您或許會以爲昨天晚上，我可以安靜地閱讀我用獎金買的那套史蒂文生的書了吧？親愛的長腿叔叔，如果您這樣想的話，那是因爲您沒上過女子大學。今天有六個同學來我房間做牛奶糖，其中一位不小心把糖滴在我們最好的地毯上，怎麼擦都擦不乾淨了。

　　我還沒跟您談到最近的讀書狀況，但我每天都在學習；偶爾放下書本和您談談生活瑣事，可以讓我轉換一下思緒。可惜我們的談話是單方面的，這都是您不好，歡迎您隨時反駁我。

　　斷斷續續寫了三天，恐怕您一定厭煩了！

　　再見，耐心的「紳士」先生！

茱蒂

長腿叔叔史密斯先生：

　　先生，剛學完立論學，和列舉論題要點的學問，我決定用下列方式給您寫信。事實俱在，冗字全無。

　　一、本週進行下列筆試：

　　　　A. 化學

　　　　B. 歷史

　　二、正在建築的新宿舍：

　　　　A. 所用材料

　　　　　（a）紅磚

　　　　　（b）灰石

　　　　B. 容量：

　　　　　（a）一位院長、五位導師

　　　　　（b）二百名女生

　　　　　（c）一位舍監、三位廚師、二十名女服務員、二十名清潔女工

三、今晚的甜點是奶凍。

四、我在寫一篇有關莎士比亞戲劇源流的論文。

五、今天下午打籃球，盧‧麥克馬洪滑倒了，她的：

　　A. 肩胛骨錯位

　　B. 膝蓋擦傷

六、我買了一頂新帽子，上面有：

　　A. 藍絲絨緞帶

　　B. 兩根藍色翎毛

　　C. 三個紅色絨球

七、現在是九點半

八、晚安

茱蒂

6月2日

親愛的長腿叔叔：

　　您絕對猜不到有什麼好事到了。馬克白太太邀請我暑假和他們一起去阿迪朗得克露營！有一個設在美麗林中湖畔的俱樂部，他們是該俱樂部的會員。會員們在林中四處蓋有自己的房子，他們可以在湖上划船，也可以在林中小徑散步到其他營區。俱樂部一星期開一次舞會——在這個暑假，吉米‧馬克白有個同學也會來玩一段時間。這樣一來，我們就有很多男舞伴了。

馬克白夫人真好，不是嗎？看來我耶誕節到她家去時，她對我的印象很好。

請原諒我這封信寫得這樣簡短。這不算是信，只是想讓您知道今年暑假有人會照顧我了。

您的

非常心滿意足的茱蒂

6月5日

親愛的長腿叔叔：

您的祕書來信告訴我，史密斯先生不希望我接受馬克白夫人的邀請；而是希望我和上個暑假一樣，前往洛克威洛農莊。

叔叔，為什麼？為什麼？為什麼？

您不明白，馬克白夫人是真心地希望我能參加這次的露營活動。我不僅不會給她們添任何麻煩，還是個好幫手。他們帶的人很少，莎莉跟我可以做很多有用的事。這是個讓我學習打理家務的好機會，也是每個女人都應該要懂的事，而我只懂得管理孤兒院。

　　露營地沒有和我們年齡相仿的女孩，馬克白夫人要我去和莎莉作伴。我們打算一起讀書，把明年英文和社會學的課本先讀完。老師說在暑假裏讀這些書，對之後會有很大的幫助，而兩個人一起讀、一起討論的話，更能加深印象。

　　光是跟莎莉的媽媽住在一起就能學到很多東西。她是全世界最有趣而且最迷人的女士，她什麼都懂，你想想，我與李皮太太一起度過了那麼多個夏天，我十分渴望擁有一個不一樣的學習對象。您也不要擔心我去會很擁擠，她們的房子是橡皮做的，彈性很大；客人多了就在露天搭建很多帳篷，把男孩子趕到那裏去睡。一切都將如此地美妙，而且戶外健康活動對身體大有裨益。吉米‧馬克白要教我騎馬、划船，還有——一堆我該懂的事情。這將會是我從未有過，並且是一段有趣而悠閒的時光；我認為每個女孩子一生都值得擁有一次這樣的機會。我當然會照您的話去做，不過，求求您，求求您讓我去。叔叔，我從沒這麼有動力想要做一件事情。

　　這不是未來的大作家喬若莎‧艾伯特，只是一個女孩子——茱蒂，寫給您的信。

6月9日

約翰‧史密斯先生：

先生，您七日的賜函收迄。據經您祕書轉達之命，我於下星期五出發，前往洛克威洛農莊度假。

希望能永遠向您致敬的
喬若莎‧艾伯特（小姐）

8月3日於洛克威洛農莊

親愛的長腿叔叔：

離我上一封信已經快兩個月了，這樣不太好，但是坦白說，這個暑假我不太喜歡您。

您無法想像放棄馬克白家的露營讓我有多難過。當然，您是我的監護人，我明白無論什麼事都必須遵照您的意見。但我真的看不出任何「理由」。對我而言，這是我遇過最美妙的一件事，如果我是叔叔您而您是茱蒂，我會說：「祝福妳，我的孩子，快去吧！玩得愉快些。多認識一些人、多學習些新事物，在戶外多住一陣子，鍛鍊得結結實實的。用功一年了，好好地放鬆一下吧！」

可是全然不是這樣！只由您的祕書寫來一行字，命令我去洛克威洛。

您的命令不近人情，使我覺得很傷心。如果您對我有一點點如我對您的感情，您至少偶爾會寫幾行字給我；而不是讓您的祕書寄來那些，用打字機打出來的可惡字條。如果我能感覺到您一絲絲的關懷，我將會願意做任何事使您高興。

我知道我應該規規矩矩地，寫一封鉅細靡遺的長信給您，且不期望任何的回覆。您遵守了您的諾言——讓我上大學——而我猜想，您一定認為我沒有信守我的承諾。

不過，叔叔，這對我而言太難了，真的太難了。我是如此寂寞，您是我唯一可以掛念的人，而您卻如幻影一般。您只是我捏造出來的想像人物——也許真實的您，一點也不如我的想像。不過您確實曾經在我生病住進醫院時，給過我一張紙條。現在，每當我感覺自己被人們遺忘時，我就會拿出您的卡片，一遍又一遍地閱讀。

我恐怕沒有說清楚起初我想表達的意思，我想要說的是：我鬱鬱寡歡，因為被一個專橫獨斷、不近人情、無所不在卻隱藏起來的上帝所支配。他使我感到很是受傷。但是，一個人能像您對我這樣好、這樣寬大、這樣體貼；我想，如果他願意的話，他有權做一個專橫獨斷、不近人情、無所不在卻隱藏起來的上帝——所以我原諒您，並試圖讓自己高興起來。可是，每當收到莎莉描述他們在露營中有多快樂的信件時，我的情緒就

變得很沮喪。

不談這件事了，讓一切都重新開始吧！

這個夏天我寫了又寫，四個短篇故事已完成並寄往四家不同的雜誌社，所以您瞧，我正努力地朝作家之路前進。我在閣樓一個角落工作，這是傑維少爺小時候下雨天玩耍的地方。那是個涼爽、空氣流通的角落，一棵楓樹的濃蔭遮蓋著兩扇天窗，楓樹上的洞裏面住了一窩紅松鼠。

過幾天會再寫一封愉快點的信，告訴您農場上的見聞。

這裏缺雨。

您始終如一的茱蒂

8月10日

親愛的長腿叔叔：

先生，我爬上牧場水池邊的一棵柳樹，並在它的第二個樹杈上給您寫信。一隻青蛙在樹下鼓噪著，樹上有一隻蚱蜢也唱個不停，兩隻小蟲上上下下地在樹幹上爬來爬去。我在這裏已經待了一個小時，我放了兩個沙發墊子在樹杈上，感覺起來更加舒適了。我帶來筆和練習簿，打算寫一篇不朽的短篇小說，卻被女主角攪得焦頭爛額。她太不聽從我的安排了，讓我只好暫時撇開她，來給您寫信。（雖然這不能給我太大的安慰，因為我也無法讓您聽從我的支配。）

如果您現在還住在可怕的紐約市，我希望能送一些可愛的、有微風吹拂的、陽光明媚的景致給您。在下了一星期的雨之後，鄉間像天堂一樣美好。

在下雨的這一個星期裏，我大部份的時間都端坐在閣樓中，如飢似渴地閱讀史蒂文生的作品。他本人比書中的任何一個角色都還要有趣，我敢說，他如果把自己寫進書中，肯定會是一位很迷人的男主角。他把父親留給自己的一萬塊美金，拿去買了一艘船暢遊南洋，您不覺得他這麼做實在是太棒了嗎？

他以冒險為生。如果我父親留給我一萬塊美元，我也會這麼做。一想到他的故事就讓我興奮。我要看看奇異而美麗的地方，我要環遊世界，叔叔，當我成為大作家、偉大的藝術家、演員或劇作家，或者其他什麼偉大人物之後，我就要去旅行。我渴望流浪，一看見地圖我就想抓起帽子、拿著雨傘、立刻起身。「我定要在有生之年，親眼看到南洋的棕櫚樹和廟宇。」

星期四傍晚，坐在門口石階上

很難再網羅什麼新聞寫在信裏了！茱蒂最近變得如此深思熟慮，想大談國家大事而不再是生活瑣事了。不過要是您一定要聽點新聞的話，那就是：

上週四我們的九隻小豬越過小溪逃跑了，只找回了八隻。我們不想冤枉誰，不過還是懷疑寡婦陶德太太的豬圈裏的豬，比原來多了一隻。

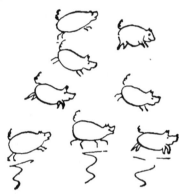

維佛先生把倉庫和兩個筒倉，漆成南瓜似的黃顏色。很難看，但他說很耐髒。

勃魯爾斯家這週有客人從俄亥俄州來了，是勃魯爾斯太太的姊姊和兩個外甥女。

我們最棒的一隻母雞下了十五個蛋，卻只孵出三隻小雞，不知問題出在哪裏。我認為是雞種不好，我喜歡奧爾平頓雞種。

長腿叔叔

郵局的新職員把庫存的牙買加薑汁啤酒（價值七美元），喝得一滴不剩時，才被人發現。

哈奇老先生的風濕病犯了，無法幹活。儘管他以前掙了不少錢，但他一點積蓄也沒有，只好靠救濟金過活了。

下週六晚上，附近的學校有一場霜淇淋晚會，敬請大家攜眷蒞臨。

我在郵局用二十五分錢買了一頂新帽子，這是我的近照——我正要去耙草。

天色已經暗得看不見了。反正，消息也更新完畢了。

晚安，茱蒂

星期五

早安！發生特大新聞了！您猜怎麼著？您永遠、永遠、永遠都猜不到，是誰要來洛克威洛了！平萊頓先生給山普太太來信，說他要開車經過柏克郡，覺得疲憊，想要在寧靜的農莊裡休息一下。他問，如果哪天晚上突然出現在門口，山普太太能否給他準備好一間房。他可能會停留一個星期，或許兩三個星期，到達後看情況而定。

我們手忙腳亂地把整個房子整理了一遍，也把所有的窗簾都洗過了。今天早晨，我去康乃爾斯買些油布舖在大門口，還用兩罐棕色地板漆把前廳和後樓都漆了一遍。明天會請陶德太太來擦窗戶（在這緊要關頭，只能放棄我們對小豬事件的猜疑了）。你聽到我所列舉的掃除項目，可能會認為這間房子還不夠整潔；不過我向您保證，它原本就很乾淨了，儘管山普太太學問不多，但對於理家還是個好手。

不過，叔叔，他真像個男人，一點也不透露自己的行蹤；不說清楚到底是今天會到，還是兩個禮拜後才到。我們將提心吊膽地等候他的到來——如果他不快點來，我們又得重新打掃一遍。

農莊雇工備好四輪馬車，和葛洛佛一起在下面等我了。我獨自駕車去——不過您只消看看老格魯夫的樣子，就不會擔心我的安全了。

我手放在胸前，向您說聲再見。

茱蒂

老格魯夫安全得很。

附記：這個結尾很不錯吧？我是從史蒂文生的書信裏借用的。

星期六

再向您道一次早安！昨天郵差來時我尚未寫好信封，所以我要再加幾行。郵件每天十二點來，鄉下郵差對農民來說極為重要。郵差不僅送信，還幫我們從城裏買東西來，每趟收費五美分。昨天他替我帶了一些鞋帶、一瓶冷霜（我沒買帽子前把鼻子曬得脫皮了），還有藍色領結和一盒黑色鞋油，一共才要十美分。會如此便宜得歸功於買得多。

　　郵差也會告訴我們許多世界大事。因為好幾家人訂了報紙，他會邊走邊看，沿路告訴那些沒有訂報紙的人，發生了什麼大事。假如是美日開戰或總統被刺，或洛克菲勒留給格利爾孤兒院一百萬美元，您不用寫信來，我一定會聽到的。

　　傑維少爺一點動靜也沒有，您真該看看我們的房子有多麼乾淨──害得我們每次進門時都會緊張兮兮地擦掉鞋底的泥巴！

　　我希望他早點來，因為我真想找個人談談。老實告訴您吧，山普太太實在有些單調，她說起話來輕鬆愉悅且滔滔不絕，卻沒有任何思想。這裏的人很奇怪，他們的天地就是這個山頂，與世界完全隔絕。您懂得我的意思吧！這點跟約翰・格利爾孤兒院一模一樣。在那兒，我們的思想也被四面鐵籬笆所囚禁，只不過那時我還很年輕，不太在意這些。每天早上等我把床鋪整理好，給孩子洗了臉，就去學校上課。傍晚放學回來再給他們洗一遍臉，把他們的襪子補好，修補弗萊迪的褲子（他一天到晚穿破），抽空做完我的作業，然後就只想上床睡覺了。所以我從不覺得社交貧乏。不過經過兩年正規的大學生活後，我想念社交活動，尤其想和有共同語言的人交流。

　　我想應該停筆了，眼下沒什麼新鮮事，下次會試著寫長一點。

　　　　　　　　　　　　　　　　　您永遠的茱蒂

附記：今年萵苣長得不好，因為前些日子的氣候太乾燥了。

8月25日

叔叔，傑維少爺終於到了，我們相處得好融洽！

至少我是這樣想的，我想他應該也是如此吧！他已經來這裏十天了，似乎還沒有要走的跡象。山普太太把他慣得不成樣子，如果他小時候就是這麼嬌生慣養，我眞不知道他怎能成爲這麼好的人。

我們一起在陽臺的小桌子上吃飯，有時候在樹下，倘若下雨或者天冷的話，就在最講究的小客廳裏吃。他隨意選一個地點，嘉麗就會搬起桌子跟在他後頭。如果來回很麻煩，或是要把菜端到很遠的地方，她就會在罐子底下發現他賞賜的一塊錢。

雖然乍看之下根本不像，但他是那種很好相處的人。第一眼看起來像是一位標準的平萊頓家族的人，但實際上並非如此。他是一位如此單純、平凡又可愛的男子——用這個詞來形容男子似乎很好笑，不過這是眞的。他對這附近的農民非常友善，以誠相待，很快就消除了他們的防備心。最初他們很不相信他，因爲看不慣他的服飾，而我也覺得他的服裝很奇特；他總穿著打褶外套、白絨衣和褲腿肥大的騎馬服。每當他穿著新服飾下樓，山普太太就帶著自豪的微笑在他周圍打轉，從各個角度欣賞他，並且小心翼翼地避免他坐下來時沾上塵土。他總是煩得不得了地對她說：

「得了，莉莉，去忙妳的，我已經長大了，不用再管我了。」

想到那個了不得、既高大又長腿的男子（他差不多跟您一樣高了，叔叔），曾經坐在山普太太的腿上讓她洗臉，真是非常好笑。尤其是看到山普太太的腿時更是滑稽，現在她的腿粗得嚇人，還有三重下巴，真是有趣。但他說她從前也曾經高高瘦瘦，很是敏捷，跑得比他還快。

我們有好多新奇的經歷！在鄉村四處遊蕩，我學會用羽絨做成小蒼蠅來當魚餌。我不僅學會用步槍和手槍射擊，還學會騎馬——老格魯夫還真有精神。我們餵了牠三天燕麥，牠還被一頭小牛嚇了好大一跳，差點帶著我逃跑了。

星期三

　　星期一下午我們去爬天山。山就在附近，並不是很高，應該吧！山峰上沒有積雪，不過爬到山頂時還是會喘不過氣來。山坡上樹木掩映，山頂則是亂石林立的荒野。我們在山上玩到日落，生了一堆火之後開始煮晚餐。傑維少爺做晚飯，他說他比我更懂得烹飪——的確如此，因為以前他常露營。我們藉著月光走下山，在幽暗的林間小徑上，全靠他口袋裏那只手電筒的光。真的很好玩！他一路上又說又笑，講了許多有趣的故事；我讀的書他全都讀過，還讀了很多其他的書，他的博學多聞讓人吃驚。

　　上午，我們走得很遠，正好碰上了暴風雨，回到家後衣服都濕透了但依然興致勃勃。山普太太看見我們落湯雞似地走進廚房，驚訝萬分，您真該看看她當時的表情。

　　「天呀，傑維少爺，茱蒂小姐！看你們濕成什麼樣子，瞧瞧！瞧瞧！這可怎麼辦才好？這麼新的大衣都被蹧蹋了。」

　　她可真有意思，好像我們都是小孩子，而她是被惹惱的母親。我甚至擔心吃茶點時她會不給我們果醬呢！

星期天

現在是星期天晚上十一點左右，我早該進入夢鄉了，可是晚餐時喝了點黑咖啡，睡不了美容覺了！

今天早上，山普太太跟平萊頓先生雙方各持己見，僵持不下。

「我們必須在十點十五分時出發，好在十一點時抵達教堂。」

「非常好，莉莉，」傑維少爺說，「妳把馬車備好，到時候我如果還沒換好衣服，妳先走就是了，別等我了！」

「我們一定得等。」她說。

「隨妳的便，」他說，「別讓馬站得太久就好。」

然後趁山普太太換衣服時，他吩咐女傭將午餐打包好，催我快點穿上便裝，帶著我從後門溜出去釣魚。

這可把全家人都給搞亂了。因為洛克威洛農場在星期天是兩點用餐，他卻吩咐七點開飯——他想幾點吃就幾點吃，好像這是一家餐館——結果阿馬薩和嘉麗就不能駕車出遊了。他說這樣更好，畢竟他們也不適合在沒有監護人的陪同下，兩個孤男寡女出去亂跑，再說，他要把馬留著才好帶我出遊。您見過這麼滑稽的事情嗎？

而可憐的山普太太相信，星期天去釣魚的人，死後一定會打入十八層地獄！她內心十分不安，責怪自己沒能趁他還小，

有機會時好好管教他。再說，她本
想在教堂裏，帶著他出出風頭。

無論如何我們去釣魚了（他釣到
四條小魚），然後我們生了營火把牠
們烤來當午餐吃。魚總是從木棒上掉
進火裏，雖然沾滿了塵土，但我們還是
吃了。我們四點回到家，五點鐘又駕車出去兜了一圈，七點吃
晚飯，十點他們叫我去睡覺──於是，我就在這兒寫信給您。

我開始有點想睡了。

晚安。

這是我釣的那隻魚的樣子。

長腿船長：

停船！停船！來一瓶蘭姆酒。猜猜我正在讀些什麼？這兩
天我們談論的話題，一直圍繞在海盜和航海上頭。《金銀島》
很有趣不是嗎？您讀過嗎？您小時候有這本書嗎？史蒂文生的
連載版權只拿到三十英鎊，當作家眞不值得。也許，我還是去
學校教書吧！

　　這封信我寫了兩個星期，已經很長了。長腿叔叔，別說我沒交代清楚。真希望您也在這兒，我們一定能相處得非常融洽，我喜歡讓我的朋友們互相認識。我想問平萊頓先生，他在紐約是否認識您──我想他可能知道。你們應該在相同的社交圈子裏活動才是，再加上也都對改革事務感興趣，但我卻無從問起，因為我根本不知道您的真名。

　　不知道您的名字真是再可笑不過了。不過李皮太太告訴我，您很奇特，我想也是。

深情滿滿的茱蒂

附記：

　　重讀此信，發現信中不全是史蒂文生，有一兩處提及了傑維少爺。

9月10日

親愛的叔叔：

　　他離開農場了，我們都很想念他！當您已經習慣某些人、某些地方或某種生活方式時，忽然被奪走的話，您的心也會感到失落、空蕩蕩的。我覺得與山普太太的談話更加沒意思了。

再過兩個星期就要開學了，我很高興又可以**繼續**上課。這個暑假我非常努力，寫了六部短篇小說和七首詩。但我寄到雜誌社的作品全被退回來了，還附有短信，非常客氣。可我並不在意，只當是在練文筆。傑維少爺看過以後（他每天收信，所以我瞞不了他），說我寫得一塌糊塗，完全不知所云（傑維少爺說話向來不拐彎抹角）。不過最後一篇描寫大學生活的短篇小說，他說還不壞，幫我用打字機打出來。我已經寄給一家雜誌社了，至今已過了兩個星期，也許他們還在考慮呢！

要變天了，一切都籠罩在奇怪的橘色光圈裡，暴風雨要來了。

鄉間的暴風雨可不是鬧著玩的，你時時刻刻都得注意露天放著的東西，免得蹧蹋了。

星期四

叔叔！叔叔！您猜怎麼著？郵差剛送來兩封信。

第一，我的小說被採用了，稿費五十美金。

喔！天啊，我是「作家」了！

第二，大學行政部來了一封信，我將獲得兩年的獎學金，包括我的食宿費和學費。這獎學金是給那些「英文特別優異及其他科目成績優良」的學生。我真的得到了！這是我離開學校前申請的，原本沒有抱太大的希望，因爲大一時沒學好數學和拉丁文，不過之後似乎就彌補過來了。我高興極了，叔叔，以後我將不再是您的負擔了，您每個月只需寄給我零用錢就行了，也許我還可以投稿、當家教什麼的來賺取零用錢。

我眞想快點回到學校念書。

您永遠的喬若莎‧艾伯特
（《當大二生贏了》之作者，刊登該文的雜誌
在每個書報攤均有銷售，售價爲十美分）

9月26日

親愛的長腿叔叔：

我已經回到學校，是高年級學生了。今年的書房更好了──有兩扇面南的大窗子，還有很多家具。茱莉亞帶著花不完的零用錢在兩天前到校了，正一心一意地佈置房間。

我們換了新壁紙，舖上雅緻的地毯，還有精巧的椅子──不再只是去年那張上紅木漆的椅子，而是貨眞價實的紅木椅，但我們也很喜歡去年的。新椅子很美麗，不過我覺得自己似乎不配坐這種椅子，總是神經緊繃，深怕在不該弄髒的地方留下污漬。

還有，叔叔，一回到學校就發現您的信——抱歉，我是指您的祕書寄來的信。

　　能否請您告訴我任何一個我可以理解的理由，解釋我為何不能接受獎學金？

　　我真的不瞭解您為什麼要反對。不過，無論您如何反對都沒有用，因為我已經接受了——也絕不改變！這聽起來似乎很不客氣，不過我不是有意的。

　　我猜想，您可能認為，一旦計劃供我上大學就不能半途而廢，非得讓我四年畢業後拿到文憑，才算大功告成。

　　不過，請從我的角度想一想，即使我接受了獎學金，我還是您所培育出來的人。您同樣為我付出四年，只不過是我欠您的債少一些罷了。我知道您並不指望我還錢，但儘管如此，只要辦得到，我還是要還您的。有了獎學金一切就會變得容易多了，我本來計劃要用一輩子來還債的，如今半輩子就夠了。

　　我希望您明白我的立場，不要生氣，我還是會充滿感恩地接受您給我的零用錢。畢竟，和茱莉亞及她的家具住在一起，需要更多的零用錢，真希望她能節儉些，或者乾脆不和我住在一起。

　　這不該算是一封信，因為我本來打算寫更多的內容。不過，我剛裝好四個窗簾和三條門簾（幸虧您看不見我的粗針線活），又用牙粉擦亮一套銅製文具（非常艱難的差事），還用指甲刀剪下掛畫用的鐵條。緊接著我拆封了四箱書，並收拾兩大箱的衣服（這似乎不可置信，喬若莎·艾伯特竟然擁有兩大箱滿滿的衣服，不過她真的有！），同時還要迎接五十位好朋友。

　　開學這一天，真是歡樂的一天。

　　晚安，親愛的叔叔，別因為您的雛鳥要獨立而生氣，她已經長成一隻精力充沛的小鳥了。不僅可以高聲地咯咯叫著，還有了這一身美麗的羽毛（這都是歸功於您）。

　　　　　　　　　　　　　　　　　　　愛您的茱蒂

11月9日

親愛的長腿叔叔：

　　茱莉亞‧平萊頓邀請我去她家過聖誕假期。史密斯先生，這沒有嚇著您吧？想像一下，約翰‧格利爾孤兒院的喬若莎‧艾伯特，跟有錢人們同坐一桌。我不知道為什麼茱莉亞要邀我，她最近似乎與我親近許多。老實說，我寧願去莎莉家，不過是茱莉亞先邀我的，因此要去只能去紐約而不是烏塞斯特。我挺害怕一次要遇見這麼多平萊頓家族的人，還得為此添置很多新衣服。所以，親愛的叔叔，如果您來信希望我安靜地留在大學，我會以非常溫順恭敬的態度，同往常般服從您的指示。

　　空閒時，我閱讀《托馬斯‧赫胥黎的生平和書信》，很輕鬆愉快，一有空就拿起來閱讀一下。您知道 archaeopteryx 是什麼嗎？是一種古代的始祖鳥。還有 stereognathus 呢？我也不懂，那好像是遺失的演化環節，如同長牙的鳥類或長翅膀的蜥蜴。啊，不是！兩者都不是，我剛剛查書了，是一種中生代的哺乳類動物。

這是僅存的一幅始祖鳥畫像。

我今年選修經濟學——很有啓發性的科目。我修完後還要選修慈善事業和改革，這樣我就知道該如何管理孤兒院了。您不覺得，如果我有投票權的話，我會是一個很棒的選民嗎？我上週滿二十一歲了，如果一個國家將我這樣一位誠實、聰明又受過教育的公民丟在一邊，豈不是太浪費了？

您永遠的茱蒂

12月7日

親愛的長腿叔叔：

感謝您批准我去拜訪茱莉亞──我想沉默就意味著贊同。

這段時間的社交活動眞是太頻繁了！上星期舉辦了一年一度的舞會，今年是第一次任何人都可以參加，以往只有高年級才行。

我邀了吉米・馬克白，而莎莉邀了吉米在普林斯頓的室友。他是去年暑假參加他們露營活動的朋友，一頭紅髮，和藹可親的樣子。茱莉亞邀請了一位從紐約來的，毫無個性的人。但從社交的角度來看也算是無懈可擊，因爲他是德拉馬特・奇切斯特家的人。這可能對您意味著什麼，對我卻毫無意義。

星期五的下午，我們的客人到齊後，在高年級生宿舍裏吃茶點，然後趕回旅館用晚餐。旅館人滿爲患，他們只好排排睡在餐桌上──他們自己這樣說的。吉米・馬克白說下一次要是再被邀請參加大學社交活動，一定把登山帳篷帶來，在校園裏紮營。

七點半，他們前來參加校長舉辦的招待會和舞會。然後我們的聯歡會提早開始了！主辦單位事先將男士們的卡片做好，然後每跳完一支曲子，就讓他們一起按照姓氏字母的順序，列隊等候，以便下一個女舞伴容易找到他們。比如，吉米・馬克白，將耐心地站在 M 裏面，直到有人來請他（至少他應該耐心等候，不過他總是晃來晃去，常常混在 R 或 S 組裏面）。我發現他眞是位難纏的客人，因爲直到舞會結束，他只和我跳了三支舞，這讓他很生氣。他說他不好意思與不認識的女孩子共舞！

第二天早上有一場合唱音樂會——您猜那首爲這場音樂會獨創的滑稽新歌是誰寫的？沒錯，是我。喔，叔叔，我告訴您，您的小棄兒現在很出名呢！

無論如何，這兩天玩得眞的很快樂，我認爲男士們也都很高興。剛開始面對一千個女孩子，有些男賓還很拘謹，不過他們很快就適應了。從普林斯頓來的兩位客人也十分開心——至少他們彬彬有禮地這麼說道，同時也邀我們明年春天參加他們的舞會。親愛的叔叔，我們答應了，所以請別反對。

茱莉亞、莎莉還有我都穿上了新衣裳，您想知道細節嗎？茱莉亞的奶油色緞子衣服上裝飾著金色刺繡，她還戴著紫色蘭花。衣服是巴黎製的，如夢似幻，至少值一百萬美元。

莎莉穿著天藍色衣服鑲有波斯花邊，與她的頭髮十分相配。雖然不值一百萬美元，也達到了同樣的效果。

我的是淡粉紅色綴著玫瑰花邊，手裏捧著吉米·馬克白送我的艷紅色玫瑰花（莎莉早告訴他要帶什麼顏色的）。我們都穿著長統絲襪、緞子鞋、圍著和衣服顏色相襯的薄紗披巾。

這些服飾的細節一定給您留下深刻的印象吧！

叔叔，我不禁爲男人枯燥乏味的生活感到悲哀。想想看，薄紗、威尼斯花邊和愛爾蘭鉤針編織，對他們毫無意義。而女人，無論她們是喜歡孩子、丈夫、微生物、詩歌、僕人、平行四邊形、花園、柏拉圖，還是喜歡橋牌，她們始終永遠且徹底地喜歡服裝。這是四海一家的天性，也讓世界更加親近（摘自莎士比亞的戲劇，並非我首創）。

此外，還有另一件事您希望我告訴您，我最近剛發現的祕密嗎？答應我不要覺得我很虛榮。請聽：

我很漂亮。

真的。房裏有三面鏡子，我不會傻到連這一點都看不出來。

一位友人

附記：這是一封您在小說裏會讀到的惡劣匿名信之一。

12月20日

親愛的長腿叔叔：

我只剩一點時間，不久後要去上兩堂課；再加上我必須收拾一個行李箱還有一個大手提袋，去趕四點的火車——不過出發前還是想寫幾句話告訴您，我對您送的聖誕禮物有多麼喜歡。

貂皮大衣、項鏈、頭巾、手套、手帕、書和手提包,所有的我都喜歡——當然最喜歡的是您!不過,叔叔,您沒有義務把我寵壞呀!我只是個平凡人,是個平凡的女孩子。您用這些塵世的花稍來誘惑我,我又怎能專心致志地讀書呢?

現在我終於能夠猜到,是哪一位理事每年給約翰‧格利爾孤兒院提供聖誕樹和每週一次的霜淇淋了。雖然他隱名埋姓,我還是能從他的所作所為,猜出他是誰。您所做的這一切好事,一定能給您帶來幸福的。

再見,祝您有一個非常愉快的耶誕節!

您永遠的茱蒂

附記:我也送給您一份禮物吧!假如您認識她的話,願您也喜歡她?

1月11日

親愛的長腿叔叔:

叔叔,原本打算在紐約寫信給您的,不過紐約實在太喧鬧了,我過了一段很美好、很有意義的日子。我慶幸自己沒有出生在這樣的家庭。我寧願在孤兒院長大,不管出身多麼低微,至少簡單誠實而不矯揉造作。我現在終於明白，為何人們總說他們被身外之物拖累。那家人的物質生活令人窒息，直到我上了特快車回到校園，我才鬆了口氣。所有的家具都雕工精細，裝飾得富麗堂皇；我所見到的人都衣著講究、彬彬有禮，低聲交談顯得品味極高。不過說實話，叔叔，自我進門一直到離去這段期間，從來沒有聽過一句真心話。我看不出那房子裏有任何的新意。

平萊頓太太滿腦子充斥著金錢珠寶、裁縫和宴會，與馬克白太太迥然不同。如果有朝一日我結婚生子，我會像馬克白家一樣培育自己的孩子；無論給我多少錢，我都不會讓他們變成像平萊頓家的孩子一樣。這樣說，對於一個剛剛接待過我的家庭是不是很不禮貌？如果是這樣，請您原諒，我不過是想和您說些悄悄話。

我僅在吃茶點的時候見到傑維少爺一次。沒有機會跟他單獨交談真是可惜，畢竟我們去年夏天相處得那麼融洽。看來他對自己的親戚沒有多大好感，而他們也不太理他。

我看到數不清的劇院、飯店和豪華巨宅；腦子裏充滿了瑪瑙、鍍金、拼花地板和棕櫚，很長時間都無法恢復過來。我很高興現在自己又回到學校和書本裏來，又變成了那個徹頭徹尾的學生。校園的寧靜比紐約的嘈雜，更令人神清氣爽，大學生活才真的可愛。書籍、學習和常規的課業使人思想活躍，一旦疲勞了，可以到體育館或操場上運動；如果腦袋和身體都累了，還有那麼多志趣相投的同學們，可以和她們暢談整個傍晚；然後帶著振奮的情緒睡覺，彷彿徹底地解決了什麼世界難題似的。在我們的談話中總能穿插許多愚蠢的笑話，還能針對一些小事胡亂開開玩笑，讓心情格外舒暢。我們對此相當地自鳴得意。

　　而最值得一談的，不是生活中大起大落的那些故事，而是一些細碎微小的愉悅。我感覺自己發現了快樂的奧祕：活在當下。不要沉浸在過去的懊悔中或僅僅是希冀著未來，而是充分享受每個當下，這就像是種田，你可以選擇粗放農業或是精耕細作。今後我要細緻地生活，享受人生的每一分、每一秒，並且在享受時能清楚地意識到自己正在享受。現實生活中有許多人不是真正在過生活，而是在賽跑，他們努力地想達到生命地平線上的某個頂點，在拚命奔跑的過程中，無暇顧及周遭美麗寧靜的景致。當他們有一天突然發現自己老了、疲憊不堪時，目標究竟是否達成，實際上也不再重要。因此，我打算漫步人生，沿途小憩，一點一滴地積累人生的樂趣；即使永遠成不了偉大的作家也無所謂。您見過像我這樣的哲學家嗎？

您的茱蒂

附記：夜裏傾盆暴雨，窗臺上剛落下些許小雨點。

2月11日

親愛的長腿叔叔：

　　請別因為這封信過短而生氣。這其實不算封信，只是想告訴您，考試一結束，我很快就會再寫封信給您。只是我現在不但要考及格還要考高分，畢竟我得保住我的獎學金。

您用功的茱蒂

3月5日

親愛的長腿叔叔：

　　柯勒校長今晚講話時，談到現代年輕人不僅過於輕率膚淺，還不懂得深思熟慮。他說我們正在逐漸失去前輩那種奮發向上和刻苦做學問的良好精神，這一點，尤其體現在不尊重權威之上，我們對長者已失去了崇敬之心。

　　從講堂回來我一直都在思考這個問題。我是不是太不拘小節了呢，叔叔？對您是否應該更敬重且疏遠些？是的，我確信我該這麼做，讓我重新開始吧！

親愛的史密斯先生：

　　我的期末考試全部通過，您聽了一定很高興，而現在我又要開始為新學年做準備了。我要停修化學——已學完了定性分析——改修生物學。不過選修這門課時我有些遲疑，因為據我所知，這堂課要解剖蚯蚓和青蛙。

　　最近我常去體育館，因為體育館有一個校友捐贈的泳池，是用水泥和大理石砌成的美麗游泳池。再加上我的好友——馬克白小姐，把她的泳衣給了我（因為縮水了她穿不下），所以我開始學游泳。

　　晚餐後的粉紅色霜淇淋真好吃。您知道嗎？這所學校出於美觀和健康的考量，禁止使用化學色素，食物只能使用蔬菜著色。

　　最近的氣候宜人，燦爛的陽光白雲與幾場瑞雪交替出現，我和同伴喜歡步行上下課，尤其是下課時。

　　親愛的史密斯先生，我希望您健康如常。

　　　　　　　　　　您最真誠的喬若莎·艾伯特致敬

4月24日

親愛的長腿叔叔：

　　春回人間！您真該來看看校園的迤邐風光。我想您應該要來親自瞧一瞧。傑維少爺上星期五順道來訪——可惜他來的時機不對，莎莉、茱莉亞和我正要去趕火車。您猜我們去哪兒了？對不起，我們去了普林斯頓參加舞會和球賽！我沒有提前徵求您的同意，是因爲我感覺您的祕書不會答應我。但是！一切都合乎規矩。我們向校方請了假，而且馬克白太太爲了照顧我們也一同前往。多麼迷人的時光——恕不詳述，事情太多、太複雜了。

星期六

拂曉前我們就出發上山了！是巡夜的人把我們六個人叫醒的。我們煮了咖啡（您絕對沒看過這麼多咖啡渣！），然後步行兩哩路到孤樹山頂看日出，連滾帶爬地登上最後一個山坡，差點趕不上看日出！我們雖然非常疲憊，不過回來吃早餐時，一樣吃得狼吞虎嚥！

天呀！長腿叔叔，這一頁充滿了驚歎號，真是感慨萬千！

原本打算多畫一些圖畫，像是樹上的新葉和遊樂場的新徑；以及寫一些明天要上的恐怖生物課、湖上的新遊船、普藍蒂絲得了肺炎，還有普列希的安哥拉小貓走丟了的事。那隻貓在佛格森大廈住了兩週才被打掃的女工發現。還有我買的三件新衣裳——有著白色、粉紅色和天藍色圓點花紋，以及搭配的帽子等等——不過我太睏了。我常用這個當成藉口，不是嗎？不過女子大學是一個忙碌的地方，一整天下來真的累壞了！況且，今天天一亮就起床了。

滿是深情的茱蒂

這就是普列希的小貓，從畫中可以看到牠的毛有多長。

5月15日

親愛的長腿叔叔：

　　附上初次發表的圖畫。它看來像是一隻蜘蛛吊在一條繩子上，其實完全不是這麼一回事，這是我在游泳池游泳的模樣。

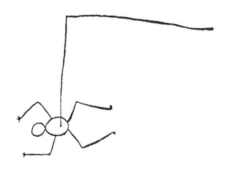

　　教練用掛在天花板滑輪上的繩子穿過我的腰帶，如果能完全信任教練，這種辦法其實還算不錯。可惜我總是怕她會把繩子鬆開，只得一隻眼睛緊張地盯著她，另一隻眼睛注意游泳，一心二用，泳技自然進步得十分緩慢。

　　近幾天，天氣變化無常，剛開始寫信時還是陰雨連綿，現在卻已經陽光普照了。莎莉邀我去打網球，這樣一來，我就可以不去體育館了。

一週後

　　早該把這封信寫完的，叔叔，您不介意吧？我寫信如此不規律。我真的很喜歡給您寫信，它使我有一種擁有親人的歸屬感。您知道嗎？您已不再是我唯一的通信對象了，還有另外兩個人喔！入冬以來，傑維少爺給我寫了一封長信（信封是用打字機印的，為了不讓茱莉亞認出他的筆跡），您有沒有被嚇到呀！然後，差不多每個星期都會有一封從普林斯頓寄來的信，信紙用的是學校的黃色信紙，字跡十分潦草。我全都及時回覆了，所以您瞧——我跟其他女孩子一樣，也會收到信了。

　　我曾告訴您，我被選為高年級戲劇社的會員了嗎？這是一個菁英組織，每千人中只有七十五人能入選。我應該成為戲劇社的會員嗎？您覺得我還會是一個始終如一的社會主義者嗎？

　　您知道，最近我在社會學中對什麼問題最感興趣嗎？我正在寫一篇〈如何照顧依賴性強的孩子〉的論文（多了不起），老師把題目寫在紙條上，而我抽到這個題目。很有趣，不是嗎？

　　晚餐鐘響了，我會在路過郵筒時把信寄出去。

滿是深情的茱蒂

6月4日

親愛的叔叔：

　　這是一個非常忙碌的時期——學校再過十天就要舉行畢業典禮；再加上明天要考試，於是大家都忙著念書、整理行裝。外面的世界如此精采，關在家裏眞是令人傷心。

　　不過沒關係，暑假就要來了。茉莉亞今年夏天要出國旅行——這是第四次了。叔叔，人各有命。莎莉跟往常一樣要去阿迪郎達克。您猜我要去哪裡？您可以猜三次，洛克威洛？錯！跟莎莉登山去？錯（我不敢奢望，畢竟去年已讓我打退堂鼓了）！您猜不到別的嗎？您太沒有想像力了，叔叔。假如您答應不會極力阻止我的話，我就告訴您，雖然我得事先向您的祕書說明，但我主意已定。

　　夏天我要跟理查‧帕特森夫人去海邊，輔導她在秋天即將上大學的女兒。我是在馬克白家認識她的，她是位非常迷人的女士。我還要教她的小女兒英語和拉丁語，雖然忙碌，不過我還是可以留一點時間給自己，這樣一來，我每個月可以賺五十美元。這不是一個小數目吧！是否有些過高了？這是她先提出來的薪資，要是我自己開價的話，我連二十五美元都難以啓齒。

　　我將在九月一日完成我在蒙格羅尼亞（那是她住的地方）的任務，接下來的三個星期，我可能會去洛克威洛——我很高興能再去看看山普夫婦和那些友善的小動物。

　　長腿叔叔，您覺得我的安排如何？您瞧，現在的我開始變得非常獨立了，您使我站穩腳步，現在我可以自己獨立行走了。

　　普林斯頓舉行畢業典禮時，我們還在考試，這真是一個沉重的打擊，莎莉和我都想去參加，然而根本不可能。

　　再見，叔叔！好好地過一個暑假吧，秋天回來時您就會精神百倍，這樣您才好投入新一年的工作。（這本該是您要寫信告訴我的事！）我根本不知道您在夏天都會做些什麼事，或是在哪裡度假和消遣。我無法想像您身處的背景。您打高爾夫嗎？還是打獵、騎馬，或者單純坐在陽光底下沉思呢？

　　做什麼都好，祝您愉快，別忘了茱蒂。

6月10日

親愛的叔叔：

　　我不知道如何落筆，但我的心意已決，絕不反悔。您說夏天想送我去歐洲旅遊，您真的對我太好、太大方了，您真的是一個好人——雖然一開始我真的十分興奮，不過三思之後只得拒絕您了。我拒絕用您的錢來繳學費，卻拿您的錢去玩樂，這太不合乎邏輯了，您不該讓我養成這種奢侈的生活習慣。從未擁有過的東西，就不會去想；可是一旦想著這些奢侈品都是他或她（英文要用兩個第三人稱）理所應得的東西時，就再也不能失去了。與莎莉和茱莉亞住在一起，對我的簡單生活是一種挑戰。她們都是從襁褓時就擁有一切，並且認為那一切都是理所當然的存在。對她們來說，她們想要的一切東西，都是世界虧欠她們的，也許真的是虧欠她們的──無論如何，這個世界似乎明白這筆債，也一直在償還她們。至於我，世界什麼都不虧欠我，一開始就毫不含糊地告訴了我這點。我無權賒欠，因為世界會駁回我的要求。

我似乎在一堆比喻中掙扎──希望您抓住要點了。總之，我深切地認為，這個夏天所能做的唯一一件正確的事──就是去教書，我必須開始自力更生。

蒙格羅尼亞四天後

剛寫完上面這些──您猜發生什麼事？女僕送來傑維少爺的名片。他今夏也要出國去，但不是和茱莉亞一家人一同前往，而是單獨一個人。我告訴他，您邀請我跟一位要照顧一群女孩子的女士同行。他知道您，叔叔。也就是說，他知道我父母雙亡，有一位好心的老先生送我上大學，但我沒有勇氣告訴他約翰‧格利爾孤兒院的林林總總。他以為您是我的監護人或家族遠親的世交，但我從未告訴他，我根本不認識您——因為這樣說似乎太奇怪了！

無論如何，他都堅持要我到歐洲去。他說我不該拒絕，因為這是我教育過程中必不可少的一部分。同時，他說此次的歐洲行他也會在巴黎，因此我們偶爾可以從夫人身邊溜走，一起到優雅、有趣的異國餐廳吃晚餐。

唉，叔叔，這真的很吸引我！我幾乎動搖了，如果他不是那麼專制的話，也許我真的會同意。我可以慢慢地被動之以情，卻無法被強迫。他說我是個愚蠢、單純、不通情理、不切實際、脾氣古怪，固執己見的小孩子（這些只是他罵我的其中幾個字眼，有好多我都記不得了）。他還說我不知好歹，我該聽從年長者的勸告，我們幾乎吵了起來——我不是很確定，不過我們的確有一番爭執。

不管怎樣，我很快地收拾行李來到蒙格羅尼亞。在我寫完信之前，希望我身後的橋、我的退路能燃燒起來，現在它們應該已經完全化為灰燼了。此刻，我在崖頂（帕特森太太海邊房子的名字），衣服已從箱子裏拿出來掛好了，而佛羅倫斯（那個小女兒）已經開始努力學習名詞的詞尾變化了。這還真不是件輕鬆的差事。她是個典型被寵壞的孩子，我得先教她如何讀書——以前，除了霜淇淋和蘇打水，她從未關心過任何東西。

我們在崖頂花園中的一個安靜角落學習——帕特森太太希望我們不要到戶外——不過說真的，我發現要在蔚藍的大海與遊船邊認真地思考，也真的是件困難的事！尤其是當我想到自己現在或許已在某艘船上，正向異國駛進的時候。不過我不會讓自己胡思亂想，我會專注於拉丁文法這些，關於孩子們功課方面的事。

您瞧！叔叔，我堅決抗拒了誘惑，專心地工作。請別生我的氣，別以為我對您的好意不知感激，我真的很感激您——永遠、永遠。我唯一能報答您的，就是當個非常有用的公民（女子也算是公民嗎？我想不是）。總之，絕對會是一個非常有用的人，在未來您會看著我說：「我讓這世界多了一個非常有用的人。」

叔叔，這聽起來很不錯，不是嗎？不過我也不想誤導您就是了。我時常覺得自己很平庸，這樣的感覺常常擊倒我。規劃未來的職涯真的很有趣，但是到頭來，我可能與其他人一樣平凡，最終也是嫁人並且帶給他工作上的靈感。

您永遠的茱蒂

8月19日

親愛的長腿叔叔：

窗外是一片美景，更確切地說是美麗的海景除了波浪、岩石，別無所有。

夏天在消逝，我花了一個早上的時間教那兩個蠢女孩學習拉丁文、英文和代數。眞不知道瑪麗恩將來如何能夠考取大學，即使考上了，又如何唸得下去；至於佛羅倫斯，更是毫無希望——不過，她們都是美女。只要她們一直這樣漂亮，蠢不蠢其實無關緊要，但我不禁想，她們無趣的談話應該會煩死她們的老公，除非她們運氣好，嫁給愚蠢的丈夫。她們很可能會嫁給愚蠢的人，這個世界上到處都是蠢人，今年夏天我就遇到了不少。

　　一到下午，我們就會去海灘散步，不漲潮時則去游泳。我現在可以很輕易地在鹽水裏游泳了——您看看，我所受的教育終於派上用場了。

　　傑維·平萊頓先生從巴黎寄來一封信，很簡短，語氣也很強硬的一封信。因爲我沒有聽他的勸告，所以他還在生氣呢！但是，如果他能及時回來的話，他會在大學開課前到洛克威洛來見我，並住上幾天。如果我又乖又甜又聽話的話，他會原諒我的所作所爲（他信上的內容給我這種感覺）。

　　還有一封莎莉寫來的信，要我九月份去她們的露營地玩兩個星期。我是否應該先徵得您的同意呢，還是我可以隨心所欲地去自己想去的地方？可以的，我相信我可以——我已經是個大四學生了，工作了一整個夏天，我覺得自己該有一些休閒娛樂。我要去看看山，去見見莎莉，還想見見莎莉的哥哥——他要帶我去划船——還有（這才是我主要的理由，我很壞）我要讓傑維少爺到了洛克威洛時，發現我不在。

我一定要讓他知道，他無權命令我，沒有人可以命令我，除了叔叔您之外——不過您也不可以老是這樣！我要出發去山林裏了。

茱蒂

9月6日於馬克白露營區

親愛的叔叔：

您的信來晚了（我很高興），如果您希望我遵循您的命令，您應該讓您的祕書至少在兩星期內把信送到我這。您瞧，我現在在莎莉這兒已經有五天了。

森林眞漂亮，無論是露營地、天氣、馬克白一家人，還有整個世界都是如此美好，我很快樂！

吉米來找我去划船了，再見——很抱歉沒有聽您的話，不過您爲什麼堅持不讓我玩一下呢？我工作了一整個夏天，應該可以放兩星期的假期。您眞殘酷，自己不玩還不許我玩。

叔叔，無論如何，我還是愛您的，儘管您多麼地不講理。

茱蒂

10月3日

親愛的長腿叔叔：

回到學校，我就是大四生了——並且當上了《月刊》的編輯。這似乎不太可能，不是嗎？這麼重要的一位人物，在幾年前居然還只是個約翰·格利爾孤兒院的孤兒？在美國，我們真的可以一舉成名！

您是怎麼看這件事的呢？洛克威洛轉來傑維少爺的一封信，他很抱歉秋天來不及趕到那兒；他受幾個朋友的邀請，乘快艇去遊玩，並祝我能有個美好的夏天，好好享受鄉間的生活。

他明明知道我所有的時間都在馬克白，因為茱莉亞告訴他了！您們男人真不如女人會耍手段，你們太不高明了。

茱莉亞有滿滿一箱令人陶醉的新衣裳——其中一件彩虹色的晚禮服，簡直是天堂裏的天使們穿的衣服。我還以為自己今年的衣服是空前的（有這個字嗎？）絕美呢！那是拜託一位普通的女裁縫師仿效帕特森太太的服裝做的，雖然無法跟原版一模一樣，但在茱莉亞打開箱子之前我都還很滿意。不過現在，我真想看看巴黎了。

親愛的叔叔，您會不會很慶幸您不是個女孩子呢？我猜您一定會覺得我們對衣服這麼小題大做，非常可笑。的確如此，這是毋庸置疑的事，不過這全是您的錯。

您聽過那位博學的赫爾教授嗎？就是那位藐視女人，並認為女人是無用裝飾的人；他認為有頭腦的婦女，應該穿合理實用的衣裳。他的妻子很順從他，也接受了他所謂的「穿著革命」。可是結果呢？他和一位歌舞團的女孩子私奔了。

您永遠的茱蒂

11月17日

親愛的長腿叔叔：

我的寫作事業受到很大的挫折，不知道是否該告訴您，不過我希望能獲得一些同情——默默地同情，請求您，別在來信時提及此事，以免觸及我的傷口。

我花了整整一個冬季的晚上，還有整個夏天教那兩個笨學生拉丁文的空檔，寫了一部長篇小說。我在開學前剛寫完就寄給了一家出版社，過了兩個月都沒有回音，我確信他們應該採納了。但是就在昨天早上，郵政快遞（欠郵資三角）把它送了回來，還附上一封出版商的信，一封很和善慈祥的信——非常坦率！他說，從我的住址來看，我應該還在讀大學，他建議我先好好讀書等到畢業後再開始寫。他引用讀者的意見如下：「小說想入非非，刻劃不夠真實，對話不夠生活化。富有幽默感但品味不高，如果她繼續努力，或許可寫出一本眞正像樣的書。」

叔叔，不完全是讚美，對嗎？我還以爲自己爲美國文學史添上了光彩的一筆呢，我眞的是這樣想的。原本我計劃在畢業之前寫本巨著，給您一個驚喜。素材是去年在茱莉亞家做客時收集的。不過我承認出版社編輯的意見確實中肯，用兩星期來觀察一個大城市的風貌和習俗是遠遠不夠的。

昨天我帶著書稿外出散步，走到煤氣站邊，進去問裏面的工人是否可以借用一下他的火爐。他很熱情地開了爐門，於是我親手把書稿丟了進去，心中覺得我將書稿丟入火爐的行爲，就像火化了我的孩子一樣。

我昨晚上床睡覺時心亂如麻，覺得自己將永遠一事無成，白白浪費了您對我的資助。可是，您猜怎麼著？今天早上醒來，一個非常美妙的新構想就出現在我的腦海裏了。一整天我都在安排我的角色，這讓我興奮得不得了，我絕對不再悲觀失望了。如果將來有一天，我的丈夫和十二個孩子全都在一場地震中喪生，第二天我還是會微笑地打起精神，重新開始新的生活。

滿是深情的茱蒂

12月14日

親愛的長腿叔叔：

　　我昨夜做了一個非常有趣的夢。我走進一家書店，店員給我一本新書，名叫《茱蒂‧艾伯特的生平與書信》。我清楚地看見它——紅色書皮上印著約翰‧格利爾孤兒院的照片，卷首是我的照片，題寫著「茱蒂‧艾伯特敬獻」。可是就在我翻到最後一頁看到自己的墓誌銘時，我就醒了過來。氣死人！我差點就可以知道自己嫁給誰，以及什麼時候死去。

　　您不覺得，能有位全知的作者，完美並真實地寫下你的一生，而你還可以讀到他所寫的這本傳記，是一件多麼有趣的事啊！假設它的閱讀條件是，你將永遠記得你讀過的內容、經歷那些你早已從書中知曉的一切、預知每一件事情的結果，更不用說，你將從書中準確知曉自己的死期。叔叔認為會有多少人有勇氣去閱讀它呢？又有多少人能克制自己的好奇心，不去翻閱這本書？即使代價是既沒有希望、也沒有驚喜地度過餘生。

　　您相信自由意志嗎？我相信，絕對相信。我一點也不相信因果論的說法，這種理論極為不道德，這樣誰都不用對任何事情負責了。那些相信宿命論的人只需要坐下來說，一切聽天由命，然後等死就好了。

　　我完全相信我的自由意志，並相信憑藉我自己的力量，一定能夠達成目標——這種信念是能夠開天闢地的。您等著瞧吧！我一定會成爲一個偉大的作家！我已經寫完新書的前四章了，另外五章的輪廓也寫出來了。

叔叔，這是封很玄奧的信——您看了會頭疼嗎？就此打住吧！我們現在要做點麥芽糖，可惜無法寄一塊給您。它眞的很好吃，因爲我們是用眞的奶油跟黃油球做的。

滿是深情的茱蒂

附記：

這是在音樂課上的優美舞姿。從附圖上看，我們就像是在跳芭蕾，最後那個優雅地用腳尖旋轉的人是我。

12月26日

我親愛親愛的叔叔：

您喪失理智了嗎？難道您不知道，不該送給一個女孩子

十七件聖誕禮物嗎？請記住，我是社會主義者。難道您想把我變成一位闊小姐嗎？

想想看，萬一我們吵架的話會有多糟糕！我得雇一輛卡車才能把您的禮物退回去。

我很抱歉我送給您的領巾織得不夠整齊，您大概看得出來，那是我親手織的。您在寒冷的日子裡，記得要將它圍上，還要將您的外衣釦子扣好。

謝謝您，叔叔，一千個謝謝，您是世上最可愛的人——也是最傻的那一個。

隨函附上一株在馬克白家露營時摘的幸運草，希望它在新的一年帶給您好運。

茱蒂

1月9日

叔叔，您願意做點什麼，來獲得永遠的救贖嗎？有一戶很窮的人家，父母身邊有四個孩子，雖然另有兩個稍長的男孩但早已離家自力更生且音訊全無。父親在一家快要倒閉的玻璃廠工作，這個工作很傷身體，已經讓他就此住進了醫院並花光他的積蓄。整個家庭的重擔，因此全落在二十四歲的大女兒肩上。她白天做針線活，一天只賺一塊五毛錢（如果找得到活時），晚上還得繡桌布。媽媽則是身體虛弱且十分虔誠，她總是雙手交疊地坐著，一臉聽天由命。所以只有女兒疲於奔命，為家庭的重擔憂慮；她不知道該如何度過剩下的冬天——我也不知道該如何是好。如果有一百塊，她就可以買些煤炭和幾雙鞋給三個孩子，好讓他們去上學，還可以留點錢。這樣她就不會因為幾天找不到工作，而愁得要死了。

您是我認識最富有的人了，您能不能省下一百塊幫幫他們呢？那個女孩比我還需要幫忙。要不是為了她，我不會開口求您，我才不想管那個母親呢！她窩囊透了。

稍晚

叔叔，我現在正在病床上寫信給您，因為我的扁桃腺發炎了。它已經讓我臥病在床兩天，現在只能喝些熱牛奶，別的全都不能吃。醫生問我：「妳小時候爸媽為什麼沒有給妳切除扁桃腺？」我怎麼會知道呢？我都懷疑他們是否真的曾為我操過心。

您的茱蒂

隔天早上

在寄出前我又重讀此信，不知為何自己在信中是如此憂傷。但我向您保證，我年輕、幸福、快樂，相信您也跟我一樣。青春與年歲無關而是在於精神，所以即使您白髮蒼蒼，叔叔，您還是可以童心未泯。

充滿感情的茱蒂

1月12日

親愛的慈善家：

昨天我收到您給那一家人的支票了，非常感謝您。午飯後，我沒去上體育課，立刻給他們送去。您真該看看那女孩的表情。她喜出望外，大大鬆了口氣，看起來似乎變得年輕許多。其實她才二十四歲，多可憐呀！

　　無論如何，最近她覺得好事接二連三地到來。不只是您的善舉，還有這兩個月她都會有工作做——因為有人要辦結婚嫁妝。

　　當那個媽媽意識到那一小張紙片代表一百塊錢時，大聲喊道：「感謝上帝啊！」

　　我對她說：「不是上帝，是長腿叔叔。」（史密斯先生，我是指您。）

　　「是上帝讓他這樣做的。」她說道。

　　「才不是！是我讓他這樣做的。」我答道。

　　不管如何，叔叔，我相信上帝會賜福給您的，您可以遠離煉獄一萬年。

最感激您的茱蒂·艾伯特

3月5日

親愛的理事：

　　明天是這個月的第一個星期三，一個對約翰·格利爾孤兒院而言，最感到厭煩的日子。當五點的鐘聲響起，您拍拍孩子

們的腦袋準備離去時，他們將會大大地鬆一口氣！您曾經拍過我的頭嗎？我想沒有，我印象中只有胖理事。

　　請轉達我對孤兒院的問候，拜託您——帶上我最真摯的問候。經過四年的滄桑生活再回想起以前，心中竟升起一股暖意。剛上大學時，我曾經因為自己被剝奪了一般女孩該有的童年，而心懷怨恨。現在，我一點也不這麼覺得了。我將之視為一段不尋常的人生經歷，它使我能站在一個旁觀者的角度審視生命。成年以後，我對世界的認識比那些家境優越的女孩們更加開闊。

　　我看到很多女孩子（例如茱莉亞）永遠都體會不到什麼叫快樂。她們已經太習慣這樣的感覺，對此早已麻木，而我非常確信自己對生命中的每一刻，都感到快樂。將來不管發生何等不愉快的事情，我都會知道自己是幸福的。我會把所有的不幸（即使是牙疼）都視為有趣的經歷，樂於去體驗；任憑風雲變幻，我都會勇敢地面對一切。

　　代我向李皮太太致意（這樣比較確切，若用「愛」這個字就太強烈了點），別忘了告訴她，我的品行變得很端正。

您深情的茱蒂

4月4日於洛克威洛

親愛的叔叔：

　　您注意到郵戳了嗎？莎莉和我在復活節來到洛克威洛。我們想找個安靜的地方度過這十天假期。在佛格森樓再多吃一次飯，都會使我們的精神崩潰。疲倦的時候，還要與四百個女孩在同一個餐廳吃飯簡直是活受罪。聲音如此嘈雜，以致於聽不到對面的人講話，除非把兩手做成話筒狀放在嘴邊大喊，這是真的。

　　我們爬山、談天、讀書、寫作，好好休息了一番。我們爬上以前傑維少爺與我煮晚餐的天山頂——真難想像那已經是兩年前的事了。因為生火而烤黑的石塊依然清晰可見，讓我開始睹物思人，總是有些地方會和什麼人聯想在一起，真是很有意思。他不在這裏，我覺得有些孤單——不過只有兩分鐘這樣想而已。

　　叔叔，您猜我最近有什麼新活動？您一定會認為我太執著了——沒錯，我正在寫一本書。三個星期前就開始著手了，進度非常快。我掌握到訣竅了，傑維少爺與那個編輯說得沒錯，只有寫自己最熟悉的東西才能寫得好。這次我寫的是我熟悉的事物——非常非常熟，猜猜背景在哪裡？就是約翰·格利爾孤兒院。而且這個故事很好，我真的認為很好——寫的都是一些日常生活瑣事。我現在是個現實主義者，雖然放棄了浪漫主義，不過將來等我自己的冒險生涯開始之後，我會再回到浪漫主義的。

　　這本新書一定得完成而且要出版，您等著瞧吧！如果下定決心想要做一件事並且鍥而不捨的話，一定會成功的。這四年來，我多麼希望能收到您一封回信，直到現在我都還沒有放棄這個希望。

　　再見，親愛的叔叔。

您深情的茱蒂

附記：

　　忘記告訴您關於農莊的消息了，真的很令人沮喪。如果您不想受刺激的話，就別看這一段了。

　　可憐的老葛洛佛死了，牠已經老得吃不下任何東西，他們只好射殺牠。上周還有九隻雞被黃鼠狼或臭鼬，抑或是老鼠咬死了。

5月17日

親愛的長腿叔叔：

　　這封信會非常非常簡短，因為我的肩膀一動筆就痛。上課時做了一整天的筆記，然後又寫了一個晚上的「不朽」巨著，我動筆的時間太長了。

三週後的星期三就要舉辦畢業典禮了，真希望您能來，好讓我們能相互認識一下——您不來我會恨您的！茱莉亞邀請傑維少爺，他代表她的家人；莎莉邀請吉米‧馬克白，他代表她的家人。我該邀請誰呢？我只有您和李皮太太，而我不想邀請她，請您來吧！

您的作家寫字寫得手都疼了。

茱蒂

6月19日於洛克威洛

親愛的長腿叔叔：

我畢業了！我的文憑跟我最好的兩件裙子放在最下面的抽屜裡。畢業典禮一如往常，在關鍵時刻掉下了幾滴眼淚。謝謝您送來的玫瑰花，真漂亮，傑維少爺和吉米也都送我玫瑰花，不過我把它們留在浴缸裏了。在畢業典禮上我選擇捧著您的花。

今年我在洛克威洛度過夏天——也許會永遠留在這裏。食宿便宜、環境清幽，有益於寫作。一個努力奮鬥的作家還能乞求什麼呢？我對自己的作品入迷，只要一張開眼就想著它，晚上也會夢到它。我需要安靜平和的環境，以及充足的時間來工作（加上富有營養的食物）。

傑維少爺八月會來這玩一個星期，而吉米‧馬克白夏天也會找時間來拜訪一下。他現在在一家證券交易所上班，要到各地向銀行兜售債券，他打算在拜訪國家農業銀行時來看望我。

您瞧，洛克威洛也並不冷清，不過我更期待您能開車經過——只是現在我知道，這輩子是不可能的了。當您沒有來參加我的畢業典禮時，我就將您從我心中抹掉並永遠地埋葬了。

茱蒂‧艾伯特文學院學士

7月24日於洛克威洛

最親愛的長腿叔叔：

工作是否樂趣無窮？——您曾經工作過嗎？尤其是當您熱愛自己的工作時就更有趣了。入夏以來，我奮筆疾書、揮灑自如，只恨時日太短，不能將自己所思所想的一切美好，都寫在紙上。

我已經完成第二稿了，明天早上七點半開始第三稿。它將會是您讀過的那些書中，最好的一本書——真的。它幾乎佔據了我全部的身心。一到早上我還來不及穿衣吃飯就想動筆，然後一寫再寫，直到筋疲力盡才跟柯林斯（新的牧羊犬）一起到田野漫步，為第二天的寫作準備素材。它將會是您所見過最好的一本書了——對不起，這些我剛才說過了。

您不會覺得我太驕傲吧，親愛的叔叔，會嗎？

我絕不是、真的不是，只是此時此刻正處於狂熱階段。也許過一會兒我就會冷靜下來，重新審視它、厭倦它。不，不會的，我確信我不會！這回我寫了本真正像樣的書，您等著拜讀吧！

談點別的事吧！我還沒有告訴過您，阿馬薩和嘉麗在五月份結婚了！他們婚後依然在這裏工作，在我看來，只要結婚誰都會變個人。以前阿馬薩腿上沾滿了泥巴，或者把煙灰弄到地板上時，嘉麗不過是笑笑而已，現在卻是破口大罵。而且她也不再用心地捲髮了。至於阿馬薩，他向來喜歡把地毯打掃乾淨和搬運木材，現在叫他幹點什麼就嘟囔個不停。他現在的裝扮也很邋遢，以前常喜歡用鮮紅色和紫色的領帶，現在不是黑色就是棕色。我決定不結婚了，顯然人一結婚就開始走下坡。

農村沒有什麼新聞，牲口很健壯、豬也很肥、牛群似乎都心滿意足、雞也下了不少蛋。你對家禽感興趣嗎？如果感興趣，我推薦你看《母雞年產蛋二百顆》，這是一本很值得看的小書。明年我想找個孵蛋機來飼養肉雞。你看，我在洛克威洛安家了。我要留在這裏直到和安東尼‧特羅洛普的母親一樣，寫上一百一十四部小說，然後我這輩子的工作就算完成了，那我就可以退休去旅遊了。

詹姆士‧馬克白先生上星期天來拜訪，晚餐吃雞肉和霜淇淋，他看起來對這兩樣餐點都很滿意。見到他我很高興，他使我意識到外面世界的存在。可憐的吉米推銷債券並不順利，儘管他肯付六％甚至七％的利息，農業銀行仍不願意接受。我想，他將不得不回到烏塞斯特，在他爸爸的工廠裡找份工作。他生性坦率、心地善良，並不適合做金融的買賣。當個成功的成衣工廠經理倒很適合他，您不覺得嗎？雖然他現在對工作服還看不上眼，但我想他慢慢地會變得現實一些。

我希望您明白，這是一個手指痙攣的人給您寫的長信。我仍然十分愛您，親愛的叔叔，我非常快樂。這裡四周都是美景，不僅有豐盛的食物，還有一張舒服的四腳床，再加上一疊白紙和一大瓶墨水——在這世間我還能奢求什麼呢？

您一如往常的茱蒂

附記：

郵差帶來一些新消息。下星期五傑維少爺要來這住一個星期，這是件令人十分高興的事——只不過我的寫作又要受到影響了，傑維少爺可不好侍候。

8月27日

親愛的長腿叔叔：

我在想，您會在哪兒呢？

我從來都不知道您在世界上的哪個角落，我希望您在這酷熱的天氣裏，別待在紐約就好。我希望您是在山頂上（不過不是瑞士，至少選近一點的地方吧）邊賞雪邊想著我。請想著我吧，我很孤單，希望能被人惦記著。喔，叔叔，要是能認識您該有多好！我們痛苦的時候就可以相互安慰了。

我真的不想在洛克威洛繼續住下去了，真想換換環境。莎莉在明年冬天要去波士頓從事社會工作，您不覺得我和她一道去會很不錯嗎？我們可以合租一個小公寓，我可以在她工作時寫作，晚上我們就可以互相作伴了。這裏除了山普夫婦、嘉麗和阿馬薩外沒有其他人可以聊天了，實在是長夜難挨。我早就猜想到您不會同意我的想法，我幾乎能想像您祕書的來信內容：

致喬若莎·艾伯特小姐：

親愛的女士，史密斯先生希望妳能留在洛克威洛。

您真摯的，

愛爾摩·H·格利茲

我討厭您的祕書，我敢肯定叫愛爾摩・H・格利茲這個名字的人，一定很討厭。不過說真的，叔叔，我希望能去波士頓。我無法留在這裏，再這樣下去，我可能會窮極無聊到跳進穀倉坑裏去了。

天啊！真熱啊！草木枯萎、小溪乾涸、道路上滿是灰塵，已經有好幾個星期沒有下雨了。

這封信裡的我看起來就像得了狂犬病一樣，不過沒有，我只是渴望能有些家的溫暖罷了。

再見，我最親愛的叔叔，我真希望認識您。

茱蒂

9月19日於洛克威洛

親愛的叔叔：

發生了一些事情，我需要聽聽您的意見。我需要的是您而不是其他人，我能去見您嗎？這件事講起來比用寫的要容易些，我擔心您的祕書會拆閱我的信。

茱蒂

附記：我很痛苦。

長腿叔叔

10月3日於洛克威洛

親愛的長腿叔叔：

收到您親手寫的字條——筆跡顫抖得很厲害，您生病了嗎？我非常掛念您。如果我能早點知道的話，就不會拿我的事情煩您了。是的，我想告訴您我的煩惱，不過這有點難以下筆，而且這是非常私人的事。看完後請不要保存，請立即燒了它吧！

在我訴說我的煩惱之前——這兒有張一千元的支票要給您。這很好笑，不是嗎？我寄給您的這張支票，您想我是從哪裡得來的呢？

沒錯，叔叔，我賣掉我的小說了。它將要分七段連載，然後出版成一本書！您可能以為我會欣喜若狂，不過我沒有，我一點也不在意這些。當然我很高興能開始回報您的幫助——我欠您二千多塊，這些都得慢慢償還。請您別吝於接受它，請求您，因為能回報您的幫助，讓我感到十分快樂。我欠您的，不僅僅是用金錢就可以償付得了的，其餘的恩惠，我會用一生的感謝與關愛來回報您。

現在，叔叔，關於另一件事，請給我您最合於人情世故的建議吧！別考慮我是否接受得了。

您知道我一直對您有種很特殊的感情，某種程度上您代表了我整個家庭。如果我告訴您，我對另一位男子有更強烈的特

156

殊情感，您不會介意吧？您不難猜出他是誰。有很長一段時間，我每封信都會提到他——他就是傑維少爺。

我希望我能讓您瞭解他是一個什麼樣的人，還有我們在一起相處是多麼快樂。我們對所有事情的看法都相同——不過也有可能是我為了迎合他，而稍微改變我的想法！

不過他幾乎都是對的。這並不奇怪，他長我十四歲。儘管如此，在其他方面他就像個大男孩，需要人照顧——譬如下雨天時他都不知道自己應該穿套雨鞋，我們常常為一些滑稽的事開懷大笑，這種情況多不勝數了。若兩人不能理解彼此的幽默，他們最終會漸行漸遠，這將對關係造成可怕的傷害。並且，我認為幽默感是天生的，即便再努力使兩人合拍，也只是徒勞而已。

他是——哦，唉！他就是他，我想他、想他、想他，我非常想念他。對我來說整個世界既空虛又痛苦。我恨月色如此美麗，而他卻無法在此與我共賞。如果您也曾愛過某人，您就會明白我的感受。如果您愛過，那我就不需要多做解釋；不過如果您沒愛過，那我也解釋不了。

無論如何，這就是我的感覺——然而我卻拒絕他的求婚。

我沒有告訴他為什麼，只是沉默無語，獨自黯然神傷。我想不出該說什麼才好。他離開了，以為我要嫁給吉米・馬克白而離開。但是我一點也不想啊，我從來不曾想過要嫁給吉米，他根本還沒長大！不過傑維少爺與我陷入了嚴重的誤會之中，我們都因此受到傷害。但我把他趕走並不是因為我不在乎他，

而是因為我太愛他了，我怕他日後會後悔與我相愛 —— 而我將
承受不了這樣的打擊！

像我這樣一個沒有來歷的女孩，嫁入他那樣的家庭太不合
適了。我從沒告訴過他約翰·格利爾孤兒院的事，也不願意解
釋我為何不知道自己的出身。您知道的，他的家庭是如此高
貴 —— 而我，雖然出身卑微，但我也是個有尊嚴的人！

還有，我認為自己對您負有一定的義務。您想將我培育成
作家，而我必須努力成就這個目標；若接受了您的教育之後又
荒廢不加以發揮，就太沒有道理了。可是，從另一方面來想，
我開始還錢了，欠您的債已經償還了一部分 —— 況且結婚以後
同樣也可以當作家，兩者並不見得相互矛盾。

我是否應該去找他，告訴他問題並不在於吉米，而是在於
約翰·格利爾孤兒院。這需要很大的勇氣，我幾乎寧願選擇悲
慘地獨自度過餘生。

這件事發生快兩個月了，他走後音訊全無。我好不容易習
慣了心碎的感覺，直到茉莉亞的來信，再度激起我的痛楚。她
無意中提到傑維少爺去加拿大打獵時在暴風雪中困了一整晚，
還因此得了肺炎，臥病不起；而我居然一點都不知情，甚至還
因為他走後完全沒有捎來隻字片語，而感到受傷！我想他一定
很痛苦，至少我知道我是！

您想我該怎麼做才好？

茱蒂

10月6日

最親愛的長腿叔叔：

　　是的，我當然會去——下星期三的下午四點半。我當然找得到地方，我已經去過紐約三次，再也不是個孩子了。我不敢相信自己真的要去見您了——多年來，我一直想像著您的存在，以至於很難意識到您是個真正的血肉之軀。

　　您真是對我太好了，叔叔，身體不好還爲我操心。請多保重，別著涼了，秋雨對健康不太好。

深情的茱蒂

附記：

　　我突然害怕了起來。您有管家嗎？我頗害怕管家的，如果是管家來開門的話，我可能會嚇昏在門口。我該對他說些什麼才好呢？您不曾告訴我您的名字，我該對他說，我是來見史密斯先生的嗎？

長腿叔叔

星期四早晨

我最最親愛的傑維少爺———長腿叔叔———平萊頓‧史密斯：

　　昨晚你睡了嗎？我沒有，一夜都沒有合眼。我太驚喜、太興奮又太困惑了，我想我再也睡不著、再也吃不下飯了。不過我希望你要睡覺，你得睡；這樣你才能快點好起來，才能快點來到我身邊。

　　親愛的，一想到你病得如此嚴重就讓我心痛不已——而我在此之前卻毫不知情。昨天醫生送我下樓上車時告訴我，這三天來，他們幾乎放棄希望了。喔，我最親愛的，若真是如此，對我而言，這世界上的希望也都將隨你而去。我想將來的某一天——在遙遠的未來——雖然我們其中一人必須先行離去，不過我們至少已經幸福地生活在一起過，有許多值得回憶的東西。

　　我想要讓你高興起來——但首先必須先讓我自己高興起來。儘管現在的我比做夢都還要快樂，但我也更加清醒。我害怕此刻會發生不好的事情，這個念頭如同陰影一般，籠罩在我的心頭。以前我總是無牽無掛，對什麼事都蠻不在乎，因為沒有什麼東西可以失去。可是從今以後，我將會無止盡地擔心著，只要你一離開我身邊，我就會想到汽車可能會撞上你，招牌可能會掉下來砸到你的頭，你可能會不小心吃下不乾淨的食物，我的心將永不安寧——不過，我一點也不渴望那種平靜的

160

安寧。

請快點好起來，快點、再快點。我要你緊靠在我身邊，讓我可以觸摸到你，確信你是真實的存在。我們在一起只有短短的半小時啊！我深怕我當時是在做夢，如果我是你家族的一員該多好（遠親也好）。這樣我就可以天天去看你、念書給你聽、為你理好靠枕、撫平你前額那兩條紋路、讓你揚起嘴角，露出你迷人的笑容。你現在心情好點了嗎？昨天我走的時候你心情很好，醫生說我一定是個好護士，你看起來一下子就年輕了十歲。戀愛可不能讓每個人都年輕十歲，如果我變回十一歲，你還在乎我嗎？

昨天是我一生中最美妙的一天，即使我活到九十九歲也忘不了這天發生的種種。清晨離開洛克威洛的那個女孩，與晚上回來的她判若兩人。山普太太四點半時叫我起床，我在黑暗中驚醒，第一個閃過腦中的念頭是：「我要去見長腿叔叔！」我藉著廚房的燭光吃過早餐，然後穿過十月裏最壯觀的景色，坐著馬車走了五哩路到火車站。我看著太陽冉冉升起，楓樹和山花鮮紅橙黃一片，石牆跟玉米田因冰霜而閃閃發亮，空氣清新、乾淨並充滿希望。我知道有好事在等著我。一路上，馬車的輪子不斷唱著：「妳就要見到長腿叔叔了。」這讓我有一種安全感。我對叔叔的處事能力有信心，我也知道在某處有另一位男士——比長腿叔叔更珍貴——正等著要見我。我有預感這次一定能見到他。結果，你瞧！

我抵達麥迪遜大街，看見那棟棕色高大的房子，著實令人生畏。我不敢貿然地走進去，因此徘徊了許久後才鼓起勇氣邁開我的腳步。其實我根本不用害怕，你的祕書是如慈父般的老人，讓我有賓至如歸的感覺。他問我：「是艾伯特小姐嗎？」我說：「是的。」讓我根本不用提起史密斯先生。他讓我在客廳等候著。這是一間莊嚴、華麗，富有男人氣息的房間。我坐在一張舒服的大椅子邊上，不斷對自己說：「我要見到長腿叔叔了！我要見到長腿叔叔了！」

　　不一會兒，管家回來請我到書房去，我激動得雙腳都快不聽使喚了。在書房門口，他回頭低聲對我說：「小姐，他病得很嚴重，醫生今天才同意他下床。請不要停留太久，使他過於激動。」從他說話的樣子就知道他很愛你，而且他也老了，容易憂心。他敲了敲門說：「艾伯特小姐來了。」接著開門讓我走進房間，並在我身後將門帶上。

　　從明亮的走廊走進黯淡的書房，一時之間我什麼東西也看不見。漸漸地我看見壁爐前有張很大的安樂椅，旁邊放著附有小椅子的茶几映著爐火。我看得出來有個人坐在大椅子裏，周圍滿是靠枕，膝上有一張毯子。我還來不及阻止他，他就已經站起身──身軀有些顫抖──扶著椅背站穩身子後不發一語地看著我。然後……然後……我才看清他的模樣，那是你啊！不過就算這樣，我還是不明白，我以為是長腿叔叔讓你來那兒見我，好給我個驚喜。

　　你笑著伸出手說：「親愛的小茱蒂，你猜不到我就是長腿叔叔嗎？」

　　這個想法瞬間掠過我的腦海。喔，我怎麼這麼笨呀！如果我夠聰明的話，那裏有一百件小事可讓我明白你就是長腿叔叔。我一定做不了好警探，是吧？叔叔……傑維？我該怎麼稱呼你？只是叫傑維顯得很不尊敬，我應該對你表示敬意的。

　　在你的醫生進來把我趕走之前，我們度過了非常甜蜜的半個小時。我恍恍惚惚地抵達車站時，差點搭上往聖路易斯的火車；而你也激動得忘了請我喝茶，但我們都非常非常快樂，不是嗎？

　　我摸黑駕車回到洛克威洛——喔，當時的夜空中閃耀著滿天的星光！

　　今早我帶著柯林斯，走遍所有我們一起去過的地方，而且我清楚記得你說過的每一句話，以及當時的樣貌。今天的樹林呈現一片青銅色，空氣冷冽清新，是登山的好天氣，我真希望你在這兒陪我一起爬山。我想你想得不得了，親愛的傑維。這是種愉快的思念，我們很快就能在一起了，從今往後我們將真真實實地屬於彼此，毫不虛假！說自己終於有了歸處，這話有點奇怪吧？不過這真的是一種非常非常甜蜜的感覺。

　　今後我不會再讓你傷心了。

你永遠並始終如一的

茱蒂

附記：這是我的第一封情書。很好玩吧？我竟然知道怎麼寫。

Daddy-Long-Legs

TO YOU

Blue Wednesday

The first Wednesday in every month was a Perfectly Awful Day--a day to be awaited with dread, endured with courage and forgotten with haste. Every floor must be spotless, every chair dustless, and every bed without a wrinkle. Ninety-seven squirming little orphans must be scrubbed and combed and buttoned into freshly starched ginghams; and all ninety-seven reminded of their manners, and told to say, "Yes, sir," "No, sir," whenever a Trustee spoke.

It was a distressing time; and poor Jerusha Abbott, being the oldest orphan, had to bear the brunt of it. But this particular first Wednesday, like its predecessors, finally dragged itself to a close. Jerusha escaped from the pantry where she had been making sandwiches for the asylum's guests, and turned upstairs to accomplish her regular work. Her special care was room F, where eleven little tots, from four to seven, occupied eleven little cots set in a row. Jerusha assembled her charges, straightened their rumpled frocks, wiped their noses, and started them in an orderly and willing line towards the dining-room to engage themselves for a blessed half hour with bread and milk and prune pudding.

Then she dropped down on the window seat and leaned throbbing temples against the cool glass. She had been on her feet since five that morning, doing everybody's bidding, scolded and hurried by a nervous matron. Mrs. Lippett, behind the scenes, did not always maintain that calm and pompous dignity with which she faced an audience of Trustees and lady visitors. Jerusha gazed out across a broad stretch of frozen lawn, beyond the tall iron paling that marked the confines of

the asylum, down undulating ridges sprinkled with country estates, to the spires of the village rising from the midst of bare trees.

The day was ended--quite successfully, so far as she knew. The Trustees and the visiting committee had made their rounds, and read their reports, and drunk their tea, and now were hurrying home to their own cheerful firesides, to forget their bothersome little charges for another month. Jerusha leaned forward watching with curiosity-- and a touch of wistfulness--the stream of carriages and automobiles that rolled out of the asylum gates. In imagination she followed first one equipage, then another, to the big houses dotted along the hillside. She pictured herself in a fur coat and a velvet hat trimmed with feathers leaning back in the seat and nonchalantly murmuring "Home" to the driver. But on the door-sill of her home the picture grew blurred.

Jerusha had an imagination--an imagination, Mrs. Lippett told her, that would get her into trouble if she didn't take care--but keen as it was, it could not carry her beyond the front porch of the houses she would enter. Poor, eager, adventurous little Jerusha, in all her seventeen years, had never stepped inside an ordinary house; she could not picture the daily routine of those other human beings who carried on their lives undiscommoded by orphans.

> *Je-ru-sha Ab-bott*
> *You are wan-ted*
> *In the of-fice,*
> *And I think you'd*
> *Better hurry up!*

Tommy Dillon, who had joined the choir, came singing up the stairs and down the corridor, his chant growing louder as he approached room F. Jerusha wrenched herself from the window and refaced the troubles of life.

"Who wants me?" she cut into Tommy's chant with a note of sharp anxiety.

> *Mrs. Lippett in the office,*
> *And I think she's mad.*
> *Ah-a-men!*

Tommy piously intoned, but his accent was not entirely malicious. Even the most hardened little orphan felt sympathy for an erring sister who was summoned to the office to face an annoyed matron; and Tommy liked Jerusha even if she did sometimes jerk him by the arm and nearly scrub his nose off.

Jerusha went without comment, but with two parallel lines on her brow. What could have gone wrong, she wondered. Were the sandwiches not thin enough? Were there shells in the nut cakes? Had a lady visitor seen the hole in Susie Hawthorn's stocking? Had--O horrors! --one of the cherubic little babes in her own room F "sauced" a Trustee?

The long lower hall had not been lighted, and as she came downstairs, a last Trustee stood, on the point of departure, in the open door that led to the porte-cochere. Jerusha caught only a fleeting impression of the man--and the impression consisted entirely of tallness. He was waving his arm towards an automobile waiting in the curved drive. As it sprang into motion and approached, head on for an instant, the glaring headlights threw his shadow sharply against the wall inside. The shadow pictured grotesquely elongated legs and arms that ran along the floor and up the wall of the corridor. It looked, for all the world, like a huge, wavering daddy-long-legs.

Jerusha's anxious frown gave place to quick laughter. She was by nature a sunny soul, and had always snatched the tiniest excuse to be amused. If one could derive any sort of entertainment out of the oppressive fact of a Trustee, it was something unexpected to the good. She advanced to the office quite cheered by the tiny episode, and presented a smiling face to Mrs. Lippett. To her surprise the matron was also, if not exactly smiling, at least appreciably affable; she wore an expression almost as pleasant as the one she donned for visitors.

"Sit down, Jerusha, I have something to say to you." Jerusha dropped into the nearest chair and waited with a touch of breathlessness. An automobile flashed past the window; Mrs. Lippett glanced after it.

"Did you notice the gentleman who has just gone?"

"I saw his back."

"He is one of our most affluential Trustees, and has given large sums of money towards the asylum's support. I am not at liberty to mention his name; he expressly stipulated that he was to remain unknown."

Jerusha's eyes widened slightly; she was not accustomed to being summoned to the office to discuss the eccentricities of Trustees with the matron.

"This gentleman has taken an interest in several of our boys. You remember Charles Benton and Henry Freize? They were both sent through college by Mr.--er--this Trustee, and both have repaid with hard work and success the money that was so generously expended. Other payment the gentleman does not wish. Heretofore his philanthropies have been directed solely towards the boys; I have never been able to interest him in the slightest degree in any of the girls in the institution, no matter how deserving. He does not, I may tell you, care for girls."

"No, ma'am," Jerusha murmured, since some reply seemed to be expected at this point.

"To-day at the regular meeting, the question of your future was brought up."

Mrs. Lippett allowed a moment of silence to fall, then resumed in a slow, placid manner extremely trying to her hearer's suddenly tightened nerves.

"Usually, as you know, the children are not kept after they are sixteen, but an exception was made in your case. You had finished our school at fourteen, and having done so well in your studies—not always, I must say, in your conduct--it was determined to let you go on in the village high school. Now you are finishing that, and of course the asylum cannot be responsible any longer for your support. As it is, you have had two years more than most."

Mrs. Lippett overlooked the fact that Jerusha had worked hard for her board during those two years, that the convenience of the asylum had come first and her education second; that on days like the present she was kept at home to scrub.

"As I say, the question of your future was brought up and your record was discussed--thoroughly discussed."

Mrs. Lippett brought accusing eyes to bear upon the prisoner in the dock, and the prisoner looked guilty because it seemed to be expected--not because she could remember any strikingly black pages in her record.

"Of course, the usual disposition of one in your place would be to put you in a position where you could begin to work, but you have done well in school in certain branches; it seems that your work in English has even been brilliant. Miss Pritchard, who is on our visiting committee, is also on the school board; she has been talking with your rhetoric teacher, and made a speech in your favour. She also read

aloud an essay that you had written entitled, ‘Blue Wednesday’ .”

Jerusha's guilty expression this time was not assumed.

“It seemed to me that you showed little gratitude in holding up to ridicule the institution that has done so much for you. Had you not managed to be funny I doubt if you would have been forgiven. But fortunately for you, Mr.--, that is, the gentleman who has just gone-- appears to have an immoderate sense of humour. On the strength of that impertinent paper, he has offered to send you to college.”

“To college?” Jerusha's eyes grew big. Mrs. Lippett nodded.

“He waited to discuss the terms with me. They are unusual. The gentleman, I may say, is erratic. He believes that you have originality, and he is planning to educate you to become a writer.”

“A writer?” Jerusha's mind was numbed. She could only repeat Mrs. Lippett's words.

“That is his wish. Whether anything will come of it, the future will show. He is giving you a very liberal allowance, almost, for a girl who has never had any experience in taking care of money, too liberal. But he planned the matter in detail, and I did not feel free to make any suggestions. You are to remain here through the summer, and Miss Pritchard has kindly offered to superintend your outfit. Your board and tuition will be paid directly to the college, and you will receive in addition during the four years you are there, an allowance of thirty-five dollars a month. This will enable you to enter on the same standing as the other students. The money will be sent to you by the gentleman's private secretary once a month, and in return, you will write a letter of acknowledgment once a month. That is--you are not to thank him for the money; he doesn't care to have that mentioned, but you are to write a letter telling of the progress in your studies and the details of your daily life. Just such a letter as you would write to your parents if they were living.”

Blue Wednesday

"These letters will be addressed to Mr. John Smith and will be sent in care of the secretary. The gentleman's name is not John Smith, but he prefers to remain unknown. To you he will never be anything but John Smith. His reason in requiring the letters is that he thinks nothing so fosters facility in literary expression as letter-writing. Since you have no family with whom to correspond, he desires you to write in this way; also, he wishes to keep track of your progress. He will never answer your letters, nor in the slightest particular take any notice of them. He detests letter-writing and does not wish you to become a burden. If any point should ever arise where an answer would seem to be imperative--such as in the event of your being expelled, which I trust will not occur--you may correspond with Mr. Griggs, his secretary. These monthly letters are absolutely obligatory on your part; they are the only payment that Mr. Smith requires, so you must be as punctilious in sending them as though it were a bill that you were paying. I hope that they will always be respectful in tone and will reflect credit on your training. You must remember that you are writing to a Trustee of the John Grier Home."

Jerusha's eyes longingly sought the door. Her head was in a whirl of excitement, and she wished only to escape from Mrs. Lippett's platitudes and think. She rose and took a tentative step backwards. Mrs. Lippett detained her with a gesture; it was an oratorical opportunity not to be slighted. "I trust that you are properly grateful for this very rare good fortune that has befallen you? Not many girls in your position ever have such an opportunity to rise in the world. You must always remember--"

"I--yes, ma'am, thank you. I think, if that's all, I must go and sew a patch on Freddie Perkins's trousers."

The door closed behind her, and Mrs. Lippett watched it with dropped jaw, her peroration in mid-air.

215 FERGUSSEN HALL
24th September

Dear Kind-Trustee-Who-Sends-Orphans-to-College,

Here I am! I travelled yesterday for four hours in a train. It's a funny sensation, isn't it? I never rode in one before.

College is the biggest, most bewildering place--I get lost whenever I leave my room. I will write you a description later when I'm feelingless muddled; also I will tell you about my lessons. Classes don't begin until Monday morning, and this is Saturday night. But I wanted to write a letter first just to get acquainted.

It seems queer to be writing letters to somebody you don't know. It seems queer for me to be writing letters at all--I've never written more than three or four in my life, so please overlook it if these are not a model kind.

Before leaving yesterday morning, Mrs. Lippett and I had a very serious talk. She told me how to behave all the rest of my life, and especially how to behave towards the kind gentleman who is doing so much for me. I must take care to be Very Respectful.

But how can one be very respectful to a person who wishes to be called John Smith? Why couldn't you have picked out a name with a little personality? I might as well write letters to Dear Hitching-Post or Dear Clothes-Prop.

I have been thinking about you a great deal this summer; having somebody take an interest in me after all these years makes me feel as though I had found a sort of family. It seems as though I belonged to somebody now, and it's a very comfortable sensation. I must say, however, that when I think about you, my imagination has very little to work upon. There are just three things that I know:

I. You are tall.
II. You are rich.
III. You hate girls.

I suppose I might call you Dear Mr. Girl-Hater. Only that's rather insulting to me. Or Dear Mr. Rich-Man, but that's insulting to you, as though money were the only important thing about you. Besides, being rich is such a very external quality. Maybe you won't stay rich all your life; lots of very clever men get smashed up in Wall Street. Butat least you will stay tall all your life! So, I've decided to call you Dear Daddy-Long-Legs. I hope you won't mind. It's just a private pet name we won't tell Mrs. Lippett.

The ten o'clock bell is going to ring in two minutes. Our day is divided into sections by bells. We eat and sleep and study by bells. It's very enlivening; I feel like a fire horse all of the time. There it goes! Lights out. Good night.

Observe with what precision I obey rules--due to my training in the John Grier Home.

Yours most respectfully,
Jerusha Abbott

To Mr. Daddy-Long-Legs Smith
1st October

Dear Daddy-Long-Legs,

I love college and I love you for sending me--I'm very, very happy, and so excited every moment of the time that I can scarcely sleep. You can't imagine how different it is from the John Grier Home.

I never dreamed there was such a place in the world. I'm feeling sorry for everybody who isn't a girl and who can't come here; I am sure the college you attended when you were a boy couldn't have been so nice.

My room is up in a tower that used to be the contagious ward before they built the new infirmary. There are three other girls on the same floor of the tower--a Senior who wears spectacles and is always asking us please to be a little more quiet, and two Freshmen named Sallie McBride and Julia Rutledge Pendleton. Sallie has red hair and a turn-up nose and is quite friendly; Julia comes from one of the first families in New York and hasn't noticed me yet. They room together and the Senior and I have singles. Usually Freshmen can't get singles; they are very scarce, but I got one without even asking. I suppose the registrar didn't think it would be right to ask a properly brought-up girl to room with a foundling. You see there are advantages!

My room is on the north-west corner with two windows and a view. After you've lived in a ward for eighteen years with twenty room-mates, it is restful to be alone. This is the first chance I've ever had to get acquainted with Jerusha Abbott. I think I'm going to like her.

Do you think you are?

Tuesday

They are organizing the Freshman basket-ball team and there's just a chance that I shall get in it. I'm little of course, but terribly quick and wiry and tough. While the others are hopping about in the air, I can dodge under their feet and grab the ball. It's loads of fun practising--out in the athletic field in the afternoon with the trees all red and yellow and the air full of the smell of burning leaves, and everybody laughing and shouting. These are the happiest girls I ever

saw--and I am the happiest of all!

I meant to write a long letter and tell you all the things I'm learning (Mrs. Lippett said you wanted to know), but 7th hour has just rung, and in ten minutes I'm due at the athletic field in gymnasium clothes. Don't you hope I'll get in the team?

Yours always,
Jerusha Abbott

PS. (9 o'clock.) Sallie McBride just poked her head in at my door. This is what she said: "I'm so homesick that I simply can't stand it. Do you feel that way?" I smiled a little and said no; I thought I could pull through. At least homesickness is one disease that I've escaped! I never heard of anybody being asylum-sick, did you?

10th October

Dear Daddy-Long-Legs,

Did you ever hear of Michael Angelo?

He was a famous artist who lived in Italy in the Middle Ages. Everybody in English Literature seemed to know about him, and the whole class laughed because I thought he was an archangel. He sounds like an archangel, doesn't he? The trouble with college is that you are expected to know such a lot of things you've never learned. It's very embarrassing at times. But now, when the girls talk about things that I never heard of, I just keep still and look them up in the encyclopedia.

I made an awful mistake the first day. Somebody mentioned Maurice Maeterlinck, and I asked if she was a Freshman. That joke has gone allover college. But anyway, I'm just as bright in class as any of the others--and brighter than some of them!

Do you care to know how I've furnished my room? It's a symphony in brown and yellow. The wall was tinted buff, and I've bought yellow denim curtains and cushions and a mahogany desk (second hand for three dollars) and a rattan chair and a brown rug with an ink spot in the middle. I stand the chair over the spot.

The windows are up high; you can't look out from an ordinary seat. But I unscrewed the looking-glass from the back of the bureau, upholstered the top and moved it up against the window. It's just the right height for a window seat. You pull out the drawers like steps and walk up. Very comfortable!

Sallie McBride helped me choose the things at the Senior auction. She has lived in a house all her life and knows about furnishing. You can't imagine what fun it is to shop and pay with a real five-dollar bill and get some change--when you've never had more than a few cents in your life. I assure you, Daddy dear, I do appreciate that allowance.

Sallie is the most entertaining person in the world--and Julia Rutledge Pendleton the least so. It's queer what a mixture the registrar can make in the matter of room-mates. Sallie thinks everything is funny--even flunking--and Julia is bored at everything. She never makes the slightest effort to be amiable. She believes that if you are a Pendleton, that fact alone admits you to heaven without any further examination. Julia and I were born to be enemies.

And now I suppose you've been waiting very impatiently to hear what I am learning?

I. Latin: Second Punic war. Hannibal and his forces pitched camp at Lake Trasimenus last night. They prepared an ambuscade for the Romans, and a battle took place at the fourth watch this morning. Romans in retreat.

II. French: 24 pages of the Three Musketeers and third conjugation, irregular verbs.

III. Geometry: Finished cylinders; now doing cones.

IV. English: Studying exposition. My style improves daily in clearness and brevity.

V. Physiology: Reached the digestive system. Bile and the pancreas next time.

Yours, on the way to being educated,
Jerusha Abbott

PS. I hope you never touch alcohol, Daddy? It does dreadful things to your liver.

Wednesday

Dear Daddy-Long-Legs,

I've changed my name.

I'm still "Jerusha" in the catalogue, but I'm "Judy" everywhere else. It's really too bad, isn't it, to have to give yourself the only pet name you ever had? I didn't quite make up the Judy though. That's what Freddy Perkins used to call me before he could talk plainly.

I wish Mrs. Lippett would use a little more ingenuity about choosing babies' names. She gets the last names out of the telephone book--you'll find Abbott on the first page--and she picks the Christian names up anywhere; she got Jerusha from a tombstone. I've always hated it; but I rather like Judy. It's such a silly name. It belongs to the kind of girl I'm not--a sweet little blue-eyed thing, petted and spoiled by all the family, who romps her way through life without any cares.

Wouldn't it be nice to be like that? Whatever faults I may have, no one can ever accuse me of having been spoiled by my family! But it's great fun to pretend I've been. In the future please always address me as Judy.

Do you want to know something? I have three pairs of kid gloves. I've had kid mittens before from the Christmas tree, but never real kid gloves with five fingers. I take them out and try them on every little while. It's all I can do not to wear them to classes. (Dinner bell. Goodbye.)

Friday

What do you think, Daddy? The English instructor said that my last paper shows an unusual amount of originality. She did, truly. Those were her words. It doesn't seem possible, does it, considering the eighteen years of training that I've had? The aim of the John Grier Home (as you doubtless know and heartily approve of) is to turn the ninety-seven orphans into ninety-seven twins.

The unusual artistic ability which I exhibit was developed at an early age through drawing chalk pictures of Mrs. Lippett on the woodshed door.

I hope that I don't hurt your feelings when I criticize the home of my youth? But you have the upper hand, you know, for if I become too impertinent, you can always stop payment of your cheques. That isn't a very polite thing to say--but you can't expect me to have any manners; a foundling asylum isn't a young ladies' finishing school.

You know, Daddy, it isn't the work that is going to be hard in college. It's the play. Half the time I don't know what the girls are talking about; their jokes seem to relate to a past that every one but me has shared. I'm a foreigner in the world and I don't understand the

language. It's a miserable feeling. I've had it all my life. At the high school the girls would stand in groups and just look at me. I was queer and different and everybody knew it. I could FEEL "John Grier Home" written on my face. And then a few charitable ones would make a point of coming up and saying something polite. I HATED EVERY ONE OFTHEM--the charitable ones most of all.

Nobody here knows that I was brought up in an asylum. I told Sallie McBride that my mother and father were dead, and that a kind old gentleman was sending me to college which is entirely true so far as it goes. I don't want you to think I am a coward, but I do want to belike the other girls, and that Dreadful Home looming over my childhood is the one great big difference. If I can turn my back on that and shut out the remembrance, I think, I might be just as desirable as any other girl. I don't believe there's any real, underneath difference, do you?

Anyway, Sallie McBride likes me!

Yours ever,

Judy Abbott (Nee Jerusha.)

Saturday morning

I've just been reading this letter over and it sounds pretty un-cheerful. But can't you guess that I have a special topic due Monday morning and a review in geometry and a very sneezy cold?

Sunday

I forgot to post this yesterday, so I will add an indignant postscript. We had a bishop this morning, and WHAT DO YOU THINK HE SAID?

"The most beneficent promise made us in the Bible is this, "The poor ye have always with you." They were put here in order to keep us charitable."

The poor, please observe, being a sort of useful domestic animal. If I hadn't grown into such a perfect lady, I should have gone up after service and told him what I thought.

25th October

Dear Daddy-Long-Legs,

I'm in the basket-ball team and you ought to see the bruise on my left shoulder. It's blue and mahogany with little streaks of orange. Julia Pendleton tried for the team, but she didn't get in. Hooray!

You see what a mean disposition I have.

College gets nicer and nicer. I like the girls and the teachers and the classes and the campus and the things to eat. We have ice-cream twice a week and we never have corn-meal mush.

You only wanted to hear from me once a month, didn't you? And I've been peppering you with letters every few days! But I've been so excited about all these new adventures that I MUST talk to somebody; and you're the only one I know. Please excuse my exuberance; I'll settle pretty soon. If my letters bore you, you can always toss them into the wastebasket. I promise not to write another till the middle of November.

Yours most loquaciously,
Judy Abbott

15th November

Dear Daddy-Long-Legs,

Listen to what I've learned to-day.

The area of the convex surface of the frustum of a regular pyramid is half the product of the sum of the perimeters of its bases by the altitude of either of its trapezoids.

It doesn't sound true, but it is--I can prove it!

You've never heard about my clothes, have you, Daddy? Six dresses, all new and beautiful and bought for me--not handed down from somebody bigger. Perhaps you don't realize what a climax that marks in the career of an orphan? You gave them to me, and I am very, very, VERY much obliged. It's a fine thing to be educated--but nothing compared to the dizzying experience of owning six new dresses. Miss Pritchard, who is on the visiting committee, picked them out--not Mrs. Lippett, thank goodness. I have an evening dress, pink mull over silk (I'm perfectly beautiful in that), and a blue church dress, and a dinner dress of red veiling with Oriental trimming (makes me look like a Gipsy), and another of rose-coloured challis, and a grey street suit, and an every-day dress for classes. That wouldn't be an awfully big wardrobe for Julia Rutledge Pendleton, perhaps, but for Jerusha Abbott--Oh, my!

I suppose you're thinking now what a frivolous, shallow little beast she is, and what a waste of money to educate a girl?

But, Daddy, if you'd been dressed in checked ginghams all your life, you'd appreciate how I feel. And when I started to the high school, I entered upon another period even worse than the checked ginghams.

The poor box.

You can't know how I dreaded appearing in school in those miserable poor-box dresses. I was perfectly sure to be put down in class next to the girl who first owned my dress, and she would whisper and giggle and point it out to the others. The bitterness of wearing your enemies' cast-off clothes eats into your soul. If I wore silk stockings for the rest of my life, I don't believe I could obliterate the scar.

LATEST WAR BULLETIN!
News from the Scene of Action.

At the fourth watch on Thursday the 13th of November, Hannibal routed the advance guard of the Romans and led the Carthaginian forces over the mountains into the plains of Casilinum. A cohort of light armed Numidians engaged the infantry of Quintus Fabius Maximus. Two battles and light skirmishing. Romans repulsed with heavy losses.

I have the honour of being,
Your special correspondent from the
front,
J. Abbott

PS. I know I'm not to expect any letters in return, and I've been warned not to bother you with questions, but tell me, Daddy, just this once--are you awfully old or just a little old? And are you perfectly bald or just a little bald? It is very difficult thinking about you in the abstract like a theorem in geometry.

Given a tall rich man who hates girls, but is very generous to one quite impertinent girl, what does he look like? R.S.V.P.

19th December

Dear Daddy-Long-Legs,

You never answered my question and it was very important.

ARE YOU BALD?

I have it planned exactly what you look like—very satisfactorily-- until I reach the top of your head, and then I AM stuck. I can't decide whether you have white hair or black hair or sort of sprinkly grey hair or maybe none at all.

Here is your portrait[1]:

But the problem is, shall I add some hair?

Would you like to know what colour your eyes are? They're grey, and your eyebrows stick out like a porch roof (beetling, they're called in novels), and your mouth is a straight line with a tendency to turn down at the corners. Oh, you see, I know! You're a snappy old thing with a temper. (Chapel bell.)

9.45 p.m.

I have a new unbreakable rule: never, never to study at night no matter how many written reviews are coming in the morning. Instead, I read just plain books--I have to, you know, because there are eighteen blank years behind me. You wouldn't believe, Daddy, what an abyss of ignorance my mind is; I am just realizing the depths myself. The things that most girls with a properly assorted family and a home and friends and a library know by absorption, I have never heard of. For example:

---

1   Please find the illustration in Chinese version.

I never read Mother Goose or David Copperfield or Ivanhoe or Cinderella or Blue Beard or Robinson Crusoe or Jane Eyre or Alice in Wonderland or a word of Rudyard Kipling. I didn't know that Henry the Eighth was married more than once or that Shelley was a poet. I didn't know that people used to be monkeys and that the Garden of Eden was a beautiful myth. I didn't know that R. L. S. stood for Robert Louis Stevenson or that George Eliot was a lady. I had never seen a picture of the "Mona Lisa" and (it's true but you won't believe it) I had never heard of Sherlock Holmes.

Now, I know all of these things and a lot of others besides, but you can see how much I need to catch up. And oh, but it's fun! I look forward all day to evening, and then I put an "engaged" on the door and get into my nice red bath robe and furry slippers and pile all the cushions behind me on the couch, and light the brass student lamp at my elbow, and read and read and read one book isn't enough. I have four going at once. Just now, they're Tennyson's poems and Vanity Fair and Kipling's Plain Tales and--don't laugh--Little Women. I find that I am the only girl in college who wasn't brought up on Little Women. I haven't told anybody though (that WOULD stamp me as queer). I just quietly went and bought it with $1.12 of my last month's allowance; and the next time somebody mentions pickled limes, I'll know what she is talking about! (Ten o'clock bell. This is a very interrupted letter.)

Saturday

Sir,

I have the honour to report fresh explorations in the field of

geometry. On Friday last we abandoned our former works in parallelopipeds and proceeded to truncated prisms. We are finding the road rough and very uphill.

Sunday

The Christmas holidays begin next week and the trunks are up. The corridors are so filled up that you can hardly get through, and everybody is so bubbling over with excitement that studying is getting left out. I'm going to have a beautiful time in vacation; there's another Freshman who lives in Texas staying behind, and we are planning to take long walks and if there's any ice--learn to skate. Then there is still the whole library to be read--and three empty weeks to do it in! Good bye, Daddy, I hope that you are feeling as happy as I am.

Yours ever,
Judy

PS. Don't forget to answer my question. If you don't want the trouble of writing, have your secretary telegraph. He can just say:

Mr. Smith is quite bald,
or
Mr. Smith is not bald,
or
Mr. Smith has white hair.

And you can deduct the twenty-five cents out of my allowance. Goodbye till January--and a merry Christmas!

Towards the end of the Christmas vacation.
Exact date unknown

Dear Daddy-Long-Legs,

Is it snowing where you are? All the world that I see from my tower is draped in white and the flakes are coming down as big as pop-corns. It's late afternoon--the sun is just setting (a cold yellow colour) behind some colder violet hills, and I am up in my window seat using the last light to write to you.

Your five gold pieces were a surprise! I'm not used to receiving Christmas presents. You have already given me such lots of things-- everything I have, you know--that I don't quite feel that I deserve extras. But I like them just the same. Do you want to know what I bought with my money?

I. A silver watch in a leather case to wear on my wrist and get me to recitations in time.
II. Matthew Arnold's poems.
III. A hot water bottle.
IV. A steamer rug. (My tower is cold.)V. Five hundred sheets of yellow manuscript paper. (I'm going to commence being an author pretty soon.)
VI. A dictionary of synonyms. (To enlarge the author's vocabulary.)
VII. (I don't much like to confess this last item, but I will.) A pair of silk stockings. And now, Daddy, never say I don't tell all!

It was a very low motive, if you must know it, that prompted the silk stockings. Julia Pendleton comes into my room to do geometry, and she sits cross-legged on the couch and wears silk stockings every night. But just wait--as soon as she gets back from vacation I shall go in and sit on her couch in my silk stockings. You see, Daddy, the miserable creature that I am but at least I'm honest; and you knew already, from my asylum record, that I wasn't perfect, didn't you?

To recapitulate (that's the way the English instructor begins every other sentence), I am very much obliged for my seven presents. I'm pretending to myself that they came in a box from my family in California. The watch is from father, the rug from mother, the hot water bottle from grandmother who is always worrying for fear I shall catch cold in this climate--and the yellow paper from my little brother Harry. My sister Isabel gave me the silk stockings, and Aunt Susan the Matthew Arnold poems; Uncle Harry (little Harry is named after him) gave me the dictionary. He wanted to send chocolates, but I insisted on synonyms.

You don't object, do you, to playing the part of a composite family?

And now, shall I tell you about my vacation, or are you only interested in my education as such? I hope you appreciate the delicate shade of meaning in "as such". It is the latest addition to my vocabulary.

The girl from Texas is named Leonora Fenton. (Almost as funny as Jerusha, isn't it?) I like her, but not so much as Sallie McBride; I shall never like any one so much as Sallie--except you. I must always like you the best of all, because you're my whole family rolled into one. Leonora and I and two Sophomores have walked 'cross country every pleasant day and explored the whole neighbourhood, dressed in short skirts and knit jackets and caps, and carrying shiny sticks to whack things with. Once we walked into town--four miles--and stopped at a restaurant where the college girls go for dinner. Broiled lobster (35cents), and for dessert, buckwheat cakes and maple syrup (15 cents).Nourishing and cheap.

It was such a lark! Especially for me, because it was so awfully different from the asylum--I feel like an escaped convict every time I leave the campus. Before I thought, I started to tell the others what an experience I was having. The cat was almost out of the bag when I grabbed it by its tail and pulled it back. It's awfully hard for me not to tell everything I know. I'm a very confiding soul by nature; ifI didn't have you to tell things to, I'd burst.

We had a molasses candy pull last Friday evening, given by the house matron of Fergussen to the left-behinds in the other halls. There were twenty-two of us altogether, Freshmen and Sophomores and juniors and Seniors all united in amicable accord. The kitchen is huge, with copper pots and kettles hanging in rows on the stone wall-- the littlest casserole among them about the size of a wash boiler. Four hundred girls live in Fergussen. The chef, in a white cap and apron, fetched out twenty-two other white caps and aprons--I can't imagine where he got so many--and we all turned ourselves into cooks.

It was great fun, though I have seen better candy. When it was finally finished, and ourselves and the kitchen and the door-knobs all thoroughly sticky, we organized a procession and still in our caps and aprons, each carrying a big fork or spoon or frying pan, we marched through the empty corridors to the officers' parlour, where half-a-dozen professors and instructors were passing a tranquil evening. We serenaded them with college songs and offered refreshments. They accepted politely but dubiously. We left them sucking chunks of molasses candy, sticky and speechless.

So you see, Daddy, my education progresses!

Don't you really think that I ought to be an artist instead of an author?

Vacation will be over in two days and I shall be glad to see the girls again. My tower is just a trifle lonely; when nine people occupy a house that was built for four hundred, they do rattle around a bit.

Eleven pages--poor Daddy, you must be tired! I meant this to be just a short little thank-you note--but when I get started I seem to have a ready pen.

Goodbye, and thank you for thinking of me--I should be perfectly happy except for one little threatening cloud on the horizon. Examinations come in February.

Yours with love,
Judy

PS. Maybe it isn't proper to send love? If it isn't, please excuse. But I must love somebody and there's only you and Mrs. Lippett to choose between, so you see--you'll HAVE to put up with it, Daddy dear, because I can't love her.

On the Eve

Dear Daddy-Long-Legs,

You should see the way this college is studying! We've forgotten weever had a vacation. Fifty-seven irregular verbs have I introduced to my brain in the past four days--I'm only hoping they'll stay till after examinations.

Some of the girls sell their text-books when they're through with them, but I intend to keep mine. Then after I've graduated I shall have my whole education in a row in the bookcase, and when I need to use any detail, I can turn to it without the slightest hesitation. So much easier and more accurate than trying to keep it in your head.

Julia Pendleton dropped in this evening to pay a social call, and stayed a solid hour. She got started on the subject of family, and ICOULDN't switch her off. She wanted to know what my mother's maiden name was--did you ever hear such an impertinent question to ask of a person from a foundling asylum? I didn't have the courage to say I didn't know, so I just miserably plumped on the first name I could think of, and that was Montgomery. Then she wanted to know whether I belonged to the Massachusetts Montgomerys or the Virginia Montgomerys.

Her mother was a Rutherford. The family came over in the ark, and were connected by marriage with Henry the VIII. On her father's side they date back further than Adam. On the topmost branches of her family tree there's a superior breed of monkeys with very fine silky hair and extra long tails.

I meant to write you a nice, cheerful, entertaining letter tonight, but I'm too sleepy--and scared. The Freshman's lot is not a happy one.

Yours, about to be examined,
Judy Abbott

Sunday

Dearest Daddy-Long-Legs,

I have some awful, awful, awful news to tell you, but I won't begin with it; I'll try to get you in a good humour first.

Jerusha Abbott has commenced to be an author. A poem entitled, "From my Tower", appears in the February Monthly--on the first page, which isa very great honour for a Freshman. My English instructor stopped me on the way out from chapel last night, and said it was a charming piece of work except for the sixth line, which had too many feet. I will send you a copy in case you care to read it.

Let me see if I can't think of something else pleasant-- Oh, yes! I'm learning to skate, and can glide about quite respectably all by myself. Also I've learned how to slide down a rope from the roof of the gymnasium, and I can vault a bar three feet and six inches high--I hope shortly to pull up to four feet.

We had a very inspiring sermon this morning preached by the Bishop of Alabama. His text was: "Judge not that ye be not judged." It was about the necessity of overlooking mistakes in others, and not discouraging people by harsh judgments. I wish you might have heard it.

This is the sunniest, most blinding winter afternoon, with icicles dripping from the fir trees and all the world bending under a weight ofsnow--except me, and I'm bending under a weight of sorrow.

Now for the news--courage, Judy! --you must tell.

Are you SURELY in a good humour? I failed in mathematics and Latin prose. I am tutoring in them, and will take another examination next month. I'm sorry if you're disappointed, but otherwise I don't care a bit because I've learned such a lot of things not mentioned in the catalogue. I've read seventeen novels and bushels of poetry— really necessary novels like Vanity Fair and Richard Feverel and Alice in Wonderland. Also, Emerson's Essays and Lockhart's Life of Scott and the first volume of Gibbon's Roman Empire and half of Benvenuto Cellini's Life--wasn't he entertaining? He used to saunter out and casually kill a man before breakfast.

So, you see, Daddy, I'm much more intelligent than if I'd just stuck to Latin. Will you forgive me this once if I promise never to fail again?

Yours in sackcloth,
Judy

Dear Daddy-Long-Legs,

This is an extra letter in the middle of the month because I'm rather lonely tonight. It's awfully stormy. All the lights are out on the campus, but I drank black coffee and I can't go to sleep.

I had a supper party this evening consisting of Sallie and Julia and Leonora Fenton--and sardines and toasted muffins and salad and fudge and coffee. Julia said she'd had a good time, but Sallie stayed to help wash the dishes.

I might, very usefully, put some time on Latin tonight but, there's no doubt about it, I'm a very languid Latin scholar. We've finished Livy and De Senectute and are now engaged with De Amicitia (pronounced DamnIcitia).

Should you mind, just for a little while, pretending you are my grandmother? Sallie has one and Julia and Leonora each two, and they were all comparing them tonight. I can't think of anything I'd rather have; it's such a respectable relationship. So, if you really don't object-- When I went into town yesterday, I saw the sweetest cap of Cluny lace trimmed with lavender ribbon. I am going to make you a present of it on your eighty-third birthday.

!!!!!!!!!!!!

That's the clock in the chapel tower striking twelve. I believe I am sleepy after all.

Good night, Granny.
I love you dearly.
Judy

The Ides of March

Dear D.-L.-L.,

I am studying Latin prose composition. I have been studying it. I shall be studying it. I shall be about to have been studying it. My re-examination comes the 7th hour next Tuesday, and I am going to pass or BUST. So you may expect to hear from me next, whole and happy and free from conditions, or in fragments.

I will write a respectable letter when it's over. Tonight I have a pressing engagement with the Ablative Absolute.

Yours--in evident haste
J. A.

26th March

Mr. D.-L.-L. Smith,

SIR: You never answer any questions; you never show the slightest interest in anything I do. You are probably the horridest one of all those horrid Trustees, and the reason you are educating me is, not because you care a bit about me, but from a sense of Duty. I don't know a single thing about you. I don't even know your name. It is very uninspiring writing to a Thing. I haven't a doubt but that you throw my letters into the waste-basket without reading them. Hereafter I shall write only about work. My re-examinations in Latin and geometry came last week. I passed them both and am now free from conditions.

Yours truly,
Jerusha Abbott

2nd April

Dear Daddy-Long-Legs,

I am a BEAST.

Please forget about that dreadful letter I sent you last week--I was feeling terribly lonely and miserable and sore-throaty the night I wrote. I didn't know it, but I was just sickening for tonsillitis and grippe and lots of things mixed. I'm in the infirmary now, and have been here for six days; this is the first time they would let me sit up and have a pen and paper. The head nurse is very bossy. But I've been thinking about it all the time and I shan't get well until you forgive me.

Here is a picture of the way I look, with a bandage tied around my head in rabbit's ears.[2]

Doesn't that arouse your sympathy? I am having sublingual gland swelling. And I've been studying physiology all the year without ever hearing of sublingual glands. How futile a thing is education!

I can't write any more; I get rather shaky when I sit up too long. Please forgive me for being impertinent and ungrateful. I was badly brought up.

Yours with love,
Judy Abbott

---

2 Please find the illustration in Chinese version.

Daddy-Long-Legs

THE INFIRMARY
4th April

Dearest Daddy-Long-Legs,

Yesterday evening just towards dark, when I was sitting up in bed looking out at the rain and feeling awfully bored with life in a great institution, the nurse appeared with a long white box addressed to me, and filled with the LOVELIEST pink rosebuds. And much nicer still, it contained a card with a very polite message written in a funny little uphill back hand (but one which shows a great deal of character). Thank you, Daddy, a thousand times. Your flowers make the first real, true present I ever received in my life. If you want to know what a baby I am I lay down and cried because I was so happy.

Now that I am sure you read my letters, I'll make them much more interesting, so they'll be worth keeping in a safe with red tape around them--only please take out that dreadful one and burn it up. I'd hate to think that you ever read it over.

Thank you for making a very sick, cross, miserable Freshman cheerful. Probably you have lots of loving family and friends, and you don't know what it feels like to be alone. But I do.

Goodbye--I'll promise never to be horrid again, because now I know you're a real person; also I'll promise never to bother you with any more questions.

Do you still hate girls?

Yours for ever,
Judy

8th hour, Monday

Dear Daddy-Long-Legs,

I hope you aren't the Trustee who sat on the toad? It went off--I was told--with quite a pop, so probably he was a fatter Trustee.

Do you remember the little dugout places with gratings over them by the laundry windows in the John Grier Home? Every spring when the hoptoad season opened we used to form a collection of toads and keep them in those window holes; and occasionally they would spill over into the laundry, causing a very pleasurable commotion on wash days. We were severely punished for our activities in this direction, but in spite of all discouragement the toads would collect.

And one day--well, I won't bore you with particulars--but somehow, one of the fattest, biggest, JUCIEST toads got into one of those big leather arm chairs in the Trustees' room, and that afternoon at the Trustees' meeting--But I dare say you were there and recall the rest?

Looking back dispassionately after a period of time, I will say that punishment was merited, and--if I remember rightly--adequate.

I don't know why I am in such a reminiscent mood except that spring and the reappearance of toads always awakens the old acquisitive instinct. The only thing that keeps me from starting a collection is the fact that no rule exists against it.

After chapel, Thursday

What do you think is my favourite book? Just now, I mean; I

change every three days. Wuthering Heights. Emily Bronte was quite young when she wrote it, and had never been outside of Haworth churchyard. She had never known any men in her life; how COULD she imagine a man like Heathcliffe?

I couldn't do it, and I'm quite young and never outside the John GrierAsylum--I've had every chance in the world. Sometimes a dreadful fear comes over me that I'm not a genius. Will you be awfully disappointed, Daddy, if I don't turn out to be a great author? In the spring when everything is so beautiful and green and budding, I feel like turning my back on lessons, and running away to play with the weather. There are such lots of adventures out in the fields! It's much more entertaining to live books than to write them.

Ow ! ! ! ! ! !

That was a shriek which brought Sallie and Julia and (for a disgusted moment) the Senior from across the hall. It was caused by a centipede like this:[3]

only worse. Just as I had finished the last sentence and was thinking what to say next--plump!--it fell off the ceiling and landed at my side. I tipped two cups off the tea table in trying to get away. Sallie whacked it with the back of my hair brush--which I shall never be able to use again--and killed the front end, but the rear fifty feet ran under the bureau and escaped.

This dormitory, owing to its age and ivy-covered walls, is full of centipedes. They are dreadful creatures. I'd rather find a tiger under the bed.

---

3   Please find the illustration in Chinese version.

Friday, 9.30 p.m.

Such a lot of troubles! I didn't hear the rising bell this morning, then I broke my shoestring while I was hurrying to dress and dropped my collar button down my neck. I was late for breakfast and also for first-hour recitation. I forgot to take any blotting paper and my fountain pen leaked. In trigonometry the Professor and I had a disagreement touching a little matter of logarithms. On looking it up, I find that she was right. We had mutton stew and pie-plant for lunch--hate 'em both; they taste like the asylum. The post brought me nothing but bills (though I must say that I never do get anything else; my family are not the kind that write). In English class this afternoon we had an unexpected written lesson. This was it:

I asked no other thing,
No other was denied.
I offered Being for it;
The mighty merchant smiled.
Brazil? He twirled a button
Without a glance my way:
But, madam, is there nothing else
That we can show today?

That is a poem. I don't know who wrote it or what it means. It was simply printed out on the blackboard when we arrived and we were ordered to comment upon it. When I read the first verse I thought I had an idea--The Mighty Merchant was a divinity who distributes blessings in return for virtuous deeds--but when I got to the second verse and found him twirling a button, it seemed a blasphemous supposition, and I hastily changed my mind. The rest of the class was in the same predicament; and there we sat for three-

quarters of an hour with blank paper and equally blank minds. Getting an education is an awfully wearing process!

But this didn't end the day. There's worse to come.

It rained so we couldn't play golf, but had to go to gymnasium instead. The girl next to me banged my elbow with an Indian club. I got home to find that the box with my new blue spring dress had come, and the skirt was so tight that I couldn't sit down. Friday is sweeping day, and the maid had mixed all the papers on my desk. We had tombstone for dessert(milk and gelatin flavoured with vanilla). We were kept in chapel twenty minutes later than usual to listen to a speech about womanly women. And then--just as I was settling down with a sigh of well-earned relief to The Portrait of a Lady, a girl named Ackerly, a dough-faced, deadly, unintermittently stupid girl, who sits next to me in Latin because her name begins with A (I wish Mrs. Lippett had named me Zabriski), came to ask if Monday's lesson commenced at paragraph 69or 70, and stayed ONE HOUR. She has just gone.

Did you ever hear of such a discouraging series of events? It isn't the big troubles in life that require character. Anybody can rise to a crisis and face a crushing tragedy with courage, but to meet the petty hazards of the day with a laugh--I really think that requires SPIRIT.

It's the kind of character that I am going to develop. I am going to pretend that all life is just a game which I must play as skilfully and fairly as I can. If I lose, I am going to shrug my shoulders and laugh-- also if I win.

Anyway, I am going to be a sport. You will never hear me complain again, Daddy dear, because Julia wears silk stockings and centipedes drop off the wall.

Yours ever,

Judy

Answer soon.

27th May

Daddy-Long-Legs, Esq.

DEAR SIR: I am in receipt of a letter from Mrs. Lippett. She hopes that I am doing well in deportment and studies. Since I probably have no place to go this summer, she will let me come back to the asylum and work for my board until college opens.

I HATE THE JOHN GRIER HOME.

I'd rather die than go back.

Yours most truthfully,
Jerusha Abbott

Cher Daddy-Jambes-Longes,

Vous etes un brick!

Je suis tres heureuse about the farm, parceque je n'ai jamais been on a farm dans ma vie and I'd hate to retourner chez John Grier, et wash dishes tout l'ete. There would be danger of quelque chose affreuse happening, parceque j'ai perdue ma humilite d'autre fois et j'ai peur that I would just break out quelque jour et smash every cup and saucer dans la maison.

Pardon brievete et paper. Je ne peux pas send des mes Nouvelles parceque je suis dans French class et j'ai peur que Monsieur le Professeur is going to call on me tout de suite. He did!

Au revoir,
je vous aime beaucoup.
Judy

Daddy-Long-Legs

30th May

Dear Daddy-Long-Legs,

Did you ever see this campus? (That is merely a rhetorical question. Don't let it annoy you.) It is a heavenly spot in May. All the shrubs are in blossom and the trees are the loveliest young green-- even the old pines look fresh and new. The grass is dotted with yellow dandelions and hundreds of girls in blue and white and pink dresses. Everybody is joyous and carefree, for vacation's coming, and with that to look forward to, examinations don't count.

Isn't that a happy frame of mind to be in? And oh, Daddy! I'm the happiest of all! Because I'm not in the asylum any more; and I'm not anybody's nursemaid or typewriter or bookkeeper (I should have been, you know, except for you).

I'm sorry now for all my past badnesses.

I'm sorry I was ever impertinent to Mrs. Lippett.

I'm sorry I ever slapped Freddie Perkins.

I'm sorry I ever filled the sugar bowl with salt. I'm sorry I ever made faces behind the Trustees' backs.

I'm going to be good and sweet and kind to everybody because I'm so happy. And this summer I'm going to write and write and write and begin to be a great author. Isn't that an exalted stand to take? Oh, I'm developing a beautiful character! It droops a bit under cold and frost, but it does grow fast when the sun shines.

That's the way with everybody. I don't agree with the theory that adversity and sorrow and disappointment develop moral strength. The happy people are the ones who are bubbling over with kindliness. I have no faith in misanthropes. (Fine word! Just learned it.) You are not a misanthrope are you, Daddy?

I started to tell you about the campus. I wish you'd come for a little visit and let me walk you about and say:

"That is the library. This is the gas plant, Daddy dear. The Gothic building on your left is the gymnasium, and the Tudor Romanesque beside it is the new infirmary."

Oh, I'm fine at showing people about. I've done it all my life at the asylum, and I've been doing it all day here. I have honestly. And a Man, too!

That's a great experience. I never talked to a man before (except occasional Trustees, and they don't count). Pardon, Daddy, I don't mean to hurt your feelings when I abuse Trustees. I don't consider that you really belong among them. You just tumbled on to the Board by chance. The Trustee, as such, is fat and pompous and benevolent. He pats one on the head and wears a gold watch chain.

That looks like a June bug, but is meant to be a portrait of any Trustee except you.[4]

However--to resume:

I have been walking and talking and having tea with a man. And with a very superior man--with Mr. Jervis Pendleton of the House of Julia; her uncle, in short (in long, perhaps I ought to say; he's as tall as you.)Being in town on business, he decided to run out to the college and call on his niece. He's her father's youngest brother, but she doesn't know him very intimately. It seems he glanced at her when she was a baby, decided he didn't like her, and has never noticed her since.

4　Please find the illustration in Chinese version.

Anyway, there he was, sitting in the reception room very proper with his hat and stick and gloves beside him; and Julia and Sallie with seventh-hour recitations that they couldn't cut. So Julia dashed into my room and begged me to walk him about the campus and then deliver him to her when the seventh hour was over. I said I would, obligingly but unenthusiastically, because I don't care much for Pendletons.

But he turned out to be a sweet lamb. He's a real human being-- not a Pendleton at all. We had a beautiful time; I've longed for an uncle ever since. Do you mind pretending you're my uncle? I believe they're superior to grandmothers.

Mr. Pendleton reminded me a little of you, Daddy, as you were twenty years ago. You see I know you intimately, even if we haven't ever met! He's tall and thinnish with a dark face all over lines, and the funniest underneath smile that never quite comes through but just wrinkles up the corners of his mouth. And he has a way of making you feel right off as though you'd known him a long time. He's very companionable.

We walked all over the campus from the quadrangle to the athletic grounds; then he said he felt weak and must have some tea. He proposed that we go to College Inn--it's just off the campus by the pine walk. I said we ought to go back for Julia and Sallie, but he said he didn't like to have his nieces drink too much tea; it made them nervous. So we just ran away and had tea and muffins and marmalade and ice-cream and cake at a nice little table out on the balcony. The inn was quite conveniently empty, this being the end of the month and allowances low.

We had the jolliest time! But he had to run for his train the minute he got back and he barely saw Julia at all. She was furious with me for taking him off; it seems he's an unusually rich and desirable uncle. It relieved my mind to find he was rich, for the tea and things cost sixty cents apiece.

This morning (it's Monday now) three boxes of chocolates came by express for Julia and Sallie and me. What do you think of that? To begetting candy from a man!

I begin to feel like a girl instead of a foundling.

I wish you'd come and have tea some day and let me see if I like you. But wouldn't it be dreadful if I didn't? However, I know I should.

Bien! I make you my compliments.

"*Jamais je ne t'oublierai.*"
Judy

PS. I looked in the glass this morning and found a perfectly new dimple that I'd never seen before. It's very curious. Where do you suppose it came from?

9th June

Dear Daddy-Long-Legs,

Happy day! I've just finished my last examination Physiology. And now:

Three months on a farm!

I don't know what kind of a thing a farm is. I've never been on one in my life. I've never even looked at one (except from the car window),but I know I'm going to love it, and I'm going to love being FREE.

I am not used even yet to being outside the John Grier Home. Whenever I think of it excited little thrills chase up and down my back. I feel as though I must run faster and faster and keep looking over my shoulder to make sure that Mrs. Lippett isn't after me with

her arm stretched out to grab me back. I don't have to mind any one this summer, do I?

Your nominal authority doesn't annoy me in the least; you are too far away to do any harm. Mrs. Lippett is dead for ever, so far as I am concerned, and the Semples aren't expected to overlook my moral welfare, are they? No, I am sure not. I am entirely grown up. Hooray!

I leave you now to pack a trunk, and three boxes of teakettles and dishes and sofa cushions and books.

Yours ever,
Judy

PS. Here is my physiology exam. Do you think you could have passed?

LOCK WILLOW FARM
Saturday night

Dearest Daddy-Long-Legs,

I've only just come and I'm not unpacked, but I can't wait to tell you how much I like farms. This is a heavenly, heavenly, HEAVENLY spot! The house is square like this:[5]

And OLD. A hundred years or so. It has a veranda on the side which I can't draw and a sweet porch in front. The picture really doesn't do it justice--those things that look like feather dusters are maple trees, and the prickly ones that border the drive are murmuring pines and hemlocks. It stands on the top of a hill and looks way off

---

5　Please find the illustration in Chinese version.

over miles of green meadows to another line of hills.

That is the way Connecticut goes, in a series of Marcelle waves; and Lock Willow Farm is just on the crest of one wave. The barns used to be across the road where they obstructed the view, but a kind flash of lightning came from heaven and burnt them down.

The people are Mr. and Mrs. Semple and a hired girl and two hired men. The hired people eat in the kitchen, and the Semples and Judy in the dining-room. We had ham and eggs and biscuits and honey and jelly-cake and pie and pickles and cheese and tea for supper--and a great deal of conversation. I have never been so entertaining in my life; everything I say appears to be funny. I suppose it is, because I've never been in the country before, and my questions are backed by an all-inclusive ignorance.

The room marked with a cross is not where the murder was committed, but the one that I occupy. It's big and square and empty, with adorable old-fashioned furniture and windows that have to be propped up on sticks and green shades trimmed with gold that fall down if you touch them. And a big square mahogany table--I'm going to spend the summer with my elbows spread out on it, writing a novel.

Oh, Daddy, I'm so excited! I can't wait till daylight to explore. It's 8.30 now, and I am about to blow out my candle and try to go to sleep. We rise at five. Did you ever know such fun? I can't believe this is really Judy. You and the Good Lord give me more than I deserve. I must be a very, very, VERY good person to pay. I'm going to be. You'll see.

Good night,
Judy

PS. You should hear the frogs sing and the little pigs squeal and you should see the new moon! I saw it over my right shoulder.

LOCK WILLOW
12th July

Dear Daddy-Long-Legs,

How did your secretary come to know about Lock Willow? (That isn't arhetorical question. I am awfully curious to know.) For listen to this: Mr. Jervis Pendleton used to own this farm, but now he has given it to Mrs. Semple who was his old nurse. Did you ever hear of such a funny coincidence? She still calls him "Master Jervie" and talks about what a sweet little boy he used to be. She has one of his baby curls

put away in a box, and it is red--or at least reddish!

Since she discovered that I know him, I have risen very much in her opinion. Knowing a member of the Pendleton family is the best introduction one can have at Lock Willow. And the cream of the whole family is Master Jervis--I am pleased to say that Julia belongs to an inferior branch.

The farm gets more and more entertaining. I rode on a hay wagon yesterday. We have three big pigs and nine little piglets, and you should see them eat. They are pigs! We've oceans of little baby chickens and ducks and turkeys and guinea fowls. You must be mad to live in a city when you might live on a farm.

It is my daily business to hunt the eggs. I fell off a beam in the barn loft yesterday, while I was trying to crawl over to a nest that the black hen has stolen. And when I came in with a scratched knee, Mrs. Semple bound it up with witch-hazel, murmuring all the time, "Dear! Dear! It seems only yesterday that Master Jervie fell off that very same beam and scratched this very same knee."

The scenery around here is perfectly beautiful. There's a valley and a river and a lot of wooded hills, and way in the distance a tall blue mountain that simply melts in your mouth.

We churn twice a week; and we keep the cream in the spring house which is made of stone with the brook running underneath. Some of the farmers around here have a separator, but we don't care for these new-fashioned ideas. It may be a little harder to separate the cream in pans, but it's sufficiently better to pay. We have six calves; and I've chosen the names for all of them.

1. Sylvia, because she was born in the woods.
2. Lesbia, after the Lesbia in Catullus.
3. Sallie.
4. Julia--a spotted, nondescript animal.
5. Judy, after me.
6. Daddy-Long-Legs. You don't mind, do you, Daddy? He's pure Jersey and has a sweet disposition. He looks like this--you can see how appropriate the name is.[6]

I haven't had time yet to begin my immortal novel; the farm keeps me too busy.

Yours always,
Judy

PS. I've learned to make doughnuts.
PS. (2) If you are thinking of raising chickens, let me recommend Buff Orpingtons. They haven't any pin feathers.
PS. (3) I wish I could send you a pat of the nice, fresh butter I churned yesterday. I'm a fine dairy-maid!

---

6   Please find the illustration in Chinese version.

PS. (4) This is a picture of Miss Jerusha Abbott, the future great author, driving home the cows.[7]

Sunday

Dear Daddy-Long-Legs,

Isn't it funny? I started to write to you yesterday afternoon, but as far as I got was the heading, "Dear Daddy-Long-Legs", and then I remembered I'd promised to pick some blackberries for supper, so I went off and left the sheet lying on the table, and when I came back today, what do you think I found sitting in the middle of the page? A real true Daddy-Long-Legs!

I picked him up very gently by one leg, and dropped him out of the window. I wouldn't hurt one of them for the world. They always remind me of you.

A nice sleepy sermon with everybody drowsily waving palm-leaf fans, and the only sound, aside from the minister, the buzzing of locusts in the trees outside. I didn't wake up till I found myself on my feet singing the hymn, and then I was awfully sorry I hadn't listened to the sermon; I should like to know more of the psychology of a man who would pick out such a hymn. This was it:

> *Come, leave your sports and earthly toys*
> *And join me in celestial joys.*
> *Or else, dear friend, a long farewell.*
> *I leave you now to sink to hell.*

---

7   Please find the illustration in Chinese version.

I find that it isn't safe to discuss religion with the Semples. Their God (whom they have inherited intact from their remote Puritan ancestors) is a narrow, irrational, unjust, mean, revengeful, bigoted Person. Thank heaven I don't inherit God from anybody! I am free to make mine up as I wish Him. He's kind and sympathetic and imaginative and forgiving and understanding--and He has a sense of humour.

I like the Semples immensely; their practice is so superior to their theory. They are better than their own God. I told them so--and they are horribly troubled. They think I am blasphemous--and I think they are! We've dropped theology from our conversation.

This is Sunday afternoon.

Amasai (hired man) in a purple tie and some bright yellow buckskin gloves, very red and shaved, has just driven off with Carrie (hired girl) in a big hat trimmed with red roses and a blue muslin dress and her hair curled as tight as it will curl. Amasai spent all the morning washing the buggy; and Carrie stayed home from church ostensibly to cook the dinner, but really to iron the muslin dress.

In two minutes more when this letter is finished I am going to settle down to a book which I found in the attic. It's entitled, On the Trail, and sprawled across the front page in a funny little-boy hand:

Jervis Pendleton
if this book should ever roam,
Box its ears and send it home.

He spent the summer here once after he had been ill, when he was about eleven years old; and he left On the Trail behind. It looks well read--the marks of his grimy little hands are frequent! Also in a corner of the attic there is a water wheel and a windmill and some

213

bows and arrows. Mrs. Semple talks so constantly about him that I begin to believe he really lives--not a grown man with a silk hat and walking stick, but a nice, dirty, tousle-headed boy who clatters up the stairs with an awful racket, and leaves the screen doors open, and is always asking for cookies. (And getting them, too, if I know Mrs. Semple!) He seems to have been an adventurous little soul--and brave and truthful. I'm sorry to think he is a Pendleton; he was meant for something better.

Sir,

I remain,

Your affectionate orphan,

Judy Abbott

PS. Indians in the first chapter and highwaymen in the second. I hold my breath. What can the third contain? "Red Hawk leapt twenty feet in the air and bit the dust." That is the subject of the frontispiece. Aren't Judy and Jervie having fun?

15th September

Dear Daddy,

I was weighed yesterday on the flour scales in the general store at the Corners. I've gained nine pounds! Let me recommend Lock Willow as a health resort.

Yours ever,

Judy

25th September

Dear Daddy-Long-Legs,

Behold me--a Sophomore! I came up last Friday, sorry to leave Lock Willow, but glad to see the campus again. It is a pleasant sensation to come back to something familiar. I am beginning to feel at home in college, and in command of the situation; I am beginning, in fact, to feel at home in the world--as though I really belonged to it and had not just crept in on sufferance.

I don't suppose you understand in the least what I am trying to say. A person important enough to be a Trustee can't appreciate the feelings of a person unimportant enough to be a foundling.

And now, Daddy, listen to this. Whom do you think I am rooming with? Sallie McBride and Julia Rutledge Pendleton. It's the truth. We have a study and three little bedrooms--VOILA![8]

Sallie and I decided last spring that we should like to room together, and Julia made up her mind to stay with Sallie--why, I can't imagine, for they are not a bit alike; but the Pendletons are naturally conservative and inimical (fine word!) to change. Anyway, here we are. Think of Jerusha Abbott, late of the John Grier Home for Orphans, rooming with a Pendleton. This is a democratic country.

Sallie is running for class president, and unless all signs fail, she is going to be elected. Such an atmosphere of intrigue you should see what politicians we are! Oh, I tell you, Daddy, when we women get our rights, you men will have to look alive in order to keep yours. Election comes next Saturday, and we're going to have a torchlight

---

8   Please find the illustration in Chinese version.

procession in the evening, no matter who wins.

I am beginning chemistry, a most unusual study. I've never seen anything like it before. Molecules and Atoms are the material employed, but I'll be in a position to discuss them more definitely next month.

I am also taking argumentation and logic.
Also history of the whole world.
Also plays of William Shakespeare.
Also French.

If this keeps up many years longer, I shall become quite intelligent. I should rather have elected economics than French, but I didn't dare, because I was afraid that unless I re-elected French, the Professor would not let me pass--as it was, I just managed to squeeze through the June examination. But I will say that my high-school preparation was not very adequate.

There's one girl in the class who chatters away in French as fast as she does in English. She went abroad with her parents when she was a child, and spent three years in a convent school. You can imagine how bright she is compared with the rest of us--irregular verbs are mere playthings. I wish my parents had chucked me into a French convent when I was little instead of a foundling asylum. Oh no, I don't either! Because then maybe I should never have known you. I'd rather know you than French.

Goodbye, Daddy. I must call on Harriet Martin now, and, having discussed the chemical situation, casually drop a few thoughts on the subject of our next president.

Yours in politics,
J. Abbott

17th October

Dear Daddy-Long-Legs,

Supposing the swimming tank in the gymnasium were filled full of lemon jelly, could a person trying to swim manage to keep on top or would he sink?

We were having lemon jelly for dessert when the question came up. We discussed it heatedly for half an hour and it's still unsettled. Sallie thinks that she could swim in it, but I am perfectly sure that the best swimmer in the world would sink. Wouldn't it be funny to be drowned in lemon jelly?

Two other problems are engaging the attention of our table. 1st. What shape are the rooms in an octagon house? Some of the girls insist that they're square; but I think they'd have to be shaped like apiece of pie. Don't you?

2nd. Suppose there were a great big hollow sphere made of looking-glass and you were sitting inside. Where would it stop reflecting your face and begin reflecting your back? The more one thinks about this problem, the more puzzling it becomes. You can see with what deep philosophical reflection we engage our leisure!

Did I ever tell you about the election? It happened three weeks ago, but so fast do we live, that three weeks is ancient history. Sallie was elected, and we had a torchlight parade with transparencies saying,

"McBride for Ever," and a band consisting of fourteen pieces (three mouth organs and eleven combs).

We're very important persons now in "258." Julia and I come in for a great deal of reflected glory. It's quite a social strain to be living in the same house with a president.

Daddy-Long-Legs

Bonne nuit, cher Daddy.

Acceptez mez compliments,
Tres respectueux,
je suis,
Votre Judy

12th November

Dear Daddy-Long-Legs,

We beat the Freshmen at basket ball yesterday. Of course we're pleased--but oh, if we could only beat the juniors! I'd be willing to be black and blue all over and stay in bed a week in a witch-hazel compress.

Sallie has invited me to spend the Christmas vacation with her. She lives in Worcester, Massachusetts. Wasn't it nice of her? I shall love to go. I've never been in a private family in my life, except at Lock Willow, and the Semples were grown-up and old and don't count. But the McBrides have a houseful of children (anyway two or three) and a mother and father and grandmother, and an Angora cat. It's a perfectly complete family! Packing your trunk and going away is more fun than staying behind. I am terribly excited at the prospect.

Seventh hour--I must run to rehearsal. I'm to be in the Thanksgiving theatricals. A prince in a tower with a velvet tunic and yellow curls. Isn't that a lark?

Yours,
J. A.

Saturday

Do you want to know what I look like? Here's a photograph of all three that Leonora Fenton took.

The light one who is laughing is Sallie, and the tall one with her nose in the air is Julia, and the little one with the hair blowing across her face is Judy--she is really more beautiful than that, but the sun was in her eyes.

"STONE GATE", WORCESTER, MASS.
31st December

Dear Daddy-Long-Legs,

I meant to write to you before and thank you for your Christmas cheque, but life in the McBride household is very absorbing, and I don't seem able to find two consecutive minutes to spend at a desk.

I bought a new gown--one that I didn't need, but just wanted. My Christmas present this year is from Daddy-Long-Legs; my family just sent love.

I've been having the most beautiful vacation visiting Sallie. She lives in a big old-fashioned brick house with white trimmings set back from the street--exactly the kind of house that I used to look at so curiously when I was in the John Grier Home, and wonder what it could be like inside. I never expected to see with my own eyes--but here I am! Everything is so comfortable and restful and homelike; I walk from room to room and drink in the furnishings.

It is the most perfect house for children to be brought up in; with shadowy nooks for hide and seek, and open fire places for pop-corn,

and an attic to romp in on rainy days and slippery banisters with a comfortable flat knob at the bottom, and a great big sunny kitchen, and a nice, fat, sunny cook who has lived in the family thirteen years and always saves out a piece of dough for the children to bake. Just the sight of such a house makes you want to be a child all over again.

And as for families! I never dreamed they could be so nice. Sallie has a father and mother and grandmother, and the sweetest three-year-old baby sister all over curls, and a medium-sized brother who always forgets to wipe his feet, and a big, good-looking brother named Jimmie, who is a junior at Princeton.

We have the jolliest times at the table--everybody laughs and jokes and talks at once, and we don't have to say grace beforehand. It's a relief not having to thank Somebody for every mouthful you eat. (I dare say I'm blasphemous; but you'd be, too, if you'd offered as much obligatory thanks as I have.)

Such a lot of things we've done--I can't begin to tell you about them. Mr. McBride owns a factory and Christmas eve he had a tree for the employees' children. It was in the long packing-room which was decorated with evergreens and holly. Jimmie McBride was dressed as Santa Claus and Sallie and I helped him distribute the presents.

Dear me, Daddy, but it was a funny sensation! I felt as benevolent as a Trustee of the John Grier home. I kissed one sweet, sticky little boy--but I don't think I patted any of them on the head!

And two days after Christmas, they gave a dance at their own house for ME.

It was the first really true ball I ever attended--college doesn't count where we dance with girls. I had a new white evening gown (your Christmas present--many thanks) and long white gloves and white satin slippers. The only drawback to my perfect, utter, absolute happiness was the fact that Mrs. Lippett couldn't see me leading the cotillion with Jimmie McBride. Tell her about it, please, the next time you visit the J. G. H.

Yours ever,
Judy Abbott

PS. Would you be terribly displeased, Daddy, if I didn't turn out to be a Great Author after all, but just a Plain Girl?

6.30, Saturday

Dear Daddy,

We started to walk to town today, but mercy! how it poured. I like winter to be winter with snow instead of rain.

Julia's desirable uncle called again this afternoon--and brought a five-pound box of chocolates. There are advantages, you see, about rooming with Julia.

Our innocent prattle appeared to amuse him and he waited for a later train in order to take tea in the study. We had an awful lot of trouble getting permission. It's hard enough entertaining fathers and grandfathers, but uncles are a step worse; and as for brothers and cousins, they are next to impossible. Julia had to swear that he was her uncle before a notary public and then have the county clerk's certificate attached. (Don't I know a lot of law?) And even then I doubt if we could have had our tea if the Dean had chanced to see how youngish and good-looking Uncle Jervis is.

Anyway, we had it, with brown bread Swiss cheese sandwiches. He helped make them and then ate four. I told him that I had spent last summer at Lock Willow, and we had a beautiful gossipy time

about the Semples, and the horses and cows and chickens. All the horses that he used to know are dead, except Grover, who was a baby colt at the time of his last visit--and poor Grove now is so old he can just limp about the pasture.

He asked if they still kept doughnuts in a yellow crock with a blue plate over it on the bottom shelf of the pantry--and they do! He wanted to know if there was still a woodchuck's hole under the pile of rocks in the night pasture--and there is! Amasai caught a big, fat, grey one there this summer, the twenty-fifth great-grandson of the one Master Jervis caught when he was a little boy.

I called him "Master Jervie" to his face, but he didn't appear to be insulted. Julia says she has never seen him so amiable; he's usually pretty unapproachable. But Julia hasn't a bit of tact; and men, I find, require a great deal. They purr if you rub them the right way and spit if you don't. (That isn't a very elegant metaphor. I mean it figuratively.) We're reading Marie Bashkirtseff's journal. Isn't it amazing? Listen to this: "Last night I was seized by a fit of despair that found utterance in moans, and that finally drove me to throw the dining-room clock into the sea."

It makes me almost hope I'm not a genius; they must be very wearing to have about--and awfully destructive to the furniture.

Mercy! how it keeps Pouring.

We shall have to swim to chapel tonight.

Yours ever,
Judy

20th Jan.

Dear Daddy-Long-Legs,

Did you ever have a sweet baby girl who was stolen from the cradle in infancy?

Maybe I am she! If we were in a novel, that would be the denouement, wouldn't it?

It's really awfully queer not to know what one is--sort of exciting and romantic. There are such a lot of possibilities. Maybe I'm not American; lots of people aren't. I may be straight descended from the ancient Romans, or I may be a Viking's daughter, or I may be the child of a Russian exile and belong by rights in a Siberian prison, or maybe I'm a Gipsy--I think perhaps I am. I have a very WANDERING spirit, though I haven't as yet had much chance to develop it.

Do you know about that one scandalous blot in my career the time I ran away from the asylum because they punished me for stealing cookies? It's down in the books free for any Trustee to read. But really, Daddy, what could you expect? When you put a hungry little nine-year girl in the pantry scouring knives, with the cookie jar at her elbow, and go off and leave her alone; and then suddenly pop in again, wouldn't you expect to find her a bit crumby? And then when you jerk her by the elbow and box her ears, and make her leave the table when the pudding comes, and tell all the other children that it's because she's a thief, wouldn't you expect her to run away?

I only ran four miles. They caught me and brought me back; and everyday for a week I was tied, like a naughty puppy, to a stake in the backyard while the other children were out at recess. Oh, dear! There's the chapel bell, and after chapel I have a committee meeting.

I'm sorry because I meant to write you a very entertaining letter this time.

Auf wiedersehen
Cher Daddy,
Pax tibi!
Judy

PS. There's one thing I'm perfectly sure of I'm not a Chinaman.

4th February

Dear Daddy-Long-Legs,

Jimmie McBride has sent me a Princeton banner as big as one end of the room; I am very grateful to him for remembering me, but I don't know what on earth to do with it. Sallie and Julia won't let me hang it up; our room this year is furnished in red, and you can imagine what an effect we'd have if I added orange and black. But it's such nice, warm, thick felt, I hate to waste it. Would it be very improper to have it made into a bath robe? My old one shrank when it was washed.

I've entirely omitted of late telling you what I am learning, but though you might not imagine it from my letters, my time is exclusively occupied with study. It's a very bewildering matter to get educated in five branches at once.

"The test of true scholarship," says Chemistry Professor, "is a painstaking passion for detail."

"Be careful not to keep your eyes glued to detail," says History Professor. "Stand far enough away to get a perspective of the whole."

You can see with what nicety we have to trim our sails between chemistry and history. I like the historical method best. If I say that William the Conqueror came over in 1492, and Columbus discovered America in 1100 or 1066 or whenever it was, that's a mere detail that the Professor overlooks. It gives a feeling of security and restfulness to the history recitation, that is entirely lacking in chemistry.

Sixth-hour bell--I must go to the laboratory and look into a little matter of acids and salts and alkalis. I've burned a hole as big as aplate in the front of my chemistry apron, with hydrochloric acid. If the theory worked, I ought to be able to neutralize that hole with good strong ammonia, oughtn't I?

Examinations next week, but who's afraid?

Yours ever,
Judy

5th March

Dear Daddy-Long-Legs,

There is a March wind blowing, and the sky is filled with heavy, black moving clouds. The crows in the pine trees are making such a clamour! It's an intoxicating, exhilarating, CALLING noise. You want to close your books and be off over the hills to race with the wind.

We had a paper chase last Saturday over five miles of squashy ' cross country. The fox (composed of three girls and a bushel or so of confetti) started half an hour before the twenty-seven hunters. I was one of the twenty-seven; eight dropped by the wayside; we ended nineteen. The trail led over a hill, through a cornfield, and into a swamp where we had to leap lightly from hummock to hummock. of

course half of us went in ankle deep. We kept losing the trail, and we wasted twenty-five minutes over that swamp. Then up a hill through some woods and in at a barn window! The barn doors were all locked and the window was up high and pretty small. I don't call that fair, do you?

But we didn't go through; we circumnavigated the barn and picked up the trail where it issued by way of a low shed roof on to the top of a fence. The fox thought he had us there, but we fooled him. Then straight away over two miles of rolling meadow, and awfully hard to follow, for the confetti was getting sparse. The rule is that it must be at the most six feet apart, but they were the longest six feet I ever saw. Finally, after two hours of steady trotting, we tracked Monsieur Fox into the kitchen of Crystal Spring (that's a farm where the girls go in bob sleighs and hay wagons for chicken and waffle suppers) and we found the three foxes placidly eating milk and honey and biscuits. They hadn't thought we would get that far; they were expecting us to stick in the barn window.

Both sides insist that they won. I think we did, don't you? Because we caught them before they got back to the campus. Anyway, all nineteen of us settled like locusts over the furniture and clamoured for honey. There wasn't enough to go round, but Mrs. Crystal Spring(that's our pet name for her; she's by rights a Johnson) brought up ajar of strawberry jam and a can of maple syrup--just made last week--and three loaves of brown bread.

We didn't get back to college till half-past six--half an hour late for dinner--and we went straight in without dressing, and with perfectly unimpaired appetites! Then we all cut evening chapel, the state of our boots being enough of an excuse.

I never told you about examinations. I passed everything with the utmost ease--I know the secret now, and am never going to fail again. I shan't be able to graduate with honours though, because of that beastly Latin prose and geometry Freshman year. But I don't care. Wot's the hodds so long as you're 'appy? (That's a quotation. I've been reading the English classics.)

Speaking of classics, have you ever read Hamlet? If you haven't, do it right off. It's PERFECTLY CORKING. I've been hearing about Shakespeare all my life, but I had no idea he really wrote so well; I always suspected him of going largely on his reputation.

I have a beautiful play that I invented a long time ago when I first learned to read. I put myself to sleep every night by pretending I'm the person (the most important person) in the book I'm reading at the moment.

At present I'm Ophelia--and such a sensible Ophelia! I keep Hamlet amused all the time, and pet him and scold him and make him wrap up his throat when he has a cold. I've entirely cured him of being melancholy. The King and Queen are both dead--an accident at sea; no funeral necessary--so Hamlet and I are ruling in Denmark without any bother. We have the kingdom working beautifully. He takes care of the governing, and I look after the charities. I have just founded some first-class orphan asylums. If you or any of the other Trustees would like to visit them, I shall be pleased to show you through. I think you might find a great many helpful suggestions.

I remain, sir,
Yours most graciously,
OPHELIA,
Queen of Denmark.

Daddy-Long-Legs

24th March, maybe the 25th

Dear Daddy-Long-Legs,

I don't believe I can be going to Heaven--I am getting such a lot of good things here; it wouldn't be fair to get them hereafter too. Listen to what has happened.

Jerusha Abbott has won the short-story contest (a twenty-five dollar prize) that the Monthly holds every year. And she's a Sophomore! The contestants are mostly Seniors. When I saw my name posted, I couldn't quite believe it was true. Maybe I am going to be an author after all. I wish Mrs. Lippett hadn't given me such a silly name-- it sounds like an author-ess, doesn't it?

Also I have been chosen for the spring dramatics--As You Like It out of doors. I am going to be Celia, own cousin to Rosalind.

And lastly: Julia and Sallie and I are going to New York next Friday to do some spring shopping and stay all night and go to the theatre the next day with "Master Jervie." He invited us. Julia is going to stay at home with her family, but Sallie and I are going to stop at the Martha Washington Hotel. Did you ever hear of anything so exciting? I've never been in a hotel in my life, nor in a theatre; except once when the Catholic Church had a festival and invited the orphans, but that wasn't a real play and it doesn't count.

And what do you think we're going to see? Hamlet. Think of that! We studied it for four weeks in Shakespeare class and I know it by heart.

I am so excited over all these prospects that I can scarcely sleep.

Goodbye, Daddy.

This is a very entertaining world.

Yours ever,
Judy

PS. I've just looked at the calendar. It's the 28th. Another postscript. I saw a street car conductor today with one brown eye and one blue. Wouldn't he make a nice villain for a detective story?

7th April

Dear Daddy-Long-Legs,

Mercy! Isn't New York big? Worcester is nothing to it. Do you mean to tell me that you actually live in all that confusion? I don't believe that I shall recover for months from the bewildering effect of two days of it. I can't begin to tell you all the amazing things I've seen; I suppose you know, though, since you live there yourself.

But aren't the streets entertaining? And the people? And the shops? I never saw such lovely things as there are in the windows. It makes you want to devote your life to wearing clothes.

Sallie and Julia and I went shopping together Saturday morning. Julia went into the very most gorgeous place I ever saw, white and gold walls and blue carpets and blue silk curtains and gilt chairs. A perfectly beautiful lady with yellow hair and a long black silk trailing gown came to meet us with a welcoming smile. I thought we were paying asocial call, and started to shake hands, but it seems we were only buying hats--at least Julia was. She sat down in front of a mirror and tried on a dozen, each lovelier than the last, and bought the two loveliest of all.

I can't imagine any joy in life greater than sitting down in front of a mirror and buying any hat you choose without having first to consider the price!

And after we'd finished our shopping, we met Master Jervie at

Sherry's. I suppose you've been in Sherry's? Picture that, then picture the dining-room of the John Grier Home with its oilcloth-covered tables, and white crockery that you CAN't break, and wooden-handled knives and forks; and fancy the way I felt!

I ate my fish with the wrong fork, but the waiter very kindly gave me another so that nobody noticed.

And after luncheon we went to the theatre--it was dazzling, marvellous, unbelievable--I dream about it every night.

Isn't Shakespeare wonderful?

"Hamlet" is so much better on the stage than when we analyze it in class; I appreciated it before, but now, dear me!

I think, if you don't mind, that I'd rather be an actress than a writer. Wouldn't you like me to leave college and go into a dramatic school? And then I'll send you a box for all my performances, and smile at you across the footlights. Only wear a red rose in your buttonhole, please, so I'll surely smile at the right man. It would bean awfully embarrassing mistake if I picked out the wrong one.

We came back Saturday night and had our dinner in the train, at little tables with pink lamps and negro waiters. I never heard of meals being served in trains before, and I inadvertently said so.

"Where on earth were you brought up?" said Julia to me. " In a village," said I meekly, to Julia.

"But didn't you ever travel?" said she to me.

"Not till I came to college, and then it was only a hundred and sixty miles and we didn't eat," said I to her.

She's getting quite interested in me, because I say such funny things. I try hard not to, but they do pop out when I'm surprised--and I'm surprised most of the time. It's a dizzying experience, Daddy, to pass eighteen years in the John Grier Home, and then suddenly to be plunged into the WORLD.

But I'm getting acclimated. I don't make such awful mistakes as I did; and I don't feel uncomfortable any more with the other girls. I used to squirm whenever people looked at me. I felt as though they saw right through my sham new clothes to the checked ginghams underneath. But I'm not letting the ginghams bother me any more. Sufficient unto yesterday is the evil thereof.

I forgot to tell you about our flowers. Master Jervie gave us each a big bunch of violets and lilies-of-the-valley. Wasn't that sweet of him? I never used to care much for men--judging by Trustees--but I'm changing my mind. Eleven pages--this is a letter! Have courage. I'm going to stop.

Yours always,
Judy

10th April

Dear Mr. Rich-Man,

Here's your cheque for fifty dollars. Thank you very much, but I do not feel that I can keep it. My allowance is sufficient to afford all of the hats that I need. I am sorry that I wrote all that silly stuff about the millinery shop; it's just that I had never seen anything like it before.

However, I wasn't begging! And I would rather not accept any more charity than I have to.

Sincerely yours,
Jerusha Abbott

11th April

Dearest Daddy,

Will you please forgive me for the letter I wrote you yesterday? After I posted it I was sorry, and tried to get it back, but that beastly mail clerk wouldn't give it back to me.

It's the middle of the night now; I've been awake for hours thinking what a Worm I am--what a Thousand-legged Worm--and that's the worst I can say! I've closed the door very softly into the study so as not to wake Julia and Sallie, and am sitting up in bed writing to you on paper torn out of my history note-book.

I just wanted to tell you that I am sorry I was so impolite about your cheque. I know you meant it kindly, and I think you're an old dear to take so much trouble for such a silly thing as a hat. I ought to have returned it very much more graciously.

But in any case, I had to return it. It's different with me than with other girls. They can take things naturally from people. They have fathers and brothers and aunts and uncles; but I can't be on any such relations with any one. I like to pretend that you belong to me, just to play with the idea, but of course I know you don't. I'm alone, really-- with my back to the wall fighting the world--and I get sort of gaspy when I think about it. I put it out of my mind, and keep on pretending; but don't you see, Daddy? I can't accept any more money than I have to, because some day I shall be wanting to pay it back, and even as great an author as I intend to be won't be able to face a PERFECTLY TREMENDOUS debt.

I'd love pretty hats and things, but I mustn't mortgage the future to pay for them.

You'll forgive me, won't you, for being so rude? I have an awful habit of writing impulsively when I first think things, and then posting the letter beyond recall. But if I sometimes seem thoughtless and ungrateful, I never mean it. In my heart I thank you always for the life and freedom and independence that you have given me. My childhood was just a long, sullen stretch of revolt, and now I am so happy every moment of the day that I can't believe it's true. I feel like a made-up heroine in a story-book.

It's a quarter past two. I'm going to tiptoe out to post this off now. You'll receive it in the next mail after the other; so you won't have a very long time to think bad of me.

Good night, Daddy,
I love you always,
Judy

4th May

Dear Daddy-Long-Legs,

Field Day last Saturday. It was a very spectacular occasion. First we had a parade of all the classes, with everybody dressed in white linen, the Seniors carrying blue and gold Japanese umbrellas, and the juniors white and yellow banners. Our class had crimson balloons— very fetching, especially as they were always getting loose and floating off--and the Freshmen wore green tissue-paper hats with long streamers. Also we had a band in blue uniforms hired from town. Also about a dozen funny people, like clowns in a circus, to keep the spectators entertained between events.

Julia was dressed as a fat country man with a linen duster and whiskers and baggy umbrella. Patsy Moriarty (Patrici really. Did you

ever hear such a name? Mrs. Lippett couldn't have done better) who is tall and thin was Julia's wife in a absurd green bonnet over one ear. Waves of laughter followed them the whole length of the course. Julia played the part extremely well. I never dreamed that a Pendleton could display so much comedy spirit--begging Master Jervie's pardon; I don't consider him a true Pendleton though, any more than I consider you a true Trustee.

Sallie and I weren't in the parade because we were entered for the events. And what do you think? We both won! At least in something. We tried for the running broad jump and lost; but Sallie won the pole-vaulting (seven feet three inches) and I won the fifty-yard sprint (eight seconds).

I was pretty panting at the end, but it was great fun, with the whole class waving balloons and cheering and yelling:

What's the matter with Judy Abbott?
She's all right.
Who's all right?
Judy Ab-bott!

That, Daddy, is true fame. Then trotting back to the dressing tent and being rubbed down with alcohol and having a lemon to suck. You see we're very professional. It's a fine thing to win an event for your class, because the class that wins the most gets the athletic cup for the year. The Seniors won it this year, with seven events to their credit. The athletic association gave a dinner in the gymnasium to all of the winners. We had fried soft-shell crabs, and chocolate ice-cream moulded in the shape of basket balls.

I sat up half of last night reading Jane Eyre. Are you old enough, Daddy, to remember sixty years ago? And, if so, did people talk that way?

The haughty Lady Blanche says to the footman, "Stop your chattering, knave, and do my bidding." Mr. Rochester talks about the metal welkin when he means the sky; and as for the mad woman who laughs like a hyena and sets fire to bed curtains and tears up wedding veils and BITES--it's melodrama of the purest, but just the same, you read and read and read. I can't see how any girl could have written such a book, especially any girl who was brought up in a churchyard. There's something about those Brontes that fascinates me. Their books, their lives, their spirit. Where did they get it? When I was reading about little Jane's troubles in the charity school, I got so angry that I had to go out and take a walk. I understood exactly how she felt. Having known Mrs. Lippett, I could see Mr. Brocklehurst.

Don't be outraged, Daddy. I am not intimating that the John Grier Home was like the Lowood Institute. We had plenty to eat and plenty to wear, sufficient water to wash in, and a furnace in the cellar. But there was one deadly likeness. Our lives were absolutely monotonous and uneventful. Nothing nice ever happened, except ice-cream on Sundays, and even that was regular. In all the eighteen years I was there I only had one adventure--when the woodshed burned. We had to get up in the night and dress so as to be ready in case the house should catch. But it didn't catch and we went back to bed.

Everybody likes a few surprises; it's a perfectly natural human craving. But I never had one until Mrs. Lippett called me to the office to tell me that Mr. John Smith was going to send me to college. And then she broke the news so gradually that it just barely shocked me.

You know, Daddy, I think that the most necessary quality for any person to have is imagination. It makes people able to put themselves in other people's places. It makes them kind and sympathetic and understanding. It ought to be cultivated in children. But the John

Grier Home instantly stamped out the slightest flicker that appeared. Duty was the one quality that was encouraged. I don't think children ought to know the meaning of the word; it's odious, detestable. They ought to do everything from love.

Wait until you see the orphan asylum that I am going to be the head of! It's my favourite play at night before I go to sleep. I plan it out to the littlest detail--the meals and clothes and study and amusements and punishments; for even my superior orphans are sometimes bad. But anyway, they are going to be happy. I think that every one, no matter how many troubles he may have when he grows up, ought to have a happy childhood to look back upon. And if I ever have any children of my own, no matter how unhappy I may be, I am not going to let them have any cares until they grow up. (There goes the chapel bell--I'll finish this letter sometime.)

Thursday

When I came in from laboratory this afternoon, I found a squirrel sitting on the tea table helping himself to almonds. These are the kind of callers we entertain now that warm weather has come and the windows stay open--

Saturday morning

Perhaps you think, last night being Friday, with no classes today, that I passed a nice quiet, readable evening with the set of Stevenson that I bought with my prize money? But if so, you've never attended a girls' college, Daddy dear. Six friends dropped in to make fudge, and one of them dropped the fudge--while it was still liquid--right in the middle of our best rug. We shall never be able to clean up the mess.

I haven't mentioned any lessons of late; but we are still having them every day. It's sort of a relief though, to get away from them and discuss life in the large--rather one-sided discussions that you and I hold, but that's your own fault. You are welcome to answer back anytime you choose.

I've been writing this letter off and on for three days, and I fear by now vous etes bien bored!

Goodbye,

nice Mr. Man,

Judy

Mr. Daddy-Long-Legs Smith,

SIR: Having completed the study of argumentation and the science of dividing a thesis into heads, I have decided to adopt the following form for letter-writing. It contains all necessary facts, but no unnecessary verbiage.

I. We had written examinations this week in:
    A. Chemistry.
    B. History.
II. A new dormitory is being built.
    A. Its material is:
      (a) red brick.
      (b) grey stone.
    B. Its capacity will be:
      (a) one dean, five instructors.
      (b) two hundred girls.
      (c) one housekeeper, three cooks, twenty waitresses,

twenty chambermaids.

III. We had junket for dessert tonight.

IV. I am writing a special topic upon the Sources of Shakespeare's Plays.

V. Lou McMahon slipped and fell this afternoon at basketball, and she:

A. Dislocated her shoulder.

B. Bruised her knee.

VI. I have a new hat trimmed with:

A. Blue velvet ribbon.

B. Two blue quills.

C. Three red pompoms.

VII. It is half past nine.

VIII. Good night.

Judy

2nd June

Dear Daddy-Long-Legs,

You will never guess the nice thing that has happened. The McBrides have asked me to spend the summer at their camp in the Adirondacks! They belong to a sort of club on a lovely little lake in the middle of the woods. The different members have houses made of logs dotted about among the trees, and they go canoeing on the lake, and take long walks through trails to other camps, and have dances once a week in the club house--Jimmie McBride is going to have a college friend visiting him part of the summer, so you see we shall have plenty of men to dance with.

Wasn't it sweet of Mrs. McBride to ask me? It appears that she liked me when I was there for Christmas. Please excuse this being short. It isn't a real letter; it's just to let you know that I'm disposed of for the summer.

Yours,
In a VERY contented frame of mind,
Judy

5th June

Dear Daddy-Long-Legs,

Your secretary man has just written to me saying that Mr. Smith prefers that I should not accept Mrs. McBride's invitation, but should return to Lock Willow the same as last summer.

Why, why, WHY, Daddy?

You don't understand about it. Mrs. McBride does want me, really and truly. I'm not the least bit of trouble in the house. I'm a help. They don't take up many servants, and Sallie an I can do lots of useful things. It's a fine chance for me to learn housekeeping. Every woman ought to understand it, and I only know asylum-keeping.

There aren't any girls our age at the camp, and Mrs. McBride wants me for a companion for Sallie. We are planning to do a lot of reading together. We are going to read all of the books for next year's English and sociology. The Professor said it would be a great help if we would get our reading finished in the summer; and it's so much easier to remember it if we read together and talk it over.

Just to live in the same house with Sallie's mother is an education. She's the most interesting, entertaining, companionable, charming

239

woman in the world; she knows everything. Think how many summers I've spent with Mrs. Lippett and how I'll appreciate the contrast. You needn't be afraid that I'll be crowding them, for their house is made of rubber. When they have a lot of company, they just sprinkle tents about in the woods and turn the boys outside. It's going to be such a nice, healthy summer exercising out of doors every minute. Jimmie McBride is going to teach me how to ride horseback and paddle a canoe, and how to shoot and--oh, lots of things I ought to know. It's the kind of nice, jolly, care-free time that I've never had; and I think every girl deserves it once in her life. Of course I'll do exactly as you say, but please, PLEASE let me go, Daddy. I've never wanted anything so much.

This isn't Jerusha Abbott, the future great author, writing to you. It's just Judy--a girl.

9th June

Mr. John Smith,

SIR: Yours of the 7th inst. at hand. In compliance with the instructions received through your secretary, I leave on Friday next to spend the summer at Lock Willow Farm.

I hope always to remain,
(Miss) Jerusha Abbott

LOCK WILLOW FARM
3rd August

Dear Daddy-Long-Legs,

It has been nearly two months since I wrote, which wasn't nice of me, I know, but I haven't loved you much this summer--you see I'm being frank!

You can't imagine how disappointed I was at having to give up the McBrides' camp. Of course I know that you're my guardian, and that I have to regard your wishes in all matters, but I couldn't see any REASON. It was so distinctly the best thing that could have happened to me. If I had been Daddy, and you had been Judy, I should have said, " Bless you my child, run along and have a good time; see lots of new people and learn lots of new things; live out of doors, and get strong and well and rested for a year of hard work."

But not at all! Just a curt line from your secretary ordering me to Lock Willow.

It's the impersonality of your commands that hurts my feelings. It seems as though, if you felt the tiniest little bit for me the way I feel for you, you'd sometimes send me a message that you'd written with your own hand, instead of those beastly typewritten secretary's notes. If there were the slightest hint that you cared, I'd do anything on earth to please you.

I know that I was to write nice, long, detailed letters without ever expecting any answer. You're living up to your side of the bargain--I'm being educated--and I suppose you're thinking I'm not living up to mine!

But, Daddy, it is a hard bargain. It is, really. I'm so awfully lonely. You are the only person I have to care for, and you are so shadowy.

You're just an imaginary man that I've made up--and probably the real YOU isn't a bit like my imaginary YOU. But you did once, when I was ill in the infirmary, send me a message, and now, when I am feeling awfully forgotten, I get out your card and read it over.

I don't think I am telling you at all what I started to say, which was this:

Although my feelings are still hurt, for it is very humiliating to be picked up and moved about by an arbitrary, peremptory, unreasonable, omnipotent, invisible Providence, still, when a man has been as kind and generous and thoughtful as you have heretofore been towards me, I suppose he has a right to be an arbitrary, peremptory, unreasonable, invisible Providence if he chooses, and so--I'll forgive you and be cheerful again. But I still don't enjoy getting Sallie's letters about the good times they are having in camp!

However--we will draw a veil over that and begin again.

I've been writing and writing this summer; four short stories finished and sent to four different magazines. So you see I'm trying to be an author. I have a workroom fixed in a corner of the attic where Master Jervie used to have his rainy-day playroom. It's in a cool, breezy corner with two dormer windows, and shaded by a maple tree with a family of red squirrels living in a hole.

I'll write a nicer letter in a few days and tell you all the farm news. We need rain.

Yours as ever,
Judy

10th August

Mr. Daddy-Long-Legs,

SIR: I address you from the second crotch in the willow tree by thepool in the pasture. There's a frog croaking underneath, a locust singing overhead and two little "devil down heads" darting up and down the trunk. I've been here for an hour; it's a very comfortable crotch, especially after being upholstered with two sofa cushions. I came up with a pen and tablet hoping to write an immortal short story, but I've been having a dreadful time with my heroine--I CAN't make her behave as I want her to behave; so I've abandoned her for the moment, and am writing to you. (Not much relief though, for I can't make you behave as I want you to, either.)

If you are in that dreadful New York, I wish I could send you some of this lovely, breezy, sunshiny outlook. The country is Heaven after a week of rain.

During our week of rain I sat up in the attic and had an orgy of reading--Stevenson, mostly. He himself is more entertaining than any of the characters in his books; I dare say he made himself into the kind of hero that would look well in print. Don't you think it was perfect of him to spend all the ten thousand dollars his father left, for a yacht, and go sailing off to the South Seas? He lived up to his adventurous creed. If my father had left me ten thousand dollars, I'd do it, too. The thought of Vailima makes me wild. I want to see the tropics. I want to see the whole world. I am going to be a great author, or artist, or actress, or playwright--or whatever sort of a great person I turn out to be. I have a terrible wanderthirst; thevery sight of a map makes me want to put on my hat and take an umbrella and start. "I shall see before I die the palms and temples of the South."

Thursday evening at twilight, sitting on the doorstep

Very hard to get any news into this letter! Judy is becoming so philosophical of late, that she wishes to discourse largely of the world in general, instead of descending to the trivial details of daily life. But if you MUST have news, here it is:

Our nine young pigs waded across the brook and ran away last Tuesday, and only eight came back. We don't want to accuse anyone unjustly, but we suspect that Widow Dowd has one more than she ought to have.

Mr. Weaver has painted his barn and his two silos a bright pumpkin yellow--a very ugly colour, but he says it will wear.

The Brewers have company this week; Mrs. Brewer's sister and two nieces from Ohio.

One of our Rhode Island Reds only brought off three chicks out of fifteen eggs. We can't imagine what was the trouble. Rhode island Reds, in my opinion, are a very inferior breed. I prefer Buff Orpingtons.

The new clerk in the post office at Bonnyrigg Four Corners drank every drop of Jamaica ginger they had in stock--seven dollars' worth—before he was discovered.

Old Ira Hatch has rheumatism and can't work any more; he never saved his money when he was earning good wages, so now he has to live on the town.

There's to be an ice-cream social at the schoolhouse next Saturday evening. Come and bring your families.

I have a new hat that I bought for twenty-five cents at the post office. This is my latest portrait, on my way to rake the hay.[9]

---

9 Please find the illustration in Chinese version.

It's getting too dark to see; anyway, the news is all used up.

Good night,
Judy

Friday

Good morning! Here is some news! What do you think? You'd never, never, never guess who's coming to Lock Willow. A letter to Mrs. Semple from Mr. Pendleton. He's motoring through the Berkshires, and is tired and wants to rest on a nice quiet farm--if he climbs out at her doorstep some night will she have a room ready for him? Maybe he'll stay one week, or maybe two, or maybe three; he'll see how restful it is when he gets here.

Such a flutter as we are in! The whole house is being cleaned and all the curtains washed. I am driving to the Corners this morning to get some new oilcloth for the entry, and two cans of brown floor paint for the hall and back stairs. Mrs. Dowd is engaged to come tomorrow to wash the windows (in the exigency of the moment, we waive our suspicions in regard to the piglet). You might think, from this account of our activities, that the house was not already immaculate; but I assure you it was! Whatever Mrs. Semple's limitations, she is a HOUSEKEEPER.

But isn't it just like a man, Daddy? He doesn't give the remotest hint as to whether he will land on the doorstep today, or two weeks from today. We shall live in a perpetual breathlessness until he comes—and if he doesn't hurry, the cleaning may all have to be done over again.

There's Amasai waiting below with the buckboard and Grover. I

drive alone--but if you could see old Grove, you wouldn't be worried as to my safety.

With my hand on my heart--farewell.

Judy

PS. Isn't that a nice ending? I got it out of Stevenson's letters.

Saturday

Good morning again! I didn't get this ENVELOPED yesterday before the postman came, so I'll add some more. We have one mail a day at twelve o'clock. Rural delivery is a blessing to the farmers! Our postman not only delivers letters, but he runs errands for us in town, at five cents an errand. Yesterday he brought me some shoe-strings and a jar of cold cream (I sunburned all the skin off my nose before I got my new hat) and a blue Windsor tie and a bottle of blacking all for ten cents. That was an unusual bargain, owing to the largeness of my order.

Also he tells us what is happening in the Great World. Several people on the route take daily papers, and he reads them as he jogs along, and repeats the news to the ones who don't subscribe. So in case a war breaks out between the United States and Japan, or the president is assassinated, or Mr. Rockefeller leaves a million dollars to the John Grier Home, you needn't bother to write; I'll hear it anyway.

No sign yet of Master Jervie. But you should see how clean our house is--and with what anxiety we wipe our feet before we step in!

I hope he'll come soon; I am longing for someone to talk to. Mrs. Semple, to tell you the truth, gets rather monotonous. She never lets ideas interrupt the easy flow of her conversation. It's a funny thing about the people here. Their world is just this single hilltop. They are not a bit universal, if you know what I mean. It's exactly the same as at the John Grier Home. Our ideas there were bounded by the four sides of the iron fence, only I didn't mind it so much because I was younger, and was so awfully busy. By the time I'd got all my beds made and my babies' faces washed and had gone to school and come home and had washed their faces again and darned their stockings and mended Freddie Perkins's trousers (he tore them every day of his life) and learned my lessons in between--I was ready to go to bed, and I didn't notice any lack of social intercourse. But after two years in a conversational college, I do miss it; and I shall be glad to see somebody who speaks my language.

I really believe I've finished, Daddy. Nothing else occurs to me at the moment--I'll try to write a longer letter next time.

Yours always,
Judy

PS. The lettuce hasn't done at all well this year. It was so dry early in the season.

25th August

Well, Daddy, Master Jervie's here. And such a nice time as we're having! At least I am, and I think he is, too--he has been here tendays and he doesn't show any signs of going. The way Mrs. Semple pampers that man is scandalous. If she indulged him as much when he was a baby, I don't know how he ever turned out so well.

He and I eat at a little table set on the side porch, or sometimes under the trees, or--when it rains or is cold--in the best parlour. He

just picks out the spot he wants to eat in and Carrie trots after him with the table. Then if it has been an awful nuisance, and she has had to carry the dishes very far, she finds a dollar under the sugar bowl.

He is an awfully companionable sort of man, though you would never believe it to see him casually; he looks at first glance like a true Pendleton, but he isn't in the least. He is just as simple and unaffected and sweet as he can be--that seems a funny way to describe a man, but it's true. He's extremely nice with the farmers around here; he meets them in a sort of man-to-man fashion that disarms them immediately. They were very suspicious at first. They didn't care for his clothes! And I will say that his clothes are rather amazing. He wears knickerbockers and pleated jackets and white flannels and riding clothes with puffed trousers. Whenever he comes down in anything new, Mrs. Semple, beaming with pride, walks around and views him from every angle, and urges him to be careful where he sits down; she is so afraid he will pick up some dust. It bores him dreadfully. He's always ssaying to her:

"Run along, Lizzie, and tend to your work. You can't boss me any longer. I've grown up."

It's awfully funny to think of that great big, long-legged man (he's nearly as long-legged as you, Daddy) ever sitting in Mrs. Semple's lap and having his face washed. Particularly funny when you see her lap! She has two laps now, and three chins. But he says that once she was thin and wiry and spry and could run faster than he.

Such a lot of adventures we're having! We've explored the country for miles, and I've learned to fish with funny little flies made of feathers. Also to shoot with a rifle and a revolver. Also to ride horseback--there's an astonishing amount of life in old Grove. We fed him on oats for three days, and he shied at a calf and almost ran away with me.

Wednesday

We climbed Sky Hill Monday afternoon. That's a mountain near here; not an awfully high mountain, perhaps--no snow on the summit--but at least you are pretty breathless when you reach the top. The lower slopes are covered with woods, but the top is just piled rocks and open moor. We stayed up for the sunset and built a fire and cooked our supper. Master Jervie did the cooking; he said he knew how better than me and he did, too, because he's used to camping. Then we came down by moonlight, and, when we reached the wood trail where it was dark, by the light of an electric bulb that he had in his pocket. It was such fun! He laughed and joked all the way and talked about interesting things. He's read all the books I've ever read, and a lot of others besides. It's astonishing how many different things he knows.

We went for a long tramp this morning and got caught in a storm. Our clothes were drenched before we reached home but our spirits not even damp. You should have seen Mrs. Semple's face when we dripped into her kitchen.

"Oh, Master Jervie--Miss Judy! You are soaked through. Dear! Dear! What shall I do? That nice new coat is perfectly ruined."

She was awfully funny; you would have thought that we were ten years old, and she a distracted mother. I was afraid for a while that we weren't going to get any jam for tea.

Sunday

It's Sunday night now, about eleven o'clock, and I am supposed to be getting some beauty sleep, but I had black coffee for dinner,

so—no beauty sleep for me!

This morning, said Mrs. Semple to Mr. Pendleton, with a very determined accent:

"We have to leave here at a quarter past ten in order to get to church by eleven."

"Very well, Lizzie," said Master Jervie, "you have the buggy ready, and if I'm not dressed, just go on without waiting."

"We'll wait," said she.

"As you please," said he, "only don't keep the horses standing too long."

Then while she was dressing, he told Carrie to pack up a lunch, and he told me to scramble into my walking clothes; and we slipped out the back way and went fishing.

It discommoded the household dreadfully, because Lock Willow of a Sunday dines at two. But he ordered dinner at seven--he orders meals whenever he chooses; you would think the place were a restaurant—and that kept Carrie and Amasai from going driving. But he said it was all the better because it wasn't proper for them to go driving without a chaperon; and anyway, he wanted the horses himself to take me driving. Did you ever hear anything so funny?

And poor Mrs. Semple believes that people who go fishing on Sundays go afterwards to a sizzling hot hell! She is awfully troubled to think that she didn't train him better when he was small and helpless and she had the chance. Besides--she wished to show him off in church.

Anyway, we had our fishing (he caught four little ones) and we cooked them on a camp-fire for lunch. They kept falling off our spiked sticks into the fire, so they tasted a little ashy, but we ate them. We got home at four and went driving at five and had dinner at seven, and at ten I was sent to bed and here I am, writing to you.

I am getting a little sleepy, though.

Good night.

Here is a picture of the one fish I caught.[10]

Ship Ahoy, Cap'n Long-Legs!

Avast! Belay! Yo, ho, ho, and a bottle of rum. Guess what I'm reading? Our conversation these past two days has been nautical and piratical. Isn't Treasure Island fun? Did you ever read it, or wasn't it written when you were a boy? Stevenson only got thirty pounds for the serial rights--I don't believe it pays to be a great author. Maybe I'll be a school-teacher.

I've been writing this letter for two weeks, and I think it's about long enough. Never say, Daddy, that I don't give details. I wish you were here, too; we'd all have such a jolly time together. I like my different friends to know each other. I wanted to ask Mr. Pendleton if he knew you in New York--I should think he might; you must move in about the same exalted social circles, and you are both interested in reforms and things--but I couldn't, for I don't know your real name.

It's the silliest thing I ever heard of, not to know your name. Mrs. Lippett warned me that you were eccentric. I should think so!

Affectionately,
Judy

PS. On reading this over, I find that it isn't all Stevenson. There are one or two glancing references to Master Jervie.

---

10 Please find the illustration in Chinese version.

Daddy-Long-Legs

10th September

Dear Daddy,

He has gone, and we are missing him! When you get accustomed to people or places or ways of living, and then have them snatched away, it does leave an awfully empty, gnawing sort of sensation. I'm finding Mrs. Semple's conversation pretty unseasoned food.

College opens in two weeks and I shall be glad to begin work again. I have worked quite a lot this summer though--six short stories and seven poems. Those I sent to the magazines all came back with the most courteous promptitude. But I don't mind. It's good practice. Master Jervie read them--he brought in the post, so I couldn't help his knowing--and he said they were DREADFUL. They showed that I didn't have the slightest idea of what I was talking about. (Master Jervie doesn't let politeness interfere with truth.) But the last one I did--just a little sketch laid in college--he said wasn't bad; and he had it typewritten, and I sent it to a magazine. They've had it two weeks; maybe they're thinking it over.

You should see the sky! There's the queerest orange-coloured light over everything. We're going to have a storm.

A storm is awfully disturbing in the country. You are always having to think of so many things that are out of doors and getting spoiled.

Thursday

Daddy! Daddy!

What do you think? The postman has just come with two letters.

1st. My story is accepted. $50.

ALORS! I'm an AUTHOR.

2nd. A letter from the college secretary. I'm to have a scholarship for two years that will cover board and tuition. It was founded for " marked proficiency in English with general excellency in other lines." And I've won it! I applied for it before I left, but I didn't have an idea I'd get it, on account of my Freshman bad work in maths and Latin. But it seems I've made it up. I am awfully glad, Daddy, because now I won't be such a burden to you. The monthly allowance will be all I'll need, and maybe I can earn that with writing or tutoring or something.

I'm LONGING to go back and begin work.

Yours ever,
Jerusha Abbott,

Author of When the Sophomores Won the Game.

For sale at all newsstands, price ten cents.

26th September

Dear Daddy-Long-Legs,

Back at college again and an upper classman. Our study is better than ever this year--faces the South with two huge windows and oh! So furnished. Julia, with an unlimited allowance, arrived two days early and was attacked with a fever for settling.

We have new wall paper and oriental rugs and mahogany chairs— not painted mahogany which made us sufficiently happy last year, but real. It's very gorgeous, but I don't feel as though I belonged in it; I'm nervous all the time for fear I'll get an ink spot in the wrong place.

And, Daddy, I found your letter waiting for me--pardon--I mean your secretary's.

Will you kindly convey to me a comprehensible reason why I should not accept that scholarship? I don't understand your objection in the least. But anyway, it won't do the slightest good for you to object, for I've already accepted it and I am not going to change! That sounds a little impertinent, but I don't mean it so.

I suppose you feel that when you set out to educate me, you'd like to finish the work, and put a neat period, in the shape of a diploma, at the end.

But look at it just a second from my point of view. I shall owe my education to you just as much as though I let you pay for the whole of it, but I won't be quite so much indebted. I know that you don't want me to return the money, but nevertheless, I am going to want to do it, if I possibly can; and winning this scholarship makes it so much easier. I was expecting to spend the rest of my life in paying my debts, but now I shall only have to spend one-half of the rest of it.

I hope you understand my position and won't be cross. The allowance I shall still most gratefully accept. It requires an allowance to live up to Julia and her furniture! I wish that she had been reared to simpler tastes, or else that she were not my room-mate.

This isn't much of a letter; I meant to have written a lot--but I've been hemming four window curtains and three portieres (I'm glad you can't see the length of the stitches), and polishing a brass desk set with tooth powder (very uphill work), and sawing off picture wire with manicure scissors, and unpacking four boxes of books, and putting away two trunkfuls of clothes (it doesn't seem believable that Jerusha Abbott owns two trunks full of clothes, but she does!) and welcoming back fifty dear friends in between.

Opening day is a joyous occasion!

Good night, Daddy dear, and don't be annoyed because your chick is wanting to scratch for herself. She's growing up into an awfully energetic little hen--with a very determined cluck and lots of beautiful feathers (all due to you).

Affectionately,
Judy

9th November

Dear Daddy-Long-Legs,

Julia Pendleton has invited me to visit her for the Christmas holidays. How does that strike you, Mr. Smith? Fancy Jerusha Abbott, of the John Grier Home, sitting at the tables of the rich. I don't know why Julia wants me--she seems to be getting quite attached to me of late. I should, to tell the truth, very much prefer going to Sallie's, but Julia asked me first, so if I go anywhere it must be to New York instead of to Worcester. I'm rather awed at the prospect of meeting Pendletons EN MASSE, and also I'd have to get a lot of new clothes--so, Daddy dear, if you write that you would prefer having me remain quietly at college, I will bow to your wishes with my usual sweet docility.

I'm engaged at odd moments with the Life and Letters of Thomas Huxley--it makes nice, light reading to pick up between times. Do you know what an archaeopteryx is? It's a bird. And a stereognathus? I'm not sure myself, but I think it's a missing link, like a bird with teeth or a lizard with wings. No, it isn't either; I've just looked in the book. It's a mesozoic mammal.

I've elected economics this year--very illuminating subject. When I finish that I'm going to take Charity and Reform; then, Mr. Trustee, I'll know just how an orphan asylum ought to be run. Don't you think I'd make an admirable voter if I had my rights? I was twenty-one last week. This is an awfully wasteful country to throw away such an honest, educated, conscientious, intelligent citizen as I would be.

Yours always,
Judy

7th December

Dear Daddy-Long-Legs,

Thank you for permission to visit Julia--I take it that silence means consent.

Such a social whirl as we've been having! The Founder's dance came last week--this was the first year that any of us could attend; only upper classmen being allowed.

I invited Jimmie McBride, and Sallie invited his room-mate at Princeton, who visited them last summer at their camp--an awfully nice man with red hair--and Julia invited a man from New York, not very exciting, but socially irreproachable. He is connected with the De la Mater Chichesters. Perhaps that means something to you? It doesn't illuminate me to any extent.

However--our guests came Friday afternoon in time for tea in the senior corridor, and then dashed down to the hotel for dinner. The hotel was so full that they slept in rows on the billiard tables, they say. Jimmie McBride says that the next time he is bidden to a social event in this college, he is going to bring one of their Adirondack tents and pitch it on the campus.

At seven-thirty they came back for the President's reception and dance. Our functions commence early! We had the men's cards all made out ahead of time, and after every dance, we'd leave them in groups, under the letter that stood for their names, so that they could be readily found by their next partners. Jimmie McBride, for example, would stand patiently under "M" until he was claimed. (At least, he ought to have stood patiently, but he kept wandering off and getting mixed with "R" s' and "S" s' and all sorts of letters.) I found him a very difficult guest; he was sulky because he had only three dances with me. He said he was bashful about dancing with girls he didn't know!

The next morning we had a glee club concert--and who do you think wrote the funny new song composed for the occasion? It's the truth. She did. Oh, I tell you, Daddy, your little foundling is getting to be quite a prominent person!

Anyway, our gay two days were great fun, and I think the men enjoyed it. Some of them were awfully perturbed at first at the prospect off acing one thousand girls; but they got acclimated very quickly. Our two Princeton men had a beautiful time--at least they politely said they had, and they've invited us to their dance next spring. We've accepted, so please don't object, Daddy dear.

Julia and Sallie and I all had new dresses. Do you want to hear about them? Julia's was cream satin and gold embroidery and she wore purple orchids. It was a DREAM and came from Paris, and cost a million dollars.

Sallie's was pale blue trimmed with Persian embroidery, and went beautifully with red hair. It didn't cost quite a million, but was just as effective as Julia's.

Mine was pale pink crepe de chine trimmed with ecru lace and

rose satin. And I carried crimson roses which J. McB. sent (Sallie having told him what colour to get). And we all had satin slippers and silk stockings and chiffon scarfs to match.

You must be deeply impressed by these millinery details.

One can't help thinking, Daddy, what a colourless life a man is forced to lead, when one reflects that chiffon and Venetian point and hand embroidery and Irish crochet are to him mere empty words. Whereas a woman--whether she is interested in babies or microbes or husbands or poetry or servants or parallelograms or gardens or Plato or bridge—is fundamentally and always interested in clothes.

It's the one touch of nature that makes the whole world kin. (That isn't original. I got it out of one of Shakespeare's plays).

However, to resume. Do you want me to tell you a secret that I've lately discovered? And will you promise not to think me vain? Then listen:

I'm pretty.

I am, really. I'd be an awful idiot not to know it with three looking-glasses in the room.

A Friend

PS. This is one of those wicked anonymous letters you read about in novels.

20th December

Dear Daddy-Long-Legs,

I've just a moment, because I must attend two classes, pack a trunk and a suit-case, and catch the four-o'clock train--but I couldn't go without sending a word to let you know how much I appreciate my Christmas box.

I love the furs and the necklace and the Liberty scarf and the gloves and handkerchiefs and books and purse--and most of all I love you! But Daddy, you have no business to spoil me this way. I'm only human—and a girl at that. How can I keep my mind sternly fixed on a studious career, when you deflect me with such worldly frivolities?

I have strong suspicions now as to which one of the John Grier Trustees used to give the Christmas tree and the Sunday ice-cream. He was nameless, but by his works I know him! You deserve to be happy for all the good things you do.

Goodbye, and a very merry Christmas.

Yours always,

Judy

PS. I am sending a slight token, too. Do you think you would like her if you knew her?

11th January

Dear Daddy-Long-Legs,

I meant to write to you from the city, Daddy, but New York is an engrossing place.

I had an interesting--and illuminating--time, but I'm glad I don't belong to such a family! I should truly rather have the John Grier Home for a background. Whatever the drawbacks of my bringing up, there was at least no pretence about it. I know now what people mean when they say they are weighed down by Things. The material

atmosphere of that house was crushing; I didn't draw a deep breath until I was on an express train coming back. All the furniture was carved and upholstered and gorgeous; the people I met were beautifully dressed and low-voiced and well-bred, but it's the truth, Daddy, I never heard one word of real talk from the time we arrived until we left. I don't think an idea ever entered the front door.

Mrs. Pendleton never thinks of anything but jewels and dressmakers and social engagements. She did seem a different kind of mother from Mrs. McBride! If I ever marry and have a family, I'm going to make them as exactly like the McBrides as I can. Not for all the money in the world would I ever let any children of mine develop into Pendletons. Maybe it isn't polite to criticize people you've been visiting? If it isn't, please excuse. This is very confidential, between you and me.

I only saw Master Jervie once when he called at tea time, and then I didn't have a chance to speak to him alone. It was really disappointing after our nice time last summer. I don't think he cares much for his relatives--and I am sure they don't care much for him!

I've seen loads of theatres and hotels and beautiful houses. My mind is a confused jumble of onyx and gilding and mosaic floors and palms. I'm still pretty breathless but I am glad to get back to college and my books--I believe that I really am a student; this atmosphere of academic calm I find more bracing than New York. College is a very satisfying sort of life; the books and study and regular classes keep you alive mentally, and then when your mind gets tired, you have the gymnasium and outdoor athletics, and always plenty of congenial friends who are thinking about the same things you are. We spend a whole evening in nothing but talk--talk--talk--and go to bed with a very uplifted feeling, as though we had settled permanently some pressing world problems. And filling in every crevice, there is always such a lot of nonsense--just silly jokes about the little things that come up but very satisfying. We do appreciate our own witticisms!

It isn't the great big pleasures that count the most; it's making a great deal out of the little ones--I've discovered the true secret of happiness, Daddy, and that is to live in the now. Not to be for ever regretting the past, or anticipating the future; but to get the most that you can out of this very instant. It's like farming. You can have extensive farming and intensive farming; well, I am going to have intensive living after this. I'm going to enjoy every second, and I'm going to KNOW I'm enjoying it while I'm enjoying it. Most people don't live; they just race. They are trying to reach some goal far away on the horizon, and in the heat of the going they get so breathless and panting that they lose all sight of the beautiful, tranquil country they are passing through; and then the first thing they know, they are old and worn out, and it doesn't make any difference whether they've reached the goal or not. I've decided to sit down by the way and pileup a lot of little happinesses, even if I never become a Great Author. Did you ever know such a philosopheress as I am developing into?

Yours ever,
Judy

PS. It's raining cats and dogs tonight. Two puppies and a kitten have just landed on the window-sill.

11th February

Dear D.-L.-L.,

Don't be insulted because this is so short. It isn't a letter; it's just a LINE to say that I'm going to write a letter pretty soon when examinations are over. It is not only necessary that I pass, but pass WELL. I have a scholarship to live up to.

Yours, studying hard,
J. A.

5th March

Dear Daddy-Long-Legs,

President Cuyler made a speech this evening about the modern generation being flippant and superficial. He says that we are losing the old ideals of earnest endeavour and true scholarship; and particularly is this falling-off noticeable in our disrespectful attitude towards organized authority. We no longer pay a seemly deference to our superiors.

I came away from chapel very sober.

Am I too familiar, Daddy? Ought I to treat you with more dignity and aloofness? --Yes, I'm sure I ought. I'll begin again.

My Dear Mr. Smith,

You will be pleased to hear that I passed successfully my mid-year examinations, and am now commencing work in the new

semester. I am leaving chemistry--having completed the course in qualitative analysis--and am entering upon the study of biology. I approach this subject with some hesitation, as I understand that we dissect angleworms and frogs.

I am attending gymnasium very regularly of late. A proctor system has been devised, and failure to comply with the rules causes a great deal of inconvenience. The gymnasium is equipped with a very beautiful swimming tank of cement and marble, the gift of a former graduate. My room-mate, Miss McBride, has given me her bathing-suit (it shrank so that she can no longer wear it) and I am about to begin swimming lessons.

We had delicious pink ice-cream for dessert last night. Only vegetable dyes are used in colouring the food. The college is very much opposed, both from aesthetic and hygienic motives, to the use of aniline dyes.

The weather of late has been ideal--bright sunshine and clouds interspersed with a few welcome snow-storms. I and my companions have enjoyed our walks to and from classes--particularly from.

Trusting, my dear Mr. Smith, that this will find you in your usual good health.

I remain, Most cordially yours,
Jerusha Abbott

24th April

Dear Daddy,

Spring has come again! You should see how lovely the campus is. I think you might come and look at it for yourself. Master Jervie dropped in again last Friday--but he chose a most unpropitious time,

for Sallie and Julia and I were just running to catch a train. And where do you think we were going? To Princeton, to attend a dance and a ball game, if you please! I didn't ask you if I might go, because I had a feeling that your secretary would say no. But it was entirely regular; we had leave-of-absence from college, and Mrs. McBride chaperoned us. We had a charming time--but I shall have to omit details; they are too many and complicated.

Saturday

Up before dawn! The night watchman called us--six of us--and we made coffee in a chafing dish (you never saw so many grounds!) and walked two miles to the top of One Tree Hill to see the sun rise. We had to scramble up the last slope! The sun almost beat us! And perhaps you think we didn't bring back appetites to breakfast!

Dear me, Daddy, I seem to have a very ejaculatory style today; this page is peppered with exclamations.

I meant to have written a lot about the budding trees and the new cinder path in the athletic field, and the awful lesson we have in biology for tomorrow, and the new canoes on the lake, and Catherine Prentiss who has pneumonia, and Prexy's Angora kitten that strayed from home and has been boarding in Fergussen Hall for two weeks until a chambermaid reported it, and about my three new dresses--white and pink and blue polka dots with a hat to match--but I am too sleepy. I am always making this an excuse, am I not? But a girls' college is a busy place and we do get tired by the end of the day! Particularly when the day begins at dawn.

Affectionately,
Judy

15th May

Dear Daddy-Long-Legs,

The accompanying illustration is hereby reproduced for the first time[11]. It looks like a spider on the end of a string, but it isn't at all; it's a picture of me learning to swim in the tank in the gymnasium.

The instructor hooks a rope into a ring in the back of my belt, and runs it through a pulley in the ceiling. It would be a beautiful system if one had perfect confidence in the probity of one's instructor. I'm always afraid, though, that she will let the rope get slack, so I keep one anxious eye on her and swim with the other, and with this divided interest I do not make the progress that I otherwise might.

Very miscellaneous weather we're having of late. It was raining when I commenced and now the sun is shining. Sallie and I are going out to play tennis--thereby gaining exemption from Gym.

A week later

I should have finished this letter long ago, but I didn't. You don't mind, do you, Daddy, if I'm not very regular? I really do love to write to you; it gives me such a respectable feeling of having some family. Would you like me to tell you something? You are not the only man to whom I write letters. There are two others! I have been receiving beautiful long letters this winter from Master Jervie (with typewritten envelopes so Julia won't recognize the writing). Did you ever hear

11 Please find the illustration in Chinese version.

anything so shocking? And every week or so a very scrawly epistle, usually on yellow tablet paper, arrives from Princeton. All of which I answer with business-like promptness. So you see--I am not so different from other girls--I get letters, too.

Did I tell you that I have been elected a member of the Senior Dramatic Club? Very recherche organization. Only seventy-five members out of one thousand. Do you think as a consistent Socialist that I ought to belong? What do you suppose is at present engaging my attention in sociology? I am writing (figurez vous!) a paper on the Care of Dependent Children. The Professor shuffled up his subjects and dealt them out promiscuously, and that fell to me. C'est drole ca n'est pas?

There goes the gong for dinner. I'll post this as I pass the box.

Affectionately,
J.

4th June

Dear Daddy,

Very busy time--commencement in ten days, examinations tomorrow; lotsof studying, lots of packing, and the outdoor world so lovely that ithurts you to stay inside.

But never mind, vacation's coming. Julia is going abroad this summer--it makes the fourth time. No doubt about it, Daddy, goods are not distributed evenly. Sallie, as usual, goes to the Adirondacks. And what do you think I am going to do? You may have three guesses. Lock Willow? Wrong. The Adirondacks with Sallie? Wrong. (I'll never attempt that again; I was discouraged last year.) Can't you guess anything else? You're not very inventive. I'll tell you, Daddy, if you'll promise not to make a lot of objections. I warn your secretary in advance that my mind is made up.

I am going to spend the summer at the seaside with a Mrs. Charles Paterson and tutor her daughter who is to enter college in the autumn. I met her through the McBrides, and she is a very charming woman. I am to give lessons in English and Latin to the younger daughter, too, but I shall have a little time to myself, and I shall be earning fifty dollars a month! Doesn't that impress you as a perfectly exorbitant amount? She offered it; I should have blushed to ask for more than twenty-five.

I finish at Magnolia (that's where she lives) the first of September, and shall probably spend the remaining three weeks at Lock Willow—I should like to see the Semples again and all the friendly animals.

How does my programme strike you, Daddy? I am getting quite independent, you see. You have put me on my feet and I think I can almost walk alone by now.

Princeton commencement and our examinations exactly coincide--which is an awful blow. Sallie and I did so want to get away in time for it, but of course that is utterly impossible.

Goodbye, Daddy. Have a nice summer and come back in the autumn rested and ready for another year of work. (That's what you ought to be writing to me!) I haven't any idea what you do in the summer, or how you amuse yourself. I can't visualize your surroundings. Do you play golf or hunt or ride horseback or just sit in the sun and meditate?

Anyway, whatever it is, have a good time and don't forget Judy.

Daddy-Long-Legs

10th June

Dear Daddy,

This is the hardest letter I ever wrote, but I have decided what I must do, and there isn't going to be any turning back. It is very sweet and generous and dear of you to wish to send me to Europe this summer—for the moment I was intoxicated by the idea; but sober second thoughts said no. It would be rather illogical of me to refuse to take your money for college, and then use it instead just for amusement! You mustn't get me used to too many luxuries. One doesn't miss what one has never had; but it's awfully hard going without things after one has commenced thinking they are his--hers (English language needs another pronoun) by natural right. Living with Sallie and Julia is an awful strain on my stoical philosophy. They have both had things from the time they were babies; they accept happiness as a matter of course. The World, they think, owes them everything they want. Maybe the World does--in any case, it seems to acknowledge the debt and pay up. But as for me, it owes me nothing, and distinctly told me so in the beginning. I have no right to borrow on credit, for there will come a time when the World will repudiate my claim.

I seem to be floundering in a sea of metaphor--but I hope you grasp my meaning? Anyway, I have a very strong feeling that the only honest thing for me to do is to teach this summer and begin to support myself.

MAGNOLIA
Four days later

I'd got just that much written, when--what do you think happened? The maid arrived with Master Jervie's card. He is going abroad too this summer; not with Julia and her family, but entirely by himself I told him that you had invited me to go with a lady who is chaperoning a party of girls. He knows about you, Daddy. That is, he knows that my father and mother are dead, and that a kind gentleman is sending me to college; I simply didn't have the courage to tell him about the John Grier Home and all the rest. He thinks that you are my guardian and a perfectly legitimate old family friend. I have never told him that I didn't know you--that would seem too queer!

Anyway, he insisted on my going to Europe. He said that it was a necessary part of my education and that I mustn't think of refusing. Also, that he would be in Paris at the same time, and that we would runaway from the chaperon occasionally and have dinner together at nice, funny, foreign restaurants.

Well, Daddy, it did appeal to me! I almost weakened; if he hadn't been so dictatorial, maybe I should have entirely weakened. I can be enticed step by step, but I WON't be forced. He said I was a silly, foolish, irrational, quixotic, idiotic, stubborn child (those are a few of his abusive adjectives; the rest escape me), and that I didn't know what was good for me; I ought to let older people judge. We almost quarrelled--I am not sure but that we entirely did!

In any case, I packed my trunk fast and came up here. I thought I'd better see my bridges in flames behind me before I finished writing to you. They are entirely reduced to ashes now. Here I am at Cliff Top(the name of Mrs. Paterson's cottage) with my trunk unpacked and Florence (the little one) already struggling with first declension nouns.

And it bids fair to be a struggle! She is a most uncommonly spoiled child; I shall have to teach her first how to study--she has never in her life concentrated on anything more difficult than ice-cream soda water.

We use a quiet corner of the cliffs for a schoolroom--Mrs. Paterson wishes me to keep them out of doors--and I will say that I find it difficult to concentrate with the blue sea before me and ships a-sailing by! And when I think I might be on one, sailing off to foreign lands--but I WON't let myself think of anything but Latin Grammar.

So you see, Daddy, I am already plunged into work with my eyes persistently set against temptation. Don't be cross with me, please, and don't think that I do not appreciate your kindness, for I do--always--always. The only way I can ever repay you is by turning out a Very Useful Citizen (Are women citizens? I don't suppose they are.) Anyway, a Very Useful Person. And when you look at me you can say, "I gave that Very Useful Person to the world."

That sounds well, doesn't it, Daddy? But I don't wish to mislead you. The feeling often comes over me that I am not at all remarkable; it is fun to plan a career, but in all probability I shan't turn out a bit different from any other ordinary person. I may end by marrying an undertaker and being an inspiration to him in his work.

Yours ever,
Judy

19th August

Dear Daddy-Long-Legs,

My window looks out on the loveliest landscape--ocean-scape, rather--nothing but water and rocks.

The summer goes. I spend the morning with Latin and English and algebra and my two stupid girls. I don't know how Marion is ever going to get into college, or stay in after she gets there. And as for Florence, she is hopeless--but oh! such a little beauty. I don't suppose it matters in the least whether they are stupid or not so longas they are pretty? One can't help thinking, though, how their conversation will bore their husbands, unless they are fortunate enough to obtain stupid husbands. I suppose that's quite possible; the world seems to be filled with stupid men; I've met a number this summer.

In the afternoon we take a walk on the cliffs, or swim, if the tide is right. I can swim in salt water with the utmost ease you see my education is already being put to use!

A letter comes from Mr. Jervis Pendleton in Paris, rather a short concise letter; I'm not quite forgiven yet for refusing to follow his advice. However, if he gets back in time, he will see me for a few days at Lock Willow before college opens, and if I am very nice and sweet and docile, I shall (I am led to infer) be received into favour again.

Also a letter from Sallie. She wants me to come to their camp for two weeks in September. Must I ask your permission, or haven't I yet arrived at the place where I can do as I please? Yes, I am sure I have-- I'm a Senior, you know. Having worked all summer, I feel like taking a little healthful recreation; I want to see the Adirondacks; I want to see Sallie; I want to see Sallie's brother--he's going to teach me to canoe-- and (we come to my chief motive, which is mean) I want Master Jervie to arrive at Lock Willow and find me not there.

I MUST show him that he can't dictate to me. No one can dictate to me but you, Daddy--and you can't always! I'm off for the woods.

Judy

CAMP MCBRIDE
6th September

Dear Daddy,

Your letter didn't come in time (I am pleased to say). If you wish your instructions to be obeyed, you must have your secretary transmit them in less than two weeks. As you observe, I am here, and have been for five days.

The woods are fine, and so is the camp, and so is the weather, and so are the McBrides, and so is the whole world. I'm very happy!

There's Jimmie calling for me to come canoeing. Goodbye--sorry to have disobeyed, but why are you so persistent about not wanting me to play a little? When I've worked all the summer I deserve two weeks. You are awfully dog-in-the-mangerish.

However--I love you still, Daddy, in spite of all your faults.

Judy

3rd October

Dear Daddy-Long-Legs,

Back at college and a Senior--also editor of the Monthly. It doesn't seem possible, does it, that so sophisticated a person, just four years ago, was an inmate of the John Grier Home? We do arrive fast in America!

What do you think of this? A note from Master Jervie directed to Lock Willow and forwarded here. He's sorry, but he finds that he can't getup there this autumn; he has accepted an invitation to go yachting with some friends. Hopes I've had a nice summer and am enjoying the country.

And he knew all the time that I was with the McBrides, for Julia told him so! You men ought to leave intrigue to women; you haven't a light enough touch.

Julia has a trunkful of the most ravishing new clothes--an evening gown of rainbow Liberty crepe that would be fitting raiment for the angels in Paradise. And I thought that my own clothes this year were unprecedentedly (is there such a word?) beautiful. I copied Mrs. Paterson's wardrobe with the aid of a cheap dressmaker, and though the gowns didn't turn out quite twins of the originals, I was entirely happy until Julia unpacked. But now--I live to see Paris!

Dear Daddy, aren't you glad you're not a girl? I suppose you think that the fuss we make over clothes is too absolutely silly? It is. No doubt about it. But it's entirely your fault.

Did you ever hear about the learned Herr Professor who regarded unnecessary adornment with contempt and favoured sensible, utilitarian clothes for women? His wife, who was an obliging creature, adopted "dress reform." And what do you think he did? He eloped with a chorus girl.

Yours ever,
Judy

17th November

Dear Daddy-Long-Legs,

Such a blight has fallen over my literary career. I don't know whether to tell you or not, but I would like some sympathy--silent

sympathy, please; don't re-open the wound by referring to it in your next letter.

I've been writing a book, all last winter in the evenings, and all the summer when I wasn't teaching Latin to my two stupid children. I just finished it before college opened and sent it to a publisher. He kept it two months, and I was certain he was going to take it; but yesterday morning an express parcel came (thirty cents due) and there it was back again with a letter from the publisher, a very nice, fatherly letter--but frank! He said he saw from the address that I was still at college, and if I would accept some advice, he would suggest that I put all of my energy into my lessons and wait until I graduated before beginning to write. He enclosed his reader's opinion. Here it is:

"Plot highly improbable. Characterization exaggerated. Conversation unnatural. A good deal of humour but not always in the best of taste. Tell her to keep on trying, and in time she may produce a real book."

Not on the whole flattering, is it, Daddy? And I thought I was making a notable addition to American literature. I did truly. I was planning to surprise you by writing a great novel before I graduated. I collected the material for it while I was at Julia's last Christmas. But I dare say the editor is right. Probably two weeks was not enough in which to observe the manners and customs of a great city.

I took it walking with me yesterday afternoon, and when I came to the gas house, I went in and asked the engineer if I might borrow his furnace. He politely opened the door, and with my own hands I chucked it in. I felt as though I had cremated my only child!

I went to bed last night utterly dejected; I thought I was never going to amount to anything, and that you had thrown away your money for nothing. But what do you think? I woke up this morning with a beautiful new plot in my head, and I've been going about all day planning my characters, just as happy as I could be. No one can ever accuse me of being a pessimist! If I had a husband and twelve children swallowed by an earthquake one day, I'd bob up smilingly the next morning and commence to look for another set.

Affectionately,
Judy

14th December

Dear Daddy-Long-Legs,

I dreamed the funniest dream last night. I thought I went into a bookstore and the clerk brought me a new book named The Life and Letters of Judy Abbott. I could see it perfectly plainly--red cloth binding with a picture of the John Grier Home on the cover, and my portrait for a frontispiece with, "Very truly yours, Judy Abbott," written below. But just as I was turning to the end to read the inscription on my tombstone, I woke up. It was very annoying! I almost found out whom I'm going to marry and when I'm going to die.

Don't you think it would be interesting if you really could read the story of your life--written perfectly truthfully by an omniscient author? And suppose you could only read it on this condition: that you would never forget it, but would have to go through life knowing ahead of time exactly how everything you did would turn out, and foreseeing to the exact hour the time when you would die. How many people do you suppose would have the courage to read it then? or how many could suppress their curiosity sufficiently to escape from reading it, even at the price of having to live without hope and

without surprises?

Do you believe in free will? I do--unreservedly. I don't agree at all with the philosophers who think that every action is the absolutely inevitable and automatic resultant of an aggregation of remote causes. That's the most immoral doctrine I ever heard--nobody would be to blame for anything. If a man believed in fatalism, he would naturally just sit down and say, "The Lord's will be done," and continue to sit until he fell over dead.

I believe absolutely in my own free will and my own power to accomplish--and that is the belief that moves mountains. You watch me become a great author! I have four chapters of my new book finished and five more drafted.

This is a very abstruse letter--does your head ache, Daddy? I think we'll stop now and make some fudge. I'm sorry I can't send you apiece; it will be unusually good, for we're going to make it with real cream and three butter balls.

Yours affectionately,

Judy

PS. We're having fancy dancing in gymnasium class. You can see by the accompanying picture how much we look like a real ballet. The one at the end accomplishing a graceful pirouette is me--I mean I.[12]

---

12 Please find the illustration in Chinese version.

26th December

My Dear, Dear,

Daddy, Haven't you any sense? Don't you KNOW that you mustn't give one girl seventeen Christmas presents? I'm a Socialist, please remember; do you wish to turn me into a Plutocrat?

Think how embarrassing it would be if we should ever quarrel! I should have to engage a moving-van to return your gifts.

I am sorry that the necktie I sent was so wobbly; I knit it with my own hands (as you doubtless discovered from internal evidence). You will have to wear it on cold days and keep your coat buttoned up tight.

Thank you, Daddy, a thousand times. I think you're the sweetest man that ever lived--and the foolishest!

Judy

Here's a four-leaf clover from Camp McBride to bring you good luck for the New Year.

9th January

Do you wish to do something, Daddy, that will ensure your eternal salvation? There is a family here who are in awfully desperate straits. A mother and father and four visible children--the two older boys have disappeared into the world to make their fortune and have not sent any of it back. The father worked in a glass factory and got consumption-- it's awfully unhealthy work--and now has been sent away toa hospital. That took all their savings, and the support of the family falls upon the oldest daughter, who is twenty-four. She dressmakes for$1.50 a

day (when she can get it) and embroiders centrepieces in the evening. The mother isn't very strong and is extremely ineffectual and pious. She sits with her hands folded, a picture of patient resignation, while the daughter kills herself with overwork and responsibility and worry; she doesn't see how they are going to get through the rest of the winter--and I don't either. One hundred dollars would buy some coal and some shoes for three children so that they could go to school, and give a little margin so that she needn't worry herself to death when a few days pass and she doesn't get work.

You are the richest man I know. Don't you suppose you could spare one hundred dollars? That girl deserves help a lot more than I ever did. I wouldn't ask it except for the girl; I don't care much what happens to the mother--she is such a jelly-fish.

Later

I address you, Daddy, from a bed of pain. For two days I've been laid up with swollen tonsils; I can just swallow hot milk, and that is all. "What were your parents thinking of not to have those tonsils out when you were a baby?" the doctor wished to know. I'm sure I haven't an idea, but I doubt if they were thinking much about me.

Yours,

J. A.

Next morning

I just read this over before sealing it. I don't know WHY I cast such a misty atmosphere over life. I hasten to assure you that I am young and happy and exuberant; and I trust you are the same. Youth has nothing to do with birthdays, only with ALIVEDNESS of spirit, so even if your hair is grey, Daddy, you can still be a boy.

Affectionately,
Judy

12th Jan.

Dear Mr. Philanthropist,

Your cheque for my family came yesterday. Thank you so much! I cut gymnasium and took it down to them right after luncheon, and you should have seen the girl's face! She was so surprised and happy and relieved that she looked almost young; and she's only twenty-four. Isn't it pitiful?

Anyway, she feels now as though all the good things were coming together. She has steady work ahead for two months--someone's getting married, and there's a trousseau to make.

"Thank the good Lord!" cried the mother, when she grasped the fact that that small piece of paper was one hundred dollars.

"It wasn't the good Lord at all," said I, "it was Daddy-Long-Legs." (Mr. Smith, I called you.)

"But it was the good Lord who put it in his mind," said she.

"Not at all! I put it in his mind myself," said I.

But anyway, Daddy, I trust the good Lord will reward you suitably. You deserve ten thousand years out of purgatory.

Yours most gratefully,
Judy Abbott

Daddy-Long-Legs

March Fifth

Dear Mr. Trustee,

Tomorrow is the first Wednesday in the month--a weary day for the John Grier Home. How relieved they'll be when five o'clock comes and you pat them on the head and take yourselves off! Did you (individually)ever pat me on the head, Daddy? I don't believe so--my memory seems to be concerned only with fat Trustees.

Give the Home my love, please--my TRULY love. I have quite a feeling of tenderness for it as I look back through a haze of four years. When I first came to college I felt quite resentful because I'd been robbed of the normal kind of childhood that the other girls had had; but now, I don't feel that way in the least. I regard it as a very unusual adventure. It gives me a sort of vantage point from which to stand aside and look at life. Emerging full grown, I get a perspective on the world, that other people who have been brought up in the thick of things entirely lack.

I know lots of girls (Julia, for instance) who never know that they are happy. They are so accustomed to the feeling that their senses are deadened to it; but as for me--I am perfectly sure every moment of my life that I am happy. And I'm going to keep on being, no matter what unpleasant things turn up. I'm going to regard them (even toothaches) as interesting experiences, and be glad to know what they feel like. "Whatever sky's above me, I've a heart for any fate."

Give my kindest regards to Mrs. Lippett (that, I think, is truthful; love would be a little strong) and don't forget to tell her what a beautiful nature I've developed.

Affectionately,
Judy

LOCK WILLOW
4th April

Dear Daddy,

Do you observe the postmark? Sallie and I are embellishing Lock Willow with our presence during the Easter Vacation. We decided that the be stthing we could do with our ten days was to come where it is quiet. Our nerves had got to the point where they wouldn't stand another meal in Fergussen. Dining in a room with four hundred girls is an ordeal when you are tired. There is so much noise that you can't hear the girls across the table speak unless they make their hands into a megaphone and shout. That is the truth.

We are tramping over the hills and reading and writing, and having a nice, restful time. We climbed to the top of "Sky Hill" this morning where Master Jervie and I once cooked supper--it doesn't seem possible that it was nearly two years ago. I could still see the place where the smoke of our fire blackened the rock. It is funny how certain places get connected with certain people, and you never go back without thinking of them. I was quite lonely without him--for two minutes.

What do you think is my latest activity, Daddy? You will begin to believe that I am incorrigible--I am writing a book. I started it three weeks ago and am eating it up in chunks. I've caught the secret. Master Jervie and that editor man were right; you are most convincing when you write about the things you know. And this time it is about something that I do know--exhaustively. Guess where it's laid? In the John Grier Home! And it's good, Daddy, I actually believe it is—just about the tiny little things that happened every day. I'm a realist now. I've abandoned romanticism; I shall go back to it later though, when

my own adventurous future begins.

This new book is going to get itself finished--and published! You see if it doesn't. If you just want a thing hard enough and keep on trying, you do get it in the end. I've been trying for four years to get a letter from you--and I haven't given up hope yet.

Goodbye, Daddy dear.

Affectionately,
Judy

PS. I forgot to tell you the farm news, but it's very distressing. Skip this postscript if you don't want your sensibilities all wrought up. Poor old Grove is dead. He got so that he couldn't chew and they had to shoot him. Nine chickens were killed by a weasel or a skunk or a rat last week.

17th May

Dear Daddy-Long-Legs,

This is going to be extremely short because my shoulder aches at the sight of a pen. Lecture notes all day, immortal novel all evening, make too much writing.

Commencement three weeks from next Wednesday. I think you might come and make my acquaintance--I shall hate you if you don't! Julia's inviting Master Jervie, he being her family, and Sallie's inviting Jimmie McB., he being her family, but who is there for me to invite? Just you and Lippett, and I don't want her. Please come.

Yours, with love and writer's cramp.
Judy

LOCK WILLOW
19th June

Dear Daddy-Long-Legs,

I'm educated! My diploma is in the bottom bureau drawer with my two best dresses. Commencement was as usual, with a few showers at vital moments. Thank you for your rosebuds. They were lovely. Master Jervie and Master Jimmie both gave me roses, too, but I left theirs in the bath tub and carried yours in the class procession.

Here I am at Lock Willow for the summer--for ever maybe. The board is cheap; the surroundings quiet and conducive to a literary life. What more does a struggling author wish? I am mad about my book. I think of it every waking moment, and dream of it at night. All I want is peace and quiet and lots of time to work (interspersed with nourishing meals).

Master Jervie is coming up for a week or so in August, and Jimmie McBride is going to drop in sometime through the summer. He's connected with a bond house now, and goes about the country selling bonds to banks. He's going to combine the "Farmers" National' at the Corners and me on the same trip.

You see that Lock Willow isn't entirely lacking in society. I'd be expecting to have you come motoring through--only I know now that that is hopeless. When you wouldn't come to my commencement, I tore you from my heart and buried you for ever.

Judy Abbott, A.B.

24th July

Dearest Daddy-Long-Legs,

Isn't it fun to work--or don't you ever do it? It's especially fun when your kind of work is the thing you'd rather do more than anything else in the world. I've been writing as fast as my pen would go everyday this summer, and my only quarrel with life is that the days aren't long enough to write all the beautiful and valuable and entertaining thoughts I'm thinking.

I've finished the second draft of my book and am going to begin the third tomorrow morning at half-past seven. It's the sweetest book you ever saw--it is, truly. I think of nothing else. I can barely wait in the morning to dress and eat before beginning; then I write and write and write till suddenly I'm so tired that I'm limp all over. Then I go out with Colin (the new sheep dog) and romp through the fields and geta fresh supply of ideas for the next day. It's the most beautiful book you ever saw--Oh, pardon--I said that before.

You don't think me conceited, do you, Daddy dear?

I'm not, really, only just now I'm in the enthusiastic stage. Maybe later on I'll get cold and critical and sniffy. No, I'm sure I won't! This time I've written a real book. Just wait till you see it.

I'll try for a minute to talk about something else. I never told you, did I, that Amasai and Carrie got married last May? They are still working here, but so far as I can see it has spoiled them both. She used to laugh when he tramped in mud or dropped ashes on the floor, but now--you should hear her scold! And she doesn't curl her hair any longer. Amasai, who used to be so obliging about beating rugs and carrying wood, grumbles if you suggest such a thing. Also his neckties are quite dingy--black and brown, where they used to be scarlet and purple. I've determined never to marry. It's a deteriorating process, evidently.

There isn't much of any farm news. The animals are all in the best of health. The pigs are unusually fat, the cows seem contented and the hens are laying well. Are you interested in poultry? If so, let me recommend that invaluable little work, 200 Eggs per Hen per Year. I am thinking of starting an incubator next spring and raising broilers. You see I'm settled at Lock Willow permanently. I have decided to stay until I've written 114 novels like Anthony Trollope's mother. Then I shall have completed my life work and can retire and travel.

Mr. James McBride spent last Sunday with us. Fried chicken and ice-cream for dinner, both of which he appeared to appreciate. I was awfully glad to see him; he brought a momentary reminder that the world at large exists. Poor Jimmie is having a hard time peddling his bonds. The "Farmers" National' at the Corners wouldn't have anything to do with them in spite of the fact that they pay six per cent. Interest and sometimes seven. I think he'll end up by going home to Worcester and taking a job in his father's factory. He's too open and confiding and kind-hearted ever to make a successful financier. But to be the manager of a flourishing overall factory is a very desirable position, don't you think? Just now he turns up his nose at overalls, but he'll come to them.

I hope you appreciate the fact that this is a long letter from a person with writer's cramp. But I still love you, Daddy dear, and I'm very happy. With beautiful scenery all about, and lots to eat and a comfortable four-post bed and a ream of blank paper and a pint of ink--what more does one want in the world?

Yours as always,

Judy

PS. The postman arrives with some more news. We are to expect Master Jervie on Friday next to spend a week. That's a very pleasant prospect--only I am afraid my poor book will suffer. Master Jervie is very demanding.

27th August

Dear Daddy-Long-Legs,

Where are you, I wonder?

I never know what part of the world you are in, but I hope you're not in New York during this awful weather. I hope you're on a mountain peak (but not in Switzerland; somewhere nearer) looking at the snow and thinking about me. Please be thinking about me. I'm quite lonely and I want to be thought about. Oh, Daddy, I wish I knew you! Then when we were unhappy we could cheer each other up.

I don't think I can stand much more of Lock Willow. I'm thinking of moving. Sallie is going to do settlement work in Boston next winter. Don't you think it would be nice for me to go with her, then we could have a studio together? I would write while she SETTLED and we could be together in the evenings. Evenings are very long when there's no one but the Semples and Carrie and Amasai to talk to. I know in advance that you won't like my studio idea. I can read your secretary's letter now:

> *"Miss Jerusha Abbott.*
> *"DEAR MADAM,*
> *"Mr. Smith prefers that you remain at Lock Willow.*

"Yours truly,

"ELMER H. GRIGGS."

I hate your secretary. I am certain that a man named Elmer H. Griggs must be horrid. But truly, Daddy, I think I shall have to go to Boston. I can't stay here. If something doesn't happen soon, I shall throw myself into the silo pit out of sheer desperation.

Mercy! but it's hot. All the grass is burnt up and the brooks are dry and the roads are dusty. It hasn't rained for weeks and weeks.

This letter sounds as though I had hydrophobia, but I haven't. I just want some family.

Goodbye, my dearest Daddy.

I wish I knew you.
Judy

LOCK WILLOW
19th September

Dear Daddy,

Something has happened and I need advice. I need it from you, and from nobody else in the world. Wouldn't it be possible for me to see you? It's so much easier to talk than to write; and I'm afraid your secretary might open the letter.

Judy

PS. I'm very unhappy.

Daddy–Long–Legs

LOCK WILLOW
3rd October

Dear Daddy-Long-Legs,

Your note written in your own hand--and a pretty wobbly hand!
—came this morning. I am so sorry that you have been ill; I wouldn't
have bothered you with my affairs if I had known. Yes, I will tell you
the trouble, but it's sort of complicated to write, and VERY
PRIVATE. Please don't keep this letter, but burn it.

Before I begin--here's a cheque for one thousand dollars. It
seems funny, doesn't it, for me to be sending a cheque to you? Where
do you think I got it?

I've sold my story, Daddy. It's going to be published serially in
seven parts, and then in a book! You might think I'd be wild with joy,
but I'm not. I'm entirely apathetic. Of course, I'm glad to begin paying
you--I owe you over two thousand more. It's coming in instalments.
Now don't be horrid, please, about taking it, because it makes me
happy to return it. I owe you a great deal more than the mere money,
and the rest I will continue to pay all my life in gratitude and affection.

And now, Daddy, about the other thing; please give me your most
worldly advice, whether you think I'll like it or not.

You know that I've always had a very special feeling towards you;
you sort of represented my whole family; but you won't mind, will
you, if I tell you that I have a very much more special feeling for
another man? You can probably guess without much trouble who he
is. I suspect that my letters have been very full of Master Jervie for a
very long time.

I wish I could make you understand what he is like and how
entirely companionable we are. We think the same about everything--I

am afraid I have a tendency to make over my ideas to match his! But he is almost always right; he ought to be, you know, for he has fourteen years' start of me. In other ways, though, he's just an overgrown boy, and he does need looking after--he hasn't any sense about wearing rubbers when it rains. He and I always think the same things are funny, and that is such a lot; it's dreadful when two people's senses of humour are antagonistic. I don't believe there's any bridging that gulf!

And he is--Oh, well! He is just himself, and I miss him, and miss him, and miss him. The whole world seems empty and aching. I hate the moonlight because it's beautiful and he isn't here to see it with me. But maybe you've loved somebody, too, and you know? If you have, I don't need to explain; if you haven't, I can't explain.

Anyway, that's the way I feel--and I've refused to marry him.

I didn't tell him why; I was just dumb and miserable. I couldn't think of anything to say. And now he has gone away imagining that I want to marry Jimmie McBride--I don't in the least, I wouldn't think of marrying Jimmie; he isn't grown up enough. But Master Jervie and I got into a dreadful muddle of misunderstanding and we both hurt each other's feelings. The reason I sent him away was not because I didn't care for him, but because I cared for him so much. I was afraid he would regret it in the future--and I couldn't stand that! It didn't seem right for a person of my lack of antecedents to marry into any such family as his. I never told him about the orphan asylum, and I hated to explain that I didn't know who I was. I may be DREADFUL, you know. And his family are proud--and I'm proud, too!

Also, I felt sort of bound to you. After having been educated to be a writer, I must at least try to be one; it would scarcely be fair to accept your education and then go off and not use it. But now that I am going to be able to pay back the money, I feel that I have partially

discharged that debt--besides, I suppose I could keep on being a writer even if I did marry. The two professions are not necessarily exclusive.

Suppose I go to him and explain that the trouble isn't Jimmie, but is the John Grier Home--would that be a dreadful thing for me to do? It would take a great deal of courage. I'd almost rather be miserable for the rest of my life.

This happened nearly two months ago; I haven't heard a word from him since he was here. I was just getting sort of acclimated to the feeling of a broken heart, when a letter came from Julia that stirred me all up again. She said--very casually--that "Uncle Jervis" had been caught out all night in a storm when he was hunting in Canada, and had been ill ever since with pneumonia. And I never knew it. I was feeling hurt because he had just disappeared into blankness without a word. I think he's pretty unhappy, and I know I am!

What seems to you the right thing for me to do?

Judy

6th October

Dearest Daddy-Long-Legs,

Yes, certainly I'll come--at half-past four next Wednesday afternoon. Of COURSE I can find the way. I've been in New York three times and am not quite a baby. I can't believe that I am really going to see you--I've been just THINKING you so long that it hardly seems as though you are a tangible flesh-and-blood person.

You are awfully good, Daddy, to bother yourself with me, when you're not strong. Take care and don't catch cold. These fall rains are very damp.

Affectionately,
Judy

PS. I've just had an awful thought. Have you a butler? I'm afraid of butlers, and if one opens the door I shall faint upon the step. What can I say to him? You didn't tell me your name. Shall I ask for Mr. Smith?

Thursday Morning

My Very Dearest Master-Jervie-Daddy-Long-Legs Pendleton-Smith,

Did you sleep last night? I didn't. Not a single wink. I was too amazed and excited and bewildered and happy. I don't believe I ever shall sleep again--or eat either. But I hope you slept; you must, you know, because then you will get well faster and can come to me.

Dear Man, I can't bear to think how ill you've been--and all the time I never knew it. When the doctor came down yesterday to put me in the cab, he told me that for three days they gave you up. Oh, dearest, if that had happened, the light would have gone out of the world for me. I suppose that some day in the far future--one of us must leave the other; but at least we shall have had our happiness and there will be memories to live with.

I meant to cheer you up--and instead I have to cheer myself. For in spite of being happier than I ever dreamed I could be, I'm also soberer. The fear that something may happen rests like a shadow on my heart. Always before I could be frivolous and care-free and

unconcerned, because I had nothing precious to lose. But now--I shall have a Great Big Worry all the rest of my life. Whenever you are away from me I shall be thinking of all the automobiles that can run over you, or the sign-boards that can fall on your head, or the dreadful, squirmy germs that you may be swallowing. My peace of mind is gone forever--but anyway, I never cared much for just plain peace.

Please get well--fast--fast--fast. I want to have you close by where I can touch you and make sure you are tangible. Such a little half hour we had together! I'm afraid maybe I dreamed it. If I were only a member of your family (a very distant fourth cousin) then I could come and visit you every day, and read aloud and plump up your pillow and smooth out those two little wrinkles in your forehead and make the corners of your mouth turn up in a nice cheerful smile. But you are cheerful again, aren't you? You were yesterday before I left. The doctor said I must be a good nurse, that you looked ten years younger. I hope that being in love doesn't make every one ten years younger. Will you still care for me, darling, if I turn out to be only eleven?

Yesterday was the most wonderful day that could ever happen. If I live to be ninety-nine I shall never forget the tiniest detail. The girl that left Lock Willow at dawn was a very different person from the one who came back at night. Mrs. Semple called me at half-past four. Is tarted wide awake in the darkness and the first thought that popped into my head was, "I am going to see Daddy-Long-Legs!" I ate breakfast in the kitchen by candle-light, and then drove the five miles to the station through the most glorious October colouring. The sun came upon the way, and the swamp maples and dogwood glowed crimson and orange and the stone walls and cornfields sparkled with hoar frost; the air was keen and clear and full of promise. I knew something was going to happen. All the way in the train the rails kept singing, "You're goingto see Daddy-Long-Legs." It made me feel secure. I had such faith in Daddy's ability to set things right. And I knew that somewhere another man--dearer than Daddy--was wanting to see me, and somehow I had a feeling that before the journey ended I should meet him, too. And you see!

When I came to the house on Madison Avenue it looked so big and brown and forbidding that I didn't dare go in, so I walked around the block to get up my courage. But I needn't have been a bit afraid; your butler is such a nice, fatherly old man that he made me feel at home at once. "Is this Miss Abbott?" he said to me, and I said, "Yes," so I didn't have to ask for Mr. Smith after all. He told me to wait in the drawing-room. It was a very sombre, magnificent, man's sort of room. I sat down on the edge of a big upholstered chair and kept saying to myself:

"I'm going to see Daddy-Long-Legs! I'm going to see Daddy-Long-Legs!"

Then presently the man came back and asked me please to step up to the library. I was so excited that really and truly my feet would hardly take me up. Outside the door he turned and whispered, "He's been very ill, Miss. This is the first day he's been allowed to sit up. You'll not stay long enough to excite him?" I knew from the way he said it that he loved you--and I think he's an old dear!

Then he knocked and said, "Miss Abbott," and I went in and the door closed behind me.

It was so dim coming in from the brightly lighted hall that for a moment I could scarcely make out anything; then I saw a big easy chair before the fire and a shining tea table with a smaller chair beside it. And I realized that a man was sitting in the big chair propped up by pillows with a rug over his knees. Before I could stop him he rose-- rather shakily--and steadied himself by the back of the chair and just

looked at me without a word. And then--and then--I saw it was you! But even with that I didn't understand. I thought Daddy had had you come there to meet me or a surprise.

Then you laughed and held out your hand and said, "Dear little Judy, couldn't you guess that I was Daddy-Long-Legs?"

In an instant it flashed over me. Oh, but I have been stupid! A hundred little things might have told me, if I had had any wits. I wouldn't make a very good detective, would I, Daddy? Jervie? What must I call you? Just plain Jervie sounds disrespectful, and I can't be disrespectful to you!

It was a very sweet half hour before your doctor came and sent me away. I was so dazed when I got to the station that I almost took a train for St Louis. And you were pretty dazed, too. You forgot to give me any tea. But we're both very, very happy, aren't we? I drove back to Lock Willow in the dark but oh, how the stars were shining! And this morning I've been out with Colin visiting all the places that you and I went to together, and remembering what you said and how you looked. The woods today are burnished bronze and the air is full of frost. It's CLIMBING weather. I wish you were here to climb the hills with me. I am missing you dreadfully, Jervie dear, but it's a happy kind of missing; we'll be together soon. We belong to each other now really and truly, no make-believe. Doesn't it seem queer for me to belong to someone at last? It seems very, very sweet.

And I shall never let you be sorry for a single instant.

Yours, for ever and ever,
Judy

PS. This is the first love-letter I ever wrote. Isn't it funny that I know how?

國家圖書館出版品預行編目資料

長腿叔叔（中英雙語典藏版）/ 珍・韋伯斯特（Jean Webster）
作；珍・韋伯斯特（Jean Webster）繪；艾柯譯. -- 二版. -- 臺
中市：晨星，2022.10
　　面；　公分. --（愛藏本；114）
中英雙語典藏版
譯自：Daddy-Long-Legs
ISBN 978-626-320-232-0（精裝）

874.596　　　　　　　　　　　　　　　　111012340

愛藏本：114

長腿叔叔（中英雙語典藏版）
Daddy-Long-Legs

作　　者｜珍・韋伯斯特（Jean Webster）
繪　　者｜珍・韋伯斯特（Jean Webster）
譯　　者｜艾柯

責任編輯｜呂曉婕、江品如
封面設計｜鐘文君
美術編輯｜黃偵瑜
原圖上色｜王思淳
文字校潤｜江品如、呂昀慶

創 辦 人｜陳銘民
發 行 所｜晨星出版有限公司
　　　　　台中市 407 工業 30 路 1 號
　　　　　TEL：04-23595820　FAX：04-23550581
　　　　　http://star.morningstar.com.tw
　　　　　行政院新聞局局版台業字第 2500 號
法律顧問｜陳思成律師

讀者專線｜TEL：02-23672044 / 04-2359-5819#212
傳真專線｜FAX：02-23635741 / 04-23595493
讀者信箱｜service@morningstar.com.tw
網路書店｜http://www.morningstar.com.tw
郵政劃撥｜15060393　知己圖書股份有限公司

初版日期｜2002 年 08 月 31 日
二版日期｜2022 年 10 月 15 日
　ISBN｜978-626-320-232-0
　定價｜新台幣 250 元

印　　刷｜上好印刷股份有限公司

填寫線上回函，立刻享有
晨星網路書店50元購書金